CW00406570

MINE CONTROL

MINE CONTROL

The Erotic Casebook of London's Foremost Female Hypnotherapist

Lilith M Clayton

Ipsissimus Press, UK

Lilith M Clayton is a qualified hypnotherapist practising from her London, UK, consultancy.

Ipsissimus Press
PO Box 1436
Cheltenham
GL50 9QE

© 2023 by Ipsissimus Press. All rights reserved.
Reproduction, distribution, and transmission of all or parts of this publication as an audio recording or in audio form is especially and strictly prohibited.

ISBN 978-1-7394939-0-5 (electronic)
ISBN 978-1-7394939-1-2 (print)

Cover art by Ipsissimus Press.

www.ipsissimus-press.com
info@ipsissimus-press.com

Disclaimer #1

This is a work of fiction. Names, characters, businesses, places, and events are the products of the author's imagination or are used in a fictitious manner. Any resemblance to actual persons, living or dead, or actual events is coincidental. Opinions expressed are those of the characters and should not be confused with the author's.

Disclaimer #2

This is a work of *hypnotic* fiction. It is authored by a hypnotist, and is about hypnotism and the power of suggestion. This book is sold in written form only because of the inclusion of hypnotic inductions. Any suggestions you receive, accept, or act upon as a result of reading *Mine Control* are wholly by your own volition. Read—and relish!— at your own risk and responsibility.

For everyone I've ever hypnotised.

"Lift not the painted veil which those who live Call Life"
  - Shelly

"There once was a girl from Nantucket"
  - Anon

CONTENTS

FOREWORD

Magpies are incredibly intelligent creatures, compared to the vast majority of the avian species. They pair up, they communicate in groups, and they plan, share, and act collectively, in order to eat well and to avoid danger. Yet this intelligence is literally the product of their sociability—learned behaviours that they cannot not do. Certainly taught from parents to fledglings, and possibly genetically inherited, each generation is deemed to repeat the same actions, tricks, and devious tips of their ancestors.

On a new housing development, a lonely cat wanders its garden and enters the open, darkened door of the garage. As magpies gather to hunt for food, a first arrival spies the cat and shouts a warning. Others follow suit, while keeping a safe distance from whence it's pointing—magpies point with their beaks, if you didn't know. The cat pretends not to notice; the magpies maintain a shouting cacophony; eventually all leave. But the open, darkened door remains in their memories.

For subsequent days, weeks, and months, the magpies observe the cat entering and exiting the open, darkened door. Every time, they point and shout. Eventually they start shouting at the door simply being open—who knows if a cat is hiding inside? Subsequent generations adopt the same vigilance, shouting at the open, darkened door. Eventually the cat dies, but the magpies continue to shout. The open, darkened door became known for danger, and reported as danger, by magpies that were not born by the time the cat had died. Even when the new (cat-free) occupants of the house provide food, the magpies are still vigilant to the open, darkened door, and shun the food out of respect for the danger being reported.

Lilith doesn't help magpies, but the people she does help often present in a similar way. Their behaviours ingrained through teaching, socialisation, and Pavlovian conditioning. While Lilith isn't a sex therapist, she sees a lot of people for sexual problems—severe issues untreatable by her contemporaries. To her, I suppose, these are just issues; but to her clients they are the open, darkened door of danger.

The case studies in this book are, to be frank, very explicit in nature. They need to be, in order to provide the greatest levels of detail of the interventions presented. We should all be grateful to Lilith for her diligent reporting of these cases, but also for her generous and caring attention to her clients. Were it not for Lilith, these people may have suffered their frustrations for the rest of their lives.

Magpies also have sex, but their intercourse lasts but for a few seconds. As you will read, the people whose internal worlds needed help have sex that is far richer than that—at least, after Lilith has helped them. And, of course, while sexual problems can be helped in non-sexual ways, so too can non-sexual issues be solved with sexual interventions. Not since the work my academic research department did with the US Central Intelligence Agency (CIA) back in the 70s with respect to hypnotism, masturbation, and 'mind-control' has anyone explored this world as deeply and gently as Lilith.

And while magpies might be known for stealing items that shine and reflect, maybe you, too, will find yourself borrowing from Lilith's case studies. There is always something illuminating in them.

Dr Charlotte Karoly, MD
Budapest, Hungary
Spring 2023

PREFACE

From hypnotism and mesmerism, to witchcraft and voodoo, people have been seeking ways to master—to control—the minds and wills of others, and of themselves, since time immemorial.

When early perimenopause triggered the end of my career as a marketing-communications professional, the prospect of marrying up all my skills and experiences to play 'kerplunk' with people's personalities—via hypnotism—uniquely appealed to my irrational hormonal rage. I could have started a cult, of course. But that's been done. And so, instead, I became a hypnotherapist.

The first 18 months of my career-pivot were unremarkable. I tackled comedy phobias and the pre-apocalyptic anxiety that plagues us all these days. I spent the spoils of my premium fees on nice wine and fancy things whilst lamenting that I wasn't born a man, which would have made starting a far more lucrative cult so much easier. But then something changed.

This book charts the course of that change through 10 intimate client case studies. I should warn you that they are of a psycho-sexual and explicit nature (entirely professional, of course, and shared for your intellectual pleasures only). I also share my own journey down this hypnotic, erotic rabbit hole, which gets curiouser and curiouser as my powers as a hypnotist grow.

So, buckle up, Dear Reader, because your glimpse into the working life of London's foremost female hypnotherapist is about to satisfy your curiosity for the secrets of hypnosis—and for the innermost thoughts and fantasies of my clients...

Lilith M Clayton
London, England
Summer 2023

CASE #126 / IAN

"Show me your penis." Or: how a client's secret burning desires stubbed out his smoking habit, and lit a (wholly professional) fire in me!

I an is a plain, pale, and slightly portly man in his mid-50s. He wears a stiff plaid shirt, Wrangler blue-washed jeans, and chunky Clarks shoes, which, together, scream: "My wife just wants me to fit in at a family barbecue." Standard-issue haircut, specs, watch; life. His is a softly appealing—reassuring—'cuddly'?—personality and appearance.

Yes, a distinct advantage of being a hypnotist is that you can truly appraise people without the inconvenience of them noticing.

Ian's wife purchased my smoking cessation package on her husband's behalf. I've endured four sessions of his sulking at the prospect of being deprived of his beloved cigarettes thus far. Four 90-minute sessions of tedium about ungrateful teenaged children, accountancy career gripes, and long, Lycra-clad bike rides with his mates being his only means of 'escape'. Ugh.

But we are living in a material world, and I am a material girl! Most of our time together has, in fact, then, been spent with Ian 'going into trance' via a hypnotic induction method I inculcated in him during session one. I simply pop on a generic, pre-recorded relaxation track churned out by any one of my hack hypnotherapist 'peers' that Spotify plays at random. This means Ian can 'do the work subconsciously' while I do Sudoku puzzles and edit my Ocado grocery order.

There *is* method in my materialistic madness, however. While Ian is resistant to change, he has also received zero quality or tangible suggestions to do so in our sessions so far—just blah blah 'relaxotherapy' blah. He's thus perfectly frustrated and primed for today, our penultimate session: the moment for me to make the necessary edits to Ian's mind before session six next week... And the moment for me to earn my total fee of £4,800 with one fell hypnotic blow!

People think they communicate in words. But it is what is unsaid—the subtext—the whole person being truly seen—that 'speaks' to the hypnotist. Ian avoids mention of his marriage when sharing the banalities of his life, but admittedly resents his wife for sending him to me. Meanwhile, smoking is a habit of both oral fixation and avoidance, and (some of a Freudian persuasion would further argue, and so I'll run with it...) cigarettes are phallic objects.

Yes, I sense, through Ian's clouds of complaining: a strained marriage... and a flaccid penis.

It doesn't even matter if I'm right. All that matters is that I provide a new narrative, and an acceptable and accepted suggestion.

Welcome, Dear Reader, to the world of hypnotherapy!

***

"Show me your penis."

Ian shifts in my tan leather recliner. I have led him through the ritual of 'going into hypnosis' with which he is familiar. But this is a departure from my usual suggestions of total amnesia for our session before I outsource myself to a pre-recording. Hypnosis is a delicate art and science—have I sufficiently established rapport, trust, expertise, and compliance for Ian to obey?

"Unbutton your jeans, Ian. Slide down your jeans and underwear. And show me your penis."

Ian shifts again in his seat and his left leg starts to jig. I have been careful to establish ours as a strictly professional, platonic relationship—I am <u>never</u> flirtatious or sexual with clients; Ian's jovial before and after 'banter' is not indulged. But I know I am taking him 'off script' here. Hypnosis is a social construct and cultural phenomenon—it's an illusion—a magic trick. Ian has the choice between breaking the spell... or experiencing real magic.

Ian's eyes are lightly shut as per the instructions of the hypnotic induction. His leg stills and he lets out a deep sigh as he mulls my suggestion. A tear rolls down his cheek. A cascade follows. He's not crying, but he gulps back big emotions. This is an abreaction; when a hypnotised subject experiences a major emotional reaction. There may be no conscious rhyme or reason for this release, and it is the hypnotist's job to help the subject make sense of it.

"You can speak, Ian," I continue firmly. "Your emotional reaction is your mind's way of telling you that there's a gap between why you *think* you're here, and why you're *really* here. And as your mind starts to process that reassuring thought, so your emotions start to subside."

I sit back and wait for Ian's tears to cease. But his mouth moves in slow, mute, useless contortions. It's no wonder this newish vocation of mine as a hypnotist has gone to my head: I might as well be a Higher Being from outer space speaking with a primitive caveman!

"The compulsion to tell me why you're here—why you're *really* here—will soon enable you to speak, Ian. Your mind will find a way to communicate with me so as to be truthful, uninhibited, and coherent. Perhaps you will speak to me as the voice inside your head self-talks to you; or as if I'm an idealised real or imagined confidante, wholly here for you. Or you may chat as if making banter with a friendly stranger in a pub, but with you detached from, ignorant of, the content. Perhaps you will draw upon all of these ideas and more, Ian. But you can, you will, speak."

I watch Ian closely as his mind and motor functions show signs of cooperating once more. There's nothing quite like seeing these behind-closed-doors hypnosis moments to make you appreciate that most people are just malfunctioning meat-robots. Finally, his face settles.

"So. Why are you here, Ian? Why are you *really* here?"

I wait—and wait—and wait!—for Ian to speak. I wonder if I should abort, but the black screen of my phone lights up at the arrival of a silent text, distracting me. I'm in the middle of messaging back to decline my ex-colleague-frenemy's coffee invite, when he starts to mumble.

"Because... because... I... can't..? Can't. Susan. She says... it's the smoking. That's why. Because I can't... get it up!"

I leave that truth hanging in the air while I sneak a peek at my ex-colleague-frenemy's LinkedIn profile. Ian fidgets and snuffles at his psychological—not physical, of course!—exposure to me. (Seriously, though: what is the meaning of this coffee invite..?) Ian shifts again in the recliner—this time relaxing back into it. Another sniffle or two... (No, I don't want to sign in! Fucking LinkedIn.)

Oh!

Ian's hands slide down to his waist... With a final small sniff, his hands linger over the buckle of his faux leather belt. Something shifts in his mind; he decisively unbuckles his belt and pops open his flies—one button, two buttons, three. He pulls them apart and I see his belly button, a trail of mousy hair, and the top of some unimaginative striped boxer shorts probably from M&S.

Oh, fuck? Hypnotised subjects take suggestions completely literally, of course, but my aim was for him to only *mentally* expose himself to me. There's still ample time for me to stop and redirect him. But he's so... keen... so... easy. So... compliant. I mean, I knew he was primed, but..!

"You're here, Ian, because you can't get 'it' up, correct?"

What are you doing, Lilith?! I have never crossed such a line before. But I feel I must follow my instincts; words can only achieve so much.

Ian nods in response to my question, full of shame, as he eases his jeans down below his waist. I see the soft mound of his penis beneath his faded old boxers. He faces off to the side, fully dissociated from this intervention.

"Show me your penis."

Ian continues facing to the side as he hooks his fingers around the waist of his boxers. Then he lifts his ass slightly off the recliner to push them down. He sinks back into the leather, his naked pink ass on the seat, his soft, pale, shrunken cock nestled amongst a frizz of mousy hair.

(Professionally, I make a mental note to give the recliner an especial clean before my next appointment. But, personally, I must confess to feeling a little giddy at Ian's obedience... The hot pang of power coursing through my pussy makes me a disgrace to my unregulated profession.)

I force myself to think of my cleaning routine while wondering how I might tailor a generic smoking-cessation hypnotherapy process to Ian's semi-nude state... Meanwhile, a silent tear dribbles down his cheek and his sad, flaccid manhood makes small twitches, too. Suddenly I realise: Ian is showing me his penis... but he isn't *showing* me his penis.

I take a deep breath—it's time to follow my hypnotic instincts into new therapeutic territory.

***

"Your wife," I continue. "Susan. Tell me. Tell me about your best fuck with your wife? When you were as big and as hard as you've ever been. Then I shall set you free." A pause for dramatic effect! "<u>Show me</u> your penis, Ian," I command. "Tell me your memory."

Ian sighs and turns his head to the ceiling, laying fully back and relaxing further. He even shimmies his jeans and underwear down further, exposing his stocky thighs and freeing his lower body more. His forehead creases and he bites his lip. His lips are voluptuous and I imagine kissing them—before dismissing this as a new professional low.

"I... I was... beneath her... I was... I..."

His cock grows stouter while he musters the means to communicate with me.

"I... My wife and I... we met in our 20s. I loved her. I love her. We had fun. We... We'd been together nearly a year. She was a bigger girl—a woman. Still is, Susan. I like that, love that. Her curves. Her shape. The way she felt, feels. I'd always wanted to... 'sixty-nine'. A man and a woman, licking, sucking... each other at the same time. But she was... She didn't... She wasn't confident in herself, her body. I'd try to persuade her, create moments where... I so wanted to..."

7

Ian shifts in the recliner again, thrusting his groin upwards. His cock is hardening, emerging from the foreskin, revealing itself. It is burly but amply long, with a curve to the right. It quivers.

"She loved me between her legs, licking her... pussy, rubbing her clit with my fingers, sucking her til she came. But I wanted her on top of me. I wanted to bury myself in her... in her pussy. That's what I wanted. That's what I...

"We went away on holiday, and, one night after dinner, we were tipsy, and we were fooling around in bed, and I sort of manoeuvred us into doing it, 'sixty-nine', side by side. But it was... frustrating. Kissing and licking and sucking each other, but it's light and awkward side by side. But you're turned on, you want it, you...

"I wanted to push my tongue inside her, but I couldn't. And she was just tonguing the tip of my cock. It was real frustrating. And so I just... I rocked us. Sort of pulled her on top of me. She had a real hang up about this position—I knew she worried she was too heavy, too big—that she'd get all up in her head—not be in the moment. But I kept my mouth on her clit, circling it with my tongue, keeping her on top with how good it felt. So she was gasping and she sunk her mouth around my cock, taking it all in. Except she wasn't relaxed. Like, she was just crouching on top of me, her body all stiff, like, focused on sucking her tummy in, staying 'light'—like... performing."

Ian goes silent as he processes that disconnect between his pure desire and his wife's body-shy, performative response. His impressively proud cock echoes his mental state, slackening off into its curvature. I know he's about to speak again when it begins bouncing back into shape.

"And that's when I did it. I flicked my tongue back from her clit up into her slit, gripping her thighs right back. I pushed my tongue inside her, hard, insistent. And I... I fucked her with my tongue. She gasped, moaned, shook. That's when it finally happened. She just... relaxed. Relaxed back. She sat on my face. I was smothered in her pussy, her juices. Oh! Mmm... I ate her pussy, lapping at her slit, thrusting my tongue in, out, and around her. Deep. Her body was relaxed on top of mine, her sucking on my cock like... like it was a... how a child sucks its thumb? We were still new together and she had her ways, her techniques, her 'performance'. But this felt—it was—real. Real. She sucked my cock while I fucked her hot, wet pussy with my tongue."

Ian's cock is red and hard. A bead of pre-cum glistens at his tip. I don't think about his voluptuous lips speaking this into my clit and slit because that would be unprofessional.

"I'm exploring her. I've been wanting to do this since we met. Wanting so much... I move a hand from caressing her hip and ass cheek to rubbing her clit while I continue poking my tongue in and out. She sucks my cock deeper, deeply, and I can feel myself getting more and more excited. She's so hot and wet and relaxed, and I don't know why... because this, this 'sixty-nine', this is my fantasy... I knew then I wanted to be with her for the rest of my life and to explore so much more together... just to explore, I guess... but I hadn't thought of it... consciously... but I slid my tongue back from her slit up... to her asshole. And I licked her beautiful, rosy asshole, round and round, and fucked it in and out with my tongue. Spontaneous, like."

(I expect, Dear Reader, that you no longer require my editorial comments as regards the unprofessional rovings of my mind at this point, hmm?)

"It was like she just couldn't concentrate on anything but that new feeling. She'd never done anything like that before! Someone rimming her asshole. So she hunched down next to my cock, not sucking me, not grinding against me, just... passive. Feeling for the first time a tongue in and around her ass. My fingers continued to stroke her clit; so fat now. I moved my other hand from spreading her ass to her slit. I slide two, then three, fingers inside her pussy. She's not perching, rocking or grinding; something beautiful is happening—I feel like I'm playing her like an instrument: my tongue on her ass, my fingers in her slit, my fingers on her clit. And then she... explodes! She cums! She vibrates, shakes. She can't speak.

"I lap at her asshole while keeping my fingers still. She nestles her face against my hard, wet cock. She wants to suck me—give me pleasure—but can't. My tongue traces down to her slit—she's dripping wet. I slide my fingers out and move the other hand away from her clit, instead gripping her gorgeous ass with both hands and pushing her cheeks aside. I hitch her upwards slightly, and tentatively lap at her clit. She cums in another big—like, shuddering—orgasm while licking, vague-like, at my cock.

"I am so hard and ready to cum. I ease her off me, onto her hands and knees. I move around behind her, kneeling, and take my cock in my hands. We've only recently stopped using johnnies, now we're proper together, and I cannot wait to shoot my cum inside her. The lips of her pussy are red, swollen, slick. Her asshole is tempting but we haven't shared that fantasy yet—I think of the future as I push myself inside her pussy. She doesn't cum again as I slowly but deeply fuck her—like she is my reward, concentrated on me and my cock, and every sensation. I cum inside her, pulling her hips back against me as I do, and she says she can feel me throb. We gasp and pant. Just collapse bedside each other and... I love her. I love my wife."

I look from Ian's ruddy, aroused face to his fat, red, fully erect cock. Tears of pre-cum drip down its throbbing shaft onto swollen, expectant balls. I feel my pussy throbbing, too —such is the hazard, I decide, for a hypnotist exposed to their clients' most intimate remembrances and imaginings. But I am a professional and so prepare to plant the potent seeds of suggestion that Ian so wants and needs.

"In a moment, Ian—not now, but when I click my fingers," I command, "you will move your hand down to your penis to touch, grip, and appreciate it. In doing so, you will feel only dissociated curiosity and the realisation of something as yet to reveal itself. When I click my fingers for a second time, any and all feelings of a sexual nature will switch off—but in the knowledge that you can turn them back on when appropriate. You will then clean yourself off using the tissues to your right, redress yourself, and close your eyes—back into a passive state of hypnosis, ready for my final instructions."

I deliver these commands clearly but quickly—Ian is on the edge of orgasm and I want to keep him there: just right there, on that edge.

Click! My sleekly manicured fingers—Chanel Rouge Noir, of course—trigger the desired response. Ian's right hand darts from the arm of the recliner to his cock. As I'd intended, he is not masturbating or making a sexual display —he is like a person feeling for something unknown-yet-known in a fleeting moment of sleepy darkness.

"Open your eyes, Ian," I command. "See yourself. See your cock."

Ian opens his eyes and drops his gaze to his glorious manhood. His mouth forms an awestruck, silent 'O'.

"Click!" A sharp second snap of my fingers freezes the moment. I congratulate myself on my timing; in spite of my carefully crafted instructions, Ian's cock was not subject to the same controls—and was clearly about to erupt. Something I'll save for him for later!

Ian slumps robotically back into the recliner, eyes glazed and with his head at a slight angle. He's panting, winding down, in a hypnotic 'nowhere-ish'—dispelling all that unspent sexual force. His cock is losing a little of its red-hot swelling and I silently bid it goodbye as Ian reaches for a tissue—precisely as I'd instructed.

I give Ian some time to right his clothes and appearance, rising from my chair to fetch a chilled Pellegrino from the fridge. I watch a spider spin its web against the outdoor windowpane above the kitchenette while I sip the cool bubbles.

Satiated, I return to my seat—an imposing wingback chair upholstered in petrol-blue-hued velvet. I chose it to be purposefully suggestive of my power over the person on the low Freudian-style recliner, and of the traditional doctor-patient dynamic. Ian is sat, eyes closed, tranquil; waiting for me and my next commands—the picture of the perfect hypnotic subject.

I smile inwardly to myself as I part my lips to weave my last suggestion of this session.

***

"And in four, three, two, one... Return to me, Ian! Awake, renewed, and ready!"

With two insistent claps of my hands, Ian is blinking in the recliner, bewildered—but, for the first time since we began working together, slowly beaming. He shifts in his seat, stretching, adjusting to the light; then, adjusting to my presence with wordless, gawky expressions of 'what...' and 'whoa...' and 'wow...'

Ian is none the wiser for what occurred here today, of course—I furnished him with complete amnesia for his sexual reawakening; he cannot fathom why this session feels so different. And so I simply smile kindly and knowingly as my eyes flick imperceptibly from his to the large wall clock strategically positioned behind him. This is all the unconscious cue Ian needs to obey social niceties; he grapples his belongings together and stumbles into my lobby.

"Please don't feel the need to rush, Ian," I say in soothing tones while following him. "Sit a while, relax, have a herbal tea."

"No, no," he replies, patting down his John Lewis jacket whilst pulling it on in search of his wallet. "I've loads to do today. But that was just... I mean, I really feel something has shifted this time, Dr Clayton––. Sorry, I mean Mrs C––. Lilith! 'Lilith'; you said to call you that. Can't shake calling you 'doctor' that first time! Anyway. Thank you. I, er... thank you."

I relieve Ian of £800 and bid him goodbye.

I wander back into my consulting room and sniff the air; does it smell of cock? Of pre-cum? Of sex? I perch on the edge of the recliner, my hand hovering over where Ian's naked, exposed body touched the leather, breathing in any lingering aroma, noting the trace of his sweat and the wetness in my knickers...

I exhale decisively and automatically set about my usual post-client routine. The detritus of mugs and bottles is hidden away; the recliner and side tables are polished; bins are emptied; refreshments are replenished; the loo, if used, is restored to its unused state; and, finally, the reeds in the fragrance diffusers are turned.

No, there must be no distractions for my next hypnotised subject—not even unconscious ones. So I open the window and breathe in the fresh air. The spider scutters across its web to the corner of the pane, the silks crossing the opening now torn asunder. I glance back at the recliner—something new happened here today...

I resist the urge to hitch up my skirt, push my knickers aside and rock my fingers against my swollen clit til I cum. Instead, I remember my pledge to keep things professional and so fetch a can of antibacterial Pledge, and set about caressing the seat of the soft leather recliner where Ian sat. How, I wonder while I clean, shall I pass the two hours before my next client arrives..? I picture myself exiting my hypnotherapy annex and crossing the gravelled driveway to the house, where my husband—Addy—is working in his home office. I will knock, enter without saying a word, sit on his lap, and kiss him to stifle objections that he has to work. Then I'll sink to my knees in front of him and wait for his mild protests that he's in the middle of something to subside as I ease down his jeans and underwear. Then I'll suck his delicious cock til it's hard and then I'll...

Mmm? How would I like to cum..?

Such are the advantages of working for yourself from home.

***

Fast-forward two weeks and it is precisely 17 minutes prior to Ian's final appointment with me. I pause from sipping my coffee—black, decaf, because: placebo, duh!—at my lobby desk and look to the phone. It rings, right on cue.

"Hello, Lilith speaking."

"Oh, um, hello... Doct—. Lilith. Sorry! It's, er, it's Ian here. I'm sorry but I can't make it to my appointment because I..."

Ian trails off. I gave him a post-hypnotic suggestion last session that, just before today's two-o-clock, he'd be struck by the realisation that he is free of his problems. He is now groping for a rationalisation for cancelling, as previously hypnotised subjects do, but, because this revelation struck him just three minutes before he felt compelled to call me, he hasn't invented one yet.

"That's quite alright, Ian," I reassure him. "You mentioned this week might be a busy one, but said you'd reschedule if that would be the case."

"Oh, I? Yes, yes. Of course."

"I'm afraid I can't offer refunds at such short notice, but I'd be happy to reschedule you at a discounted rate."

A pause. I wish I had a window into my subjects' minds at moments like these; I imagine them making my new narrative fit as a skipping record—the distorted 'music' of their mind goes slow-fast-slow before the stuck needle skips back into its proper beat.

He mumbles the beginnings of an apology before blurting out: "No." His tempo and tone are off. "No. That won't be necessary. I don't need..." His need for social pleasantries kicks in—slow-fast-slow. "I'm sorry but I... busy... busy?"

"Ian. Why don't you pass the time by playing a little solitaire?"

Ah, a hypnotist's 'in'-joke, of course! I like to install a complexity of post-hypnotic suggestions, with this *Manchurian Candidate* reference acting as my 'back door' into a client's subconscious mind. Hypnotism can be a lonely vocation, so I hope you, Dear Reader, will allow me my fun?

"Yes, Lilith," says Ian, in a monotonic voice. "Yes. I am here."

"Good, Ian. Good."

I extract from Ian a most satisfying report on his past fortnight. He found himself peculiarly disinterested in cigarettes, leading to increasingly cordial relations with his wife, Susan. This culminated in a Prosecco-fuelled night in a neighbouring couple's sauna the weekend prior to today's Tuesday appointment, which... completely cured him of his addiction to cigarettes.

My maverick success convinced me that I must write of Ian's case to Dr Charlotte Karoly, a renowned clinical psychiatrist and psychologist based in Budapest. Dr Karoly has a special interest in hypnotism and conducted some most interesting studies of a psychosexual nature back in the 1970s before universities invented ethics boards. And so I share the following, Dear Reader, in Ian's own words— purely in the interests of professional learning and completeness.

***

"It was getting late. We'd had a fair bit to drink. Bob and Geeta went inside to get towels. Susan and I, we'd been closer and cosier all evening, my arm around her, a little touch and squeeze here and there. Well, when we were alone, she leaned forward to finish her glass on the side. And—I don't know why—but I had this sudden memory from way back, of us... I just reached my hand forward and... lightly touched two fingers over the crotch of her swimming costume, grazing from the tip of her clit, back across her slit, up to her asshole. She did a little gasp, making her cough her drink, and she turned back to me—I thought she was cross! But then she looked down at my trunks—and so did I

—and we could both see I was rock hard! Just as the neighbours came back! Susan was giggling, trying to help me out the tub and with my towel to hide my hard-on so they wouldn't see. We got away with it and headed home across the way.

"Inside, we looked at each other, like, 'huh?!', in the hallway. If it weren't for the three moody teenagers around, we'd have ripped our clothes off there and then—it was... electric... But we crept upstairs to our room and closed the door behind us. Susan was still looking at me funny—not sure what might happen; if anything would happen.

"'I want you to sit on my face,' I said—the words came out, automatic, like. She blinked, but I just stripped off my clothes and lay, ready, on the bed. I looked over to her and she was staring at my cock, transfixed—it was so big and hard. I reached down and stroked it gently. 'I want you to sit of my face, Susan... And then I want to fuck you in the ass.'

"She was sort of... passive. She pulled off her summer dress and underwear, and walked over to me. She always wants the lights off—when we managed to, before things got... lights off, always. But she stood in front of me, naked, in the light. Ah, I love my wife! I ran a hand down her belly to her pubes, twirling soft hairs in my fingers, and I leaned over to kiss her thighs. Little kisses, with a flick of my tongue—I was so hungry for her. She leaned over and caressed my cock with her hand—like she couldn't quite believe my hard-on was real. And then she just climbed on top of me—still transfixed on my cock, cupping my balls, kissing my shaft—while I pulled her hips back and buried my face in her cunt.

"I gently licked and sucked around her clit, spreading wetness from my mouth and from her moistening slit. She relaxed against me, still sort of... worshipping, like... my cock. I could feel her hot breath against it as she got more and more turned on, brushing her lips against it, a lick here and there, but not taking me in her mouth. I continued working her pussy lips, but I'd yet to lick her clit. She was moaning and moving; after all this time together, I knew I could bring her off in moments once my mouth reached her clit. But I wanted this to last. And I wanted it to be new.

"She was getting frustrated. 'Please! Please!' But I gently pushed her ass cheeks down and moved my head up, licking up from her slit—to her asshole. She gasped. I circled my tongue slowly round and round. Her juices and my saliva were dripping down her pussy and my chin onto my chest. I was so glad she wasn't sucking on my cock—her knowing my every like and kink—or I'd have cum by now!

"I pushed her hips up and forwards; I wanted to see her—gaze at her dripping, plump, hot cunt in the light. She knelt over me, passive, waiting. I skimmed two fingers either side of her labia, then up and together over her asshole, making it slippery wet as I circled it, so rosy and pink—and inviting. 'Please?'

"'Is this what you want?', I asked, moving back down to her slit—sort of teasing, sort of assuming she might not be up for... Then I slid two, then three, fingers inside her pussy, pumping them slowly back and forth, pressing down against her g-spot. She sighed in slight relief, and fucked back against my fingers, pushing harder and deeper against my hand, wanting to feel full of me. 'No, no,' she murmured. 'This isn't what you want?' 'No.' 'What then?' 'In my ass. Fuck my ass. Please.'

"I slide my hands to her hips and gesture her up, her following the movement til she's laying on her back. I look into her eyes as I wipe her juices from my mouth and chin. We kiss passionately and she writhes with frustrated pleasure, her hand edging down to her mound of hair, desperate to touch her clit and cum. 'No', I say, kissing her. 'I want to.'

"I take a pillow and place it beneath her hips, then push her legs back and up, resting her ankles on my shoulders. My cock is wet with my own juices from her teasing me, but I can't resist her soaking wet cunt—I push myself inside her. We both moan as I drive myself in as deep as I can get from this upright kneeling position. I watch as she grinds against my cock, her clit still neglected; I could so easily lean forwards into our usual embrace so that we can fuck to the hardest orgasms we've had in years. But I want her ass.

"I gently pull out and back, and nestle my cock against her asshole. 'Yes, yes,' she moans, pressing against it. We are both so slick and wet; we press and nudge until I'm past that first, second bit of tightness, then I glide inside. She lets out a small cry as I let out a breath, her relaxing and pulling me forwards til I'm fully, deeply inside her. Her legs wrap around my hips, pulling me down onto her chest so that we can kiss while I gently fuck her ass.

"She grinds her clit against me and cums—quietly climaxing, quivering—so, so hard and long. I don't know how I'm still lasting, I'm so turned on. But I move back to kneeling so I can watch her, her body now soft and still, while I fuck her—harder, faster, deeper—until I explode inside her with a cry. I pump and pant a little more as my orgasm subsides; she reaches for her clit and strokes herself to another climax while we gaze into each other's eyes. And then..."

***

"Ian," I interject. "Do you see The Red Queen?"

Another *Manchurian Candidate* 'in'-joke for no one's amusement but my own to bring Ian back to conscious operation.

"And then..." he continues, his now-conscious mind trying to segue into a socially acceptable missed-appointment-reasoning he'd been fumbling for prior to my activating hypnosis.

"You were saying: and then you realised on the way here that you're already a non-smoker. Because you haven't smoked since last week and didn't even think about it over the weekend even though you were socialising. But your wife was worried you'd, what, relapse?"

"Yes, yes! That's exactly it! I was worried about the waste of time and money, and mucking you about. But Susan said there's no point doing a hypnosis session you don't need. 'What if it undoes the magic?!' So I just suddenly realised..."

"I can assure you, Ian, there's no undoing my magic," comes my reply. "But I understand and wish you all the best now that you're free of the problems you came to me with."

Ian expresses gratitude and pledges to recommend my hypnotherapy to all who cross his path.

I replace the phone receiver and stifle a triumphant smile. Personally, I cannot imagine anything less erotic than wallowing in a suburban soup with people otherwise warring over recycling and cats. But, aside from that, my prescription for Ian played out precisely as I'd designed. He became a non-smoker the moment he shot his load into his wife's eager ass. And so I mark him as a completed case on my client management system, then sleep (lol) my Mac.

Since it would be unprofessional to masturbate in my workplace, and since my husband is away on a site visit, I resolve to draw myself a bath and relax in it with a nice glass of Chablis. No more clients today! And another £800 well earned.

CASE #139 / NEVE

Filling a wannabe-mum's void in more ways than one with a strict—and strictly professional!—new hypnotherapy approach.

Today's 2pm is Neve, a primly attractive human resources professional aged 39, who is absolutely riddled with neuroses. Chief amongst these is her longing to have a baby—alas, so far, without success. Neve is now contemplating IVF and so has arranged four de-stressing hypnotherapy sessions with moi.

I greet Neve in my lobby waiting area for her second session. She finishes flicking absent-mindedly through a high-end fashion magazine—my coffee table proffers an eclectic range of periodicals to help me establish identity and conformity—and returns my pleasantries.

She rises from the low, squashy sofa, fiddling with her ridden-up skirt and neat brown bob, and follows me into my consulting room. I note with irritation the half-slurped green juice in her right hand and the Lululemon yoga bag clutched in her left. My hypnotic powers would, indeed, aid Neve if it weren't for the strict 'wellness' curriculum she's embarked upon to ensure maximal stress about The Baby Project.

She shall have to be punished...

Neve settles down onto the recliner and I seat myself in my wingback chair. She fusses with an eyelash and smooths down her silk blouse while sighing about the inconveniences of her Tube journey here. I smile and nod benevolently, and pretend to jot preparatory notes in my 'client' notebook— but where I, in fact, write stuff like this and sometimes doodle.

I casually tap my pen against my notebook a couple of times to signal to Neve to wrap up her complaints against London's lesser privileged. She takes a last sip of her greying green goo and places the cup on the side table. Then she 'relaxes', as best a woman as uptight as Neve ever can, into the tan leather and awaits me.

I ask Neve for a progress report since we last met. I'm surprised to note I actually am intrigued! This is because our first session was most disagreeable to me... Neve sought me out for my collaborative approach, but our agreement to co-create a 'de-stressing' process was bastardised into some dismal hypnotic script to give her hostile womb and reluctant baby a pep-talk.

I don't approve of babies or most women who consciously plan to have them, but I needed the cash, and so had to psychically cleanse myself of this experience with a post-work bucket of Chardonnay and a generous donation to an abortion charity.

But a moment I did relish was Neve's realisation, while deep in hypnosis, that The Baby Project was destroying her marriage to Lars, a successful ad man. She described to me their regimented, bleak sex sessions. Imagine: Neve and Lars upon their be-cushioned queen-sized bed in their Richmond home; Lars punctually pumping away at Neve's lubed-up pussy, with only the aim *to impregnate* in mind—both hollow slaves to the vanity of white upper-middle-class procreativity.

What particularly impressed me was an irrational fear that Neve was cultivating: that sexually-sad Lars was secretly masturbating into the shower—and... thus... washing her baby down the drain. How novel! She finds reasons to burst into their ensuite during his morning ablutions. She imagines hearing a baby's cries emitting from the depths of the drain.

In a rare moment of pity, I prescribed for Neve a sophisticated dose of post-hypnotic suggestions. In crude terms: she and Lars should go out for an unhealthy dinner, get drunk on a bottle or two of red, go home, drink some more, and then, for afters, have a good, fun fuck. Specifically, Neve was to finish her husband in her mouth. Then a follow-up course of blowjobs and hand-jobs was necessary; Neve was to deprive her cunt of baby-making cum, and to spend the week between sessions filling her mouth and hands with whatever insights came up.

I tap my pen expectantly on my notebook to cue Neve's answer. She sighs about some petty work conflict she's manufactured to enhance her stress narrative. Then she slides a hand down to cup her empty belly—one of those faux subconscious moves with which I'm so familiar—and muses that a friend has recommended reiki to help with the stress.

Reiki! I appreciate Franz Mesmer and his mesmerist and animal magnetist followers of the 1780s and beyond aren't the exclusive or original inventors of the theatrical 'passing of hands' to manipulate 'energies' and cure all ills. But I have no respect for modern practitioners who do not avail themselves of the science. Mesmerism, and early hypnotism, is proven to be imagination, suggestion, placebo—and a superb excuse for getting up close to women's heaving bosoms. How can you help, let alone heal, people if you're still too preoccupied with shooting imaginary 'fluids', 'fields', and 'forces' from your hands to worry about what comes out of your mouth?!

Neve does have bad energy, though—and, I also must admit, excellent tits. So I switch on my trusty metronome—an old-fashioned but, in my opinion, stylish accoutrement to hypnosis that steadily tick-tick-ticks a client into trance at 30 beats-per-minute. (Yes, yes—I know I'm a hypocrite, wittingly mixing science and magick; it's called 'being meta', Dear Reader.)

***

"Let us begin the hypnosis procedure now," I say.

Tick, tick, tick, tick...

Neve's eyes begin to glaze, and, soon, her eyelids grow heavy. We practised this induction last session, but even I'm surprised how keen she seems to check-out of reality. Who can blame her, though?! Desiring a baby at this point in capitalism's death throes is clearly deranged and the source of much cognitive dissonance amongst great swathes of the global population. But, hey, it's all gravy to us hypnotists!

Neve's eyelids quickly flutter closed, and her breathing becomes deep and slow. Dedicated professional that I am, I watch her silk-draped breasts rise and fall with increasing serenity. She makes a dreamy "mmhm..." sound and raises her right finger.

"I'm ready."

My cue. I pluck the hypnotherapy script that Neve and I 'co-created' last session from the back of my notebook, stifling my nausea as I peruse the words I must now recite. Oh, how I long for a return to the days of Svengali 'power hypnotists' and CIA mindfuckery—albeit in more femme and freaky guises! But client rapport and Neve's belief that she's in full charge of surrendering her subconscious to me are what matter here.

So I swallow my pride—and a little bit of sick—and softly recite the cliched beach visualisation required to lure Neve deeper into trance...

***

"Imagine yourself stepping out onto a beautiful, calm, sun-kissed beach. You are surrounded by lush palm trees and grasses nestled in undulating sand dunes. Ahead of you is a sparkling deep-blue ocean—its inviting waves lap gently at the shore. There is not a cloud in the blue sky; just the hazily warm sun basking down on this scene.

"Take a moment to feel the warm sand beneath your bare feet; its soft, pale grains moving between and around your toes. Now breathe in the warm sea air; taste the subtle saltiness in the atmosphere. Feel the comfortable, blissful warmth of the sun basking down on your exposed skin. Hear the gentle breeze flickering through the palms and grasses; feel that same breeze caressing your face and body, and fluttering through your loose hair.

"Now tune into the sounds of the ocean. The waves—lapping, rolling, crashing; back and forth, in and out. You feel compelled to walk towards the water. With each step you take, with each footprint you leave in the soft, pristine sand, you imagine the bliss that awaits you in the warm, gentle ocean.

"Step by step, more and more... until your toes, your feet, reach the moist, slickening sand nearing the tide. Feel your toes, your feet—yourself—sink that little bit deeper. Your footsteps into the lapping tide, and farther still into the shallow waters, feel heavier. As the water stirs at your ankles, you realise you cannot resist going deep into this warm, gentle, blissful ocean.

"You move forwards, the water reaching your thighs, then up, up—enveloping your hips, waist, chest; lapping and lapping. Such is this bliss that you surrender your footing on the ocean floor. And now you're gliding through these waters, floating next, being taken comfortably and willingly by the current, deeper and deeper..."

***

Neve's head is lolled forwards and her body has melted into the recliner—she is deep in her desired somnambulistic trance. She pitched this beach visualisation as some sort of reverse-birth—a return to the universal womb. I couldn't resist making it a bit more 'sexy influencer in a bikini in Dubai'. If she must insist on breeding, then let's limit her inevitable post-natal depression to the superficialities of stretch marks and sagging boobs, eh?

I take a moment to savour the silence (as should she before all she hears are baby screams), because now comes her wearisome womb-baby pep-talk...

"You are in the place now, Neve," I state. "Speak."

Neve's head stirs just a little and I note her eyeballs darting back and forth beneath their lids. She speaks in a slow, drowsy way—eyes closed and between deep breaths. To her reproductive system, she pledges to maintain a positive mindset, to minimise stress, and to be as physically healthy as she can to increase the chances of the IVF being successful. To her baby, she promises how wanted, needed, and loved it is.

A monologue about nursery decor ensues. I take the opportunity to rummage Neve's bags for snacks. Last session, I was aghast to find only a vegan energy ball—which I deemed inedible—and so I left Neve with the suggestion to bring something nice today. I begrudgingly devour the 'healthy' muffin I find in her yoga kit. I make a mental note to suggest a full contingent of sugar and gluten for session three—a snack for which she will, of course, again have amnesia.

Neve is becoming emotional about some tiny socklets she's reportedly bought for the non-existent baby. To prevent an abreaction, I make soothing, affirming statements about impending parenthood between mouthfuls of muffin. She rankles at my use of words like 'toddler', 'child' or 'teenager' in imagining a future family— anything that's suggestive of an adult human. I'm well aware that her language is restricted to only 'baby'—"baby, baby, baby"!

I feel conflicted about delivering results for Neve. Is the knowledge that she is seeking to fill a void rather than bring a someday independent adult human into this world worth £800 per pop of my time and expertise..? She likely rejected my last—brief and pretty chaste—suggestions for a date-night with Lars. Perhaps I should chalk this up as a rare failure..? Cancel her next sessions?

But then I reflect on my recent, far more satisfying sessions with Ian... Could a similarly, umm, maverick method stick in Neve's subconscious mind, loosen her up, and prompt a successfully virile fuck with her husband..?

I swallow the last bite of muffin, lick my teeth clean of all that wholegrain carroty goodness, and feel a grin spread across my face. I reach for my phone and prepare to hit play on a special track at the precise moment I pinch the metronome to stop its steady ticking with my fingers.

Tick, tick, tick, t––. Then: "... / .-.. / . / . / .—.".

'SLEEP!' in Morse Code. It amuses me to embed this classic command into the minds of my most controlling and rigid of clients! Few modern subjects will accept such a Svengali-esque direct demand—especially from a woman. But I am the vampire you invite inside in hopes of herbal tea and sympathy. Perhaps, if you are worthy and good company, I will bestow some of my powers upon you; or perhaps you are simply... prey. Time to discover which Neve is...

Responding to the Morse Code interruption, she rouses from her emotional stupor and rearranges herself on the recliner. Meanwhile, I end the 'SLEEP' track and reset the metronome—this time to a much slower 10 beats-per-minute. Neve lays there, eyes closed, calm and neat—falling deeper and deeper into hypnosis to that languid ticking—in wait.

Sooo... I decide to extract from Neve her 'go-to' sexual fantasy—the one she consistently and reliably gets herself moist and/or off to. (Yes, you know what I mean, Dear Reader: *that* fantasy. *I see you.*) Channeling the excellent Dr Karoly, I spin it to Neve that Freud 2.0 psychotherapeutic innovation is very much in vogue, and that this is just the tonic she—and Lars—need to beat stress, fuck more, and bring their void-filler into being.

I sit back in my chair, luxuriating in its velvet upholstery, watching Neve's silken mounds rise and fall as if she were deep asleep, wondering whether she'll accept my suggestion...

She makes a dreamier "hmmnhmmm" sound and s-l-o-w-l-y lifts her right finger.

"I'm ready."

***

Neve has just turned 16 years old; a young, nubile, pretty schoolgirl at a private, same-sex school. She pictures herself in a classroom, with a maths lesson in progress. She's struggling; numbers aren't her forte. But she masks this by being disruptive—passing notes to friends, gossiping, giggling; up to her usual tricks.

A brusque but handsome teacher—let's call him 'Sir'—is distracted by her behaviour. He pauses from bellowing out equations he chalks upon the blackboard to call her out instead.

"I see that note is more worthy of your attentions than me, Neve. Care to share with the class?"

Neve blushes but chats back to him; detention is better than the exposure of her inability to grasp algebra. Sir flushes at her impudence—this has become a pattern with this problem student. He marches up to young Neve's desk and stares down at her. She shoots him a defiant look back and, sure enough, is dismissed from class, on orders to report to his study after school for detention.

Cut to Sir's study—all wood panelling, bottle-green leather, and shelves filled with fusty books. He sits at his grand desk glowering at Neve, who is sat in the chair opposite. He rails against her rebellious streak and the lack of discipline in her life. His face is flushed with crossness and his manner is agitated. Neve feels small and intimidated, but masks by answering back sarcastically.

BAM! Sir bangs his fist on his desk and rises abruptly. He's at the end of his tether with young Neve... and has no choice but to... teach her a lesson.

He moves to her side of the desk, looming over her. Neve becomes conscious that he might be able to glimpse down her blouse to her blossoming little breasts from this angle.

She shrinks into her seat, and lowers her gaze, but Sir moves closer.

"Stand up, Neve. I said: stand up!"

She rises to her feet, unsure what is to happen next.

Sir pulls the chair she was seated on out the way.

"Lean forward and place your hands on the desk."

She feels frozen to the spot. She'd heard rumours of some teachers using corporal punishment from older girls, but she can't believe..? Is this really..? Is he really going to..?

Sir's hand is on her back, guiding her forwards. Her hands instinctively grip the edge of the desk—and there she is: leaning onto the desk, her pert bottom forced outwards and upwards beneath her pleated grey skirt, awaiting her punishment.

Sir solemnly takes a long wooden ruler and makes a short statement about how he doesn't want to resort to such draconian measures as this, but girls like young Neve must be schooled.

Then... Sir beats her 10 times across the buttocks with his ruler. Thwack! Thwack! Thwack! The pain is dull—the blows administered over the skirt. But Neve smarts from the humiliation. Hot tears well in her eyes, and she pants and gasps to keep her emotions in check while the ruler bears down on her backside.

Having dispensed the last strike, Sir composes himself, and then instructs Neve to stand and face him. He sees the wetness in her eyes and offers words of comfort that she can, and must, mend her wicked ways.

Neve gathers her things and leaves detention. Her bottom feels warm and tingly, and she must have sweated into her panties from the experience. She feels something inside of her has stirred... Maybe this means she'll be a good pupil now and not provoke Sir's anger?

***

Oh, how Neve tried to apply herself and not be cheeky to teachers when she doesn't grasp the work! But now, here she is, back in Sir's study. Him, quaking in anger at her impudence... Her, palms pressed flat on the desk, her body leaning forwards, and her round little bottom ready for the ruler...

Sir sternly informs her that he must resort to more extreme measures for a pupil as troublesome as she.

Neve sees him reach—not for the long wooden ruler—but a short, flexible, plastic one..?

"Hitch up your skirt, Neve. Hitch up your skirt!"

Neve takes a moment to process the order. Then, hesitatingly, reaches one hand back to the hem of her grey pleated skirt. She eases it up just an inch, unsure if this is really what he means.

"Yes. Yes. Good girl. Right up."

She grapples the fabric up in her fist and draws her skirt up, revealing her lily-white thighs and white cotton panties. She takes in a breath as she feels her teacher's eyes upon her backside.

Rap! Rap! Rap! The ruler smacks against her, again and again. It stings her flesh, the thin cotton of her knickers offering no protecting from its bites. She gasps with each of the 10 strikes she is expecting, her flesh hot and her eyes hotter with forming tears.

But Sir seems dissatisfied with his work; he suddenly pulls her a little farther backwards, pushing her bottom up yet more. Then he pulls one side of her knickers a little further aside, exposing more of her bare buttock cheek. Rap! Rap! Rap! Three more quick, sharp, hard strikes of the ruler.

Neve gives a little cry and her quaking legs almost give way. She grips the desk hard with one hand and her skirt with the other as Sir dispenses two final slaps. The crotch of her displaced panties chafes against her innocent pussy as she moves with the blows.

Sir places the ruler back into his pen pot and places a comforting hand on the small of Neve's back. His voice is kindly as he encourages her to straighten her appearance and quell her tears; this is all in her best interests; this school has saved many a young girl like Neve from their wayward ways with bodily punishment.

As Neve clutches up her things, she thinks she notices something different about Sir—something about the shape in his trousers...

She hurries out his study—and out the school gates. The cool spring air feels good on her skin, soothing not only her smarting thighs and buttocks, but also the heat that seems to be radiating through her whole body... She scans her body for the source of these hot throbs...

And she realises: her panties are sopping wet, too.

***

Neve manages a full fortnight of model behaviour... until a minor school uniform infraction catches Sir's attention in the hallway on the way back from mid-morning break. Neve spends all day wondering what her after-school detention might entail—surely an untucked shirt is worthy of gentler punishment than her failings in class?

Soon the bell strikes 3.45 and, while her fellow pupils spill out the school, Neve reports to Sir's study. She knocks on the door.

"Enter."

She finds Sir sitting at his desk marking workbooks. Closing the door behind her, she senses with relief that he seems to be in a neutral mood. Perhaps she is right about this minor misstep; perhaps he'll just give her a telling off and make her write lines..?

"Ah, Neve. Yes, yes," he says, appraising her over his reading glasses. Neve smooths her shirt, paranoid that it may have become untucked again.

"You've been such a good girl in class that I'd hoped not to have to summon you here again, Neve. But then I see you, running the halls of this fine institution looking dishevelled... looking like... like a... like a—slut!"

He spits the word at her, full of his usual ire now, and rises from his chair to approach her.

"Is that what you are, Neve? A slut?"

Hot tears blister in Neve's eyes... but she feels a hot pang of anticipation course through her body, too. She can't answer—just shakes her head in a confused, weak protest.

Sir places his glasses on the desk and strides to face her. He towers over her, taking her chin in his large hand to have her look up at him. His eyes scan her face, and then move down to her chest and down over her body. Neve feels penetrated by his gaze, yet strangely soothed by his commanding touch.

"Yes. That's what you are. A slut. I shall have to teach you what a bad little slut you are—before you're ruined by all those boys you'll be sucking and fucking this summer. Yes, I know girls like you—sluts, and only just 16. I shall teach you a lesson so you don't let those boys ruin you."

The words 'sucking and fucking' stab in Neve's mind and body. She has barely kissed a boy, but she has crushes and curiosity... She touches herself at night, revivifying gossip of what other, older girls get up to with the local boys they hang out with at the park. What if she is... a slut..?

Sir seems to sense this epiphany, withdrawing his hand from her face and giving her a little nod.

"Now. Get down on your knees."

Neve searches his face, unsure, hesitant.

"Kneel down, please, Neve. In front of me. Kneel down."

Neve sinks down to the ground. She faces his crotch, seeing his shape—that swollen bulge—and feeling his musty, insistent warmth radiating towards her lips.

'Sucking...'

She has stroked herself til she pulsated—exploded—with accidental pleasure imagining herself in gossiped-about teen fumbles... blowjobs. And now she realises how Sir intends to punish her. But he is a man, not a boy? How..? What if..? Do you..?

Neve's panicked mind is silenced as Sir reaches for his belt. She stares, mesmerised, as he unbuckles himself, bursts the fastening of his trousers apart... and slowly unzips himself. Neve gasps as he reaches inside his underwear—and releases his hard, throbbing manhood. It is bigger and scarier than she imagined, but also alluring. It bobs before her: pink, veiny, pulsating.

Sir moves forwards a little, causing the tip of his penis to brush her awestruck lips. She feels heat and a dab of wetness on her lips, and draws back in shock. She licks her lips—salty?

Sir strokes his big fingers through the back of her hair, easing her head—her rosy lips—back towards his cock.

"Take me in your mouth, Neve."

His penis nudges against her lips; she parts them just a little, remembering the thrill of a boy's tongue exploring, penetrating, her mouth when they kissed at a party—the thrill of him being inside her... She sighs at the memory and feels her panties getting damp. At this momentary lapse into a sweet memory, Sir slides himself inside her mouth. Shocked, Neve grips the backs of his muscular thighs at this invasion; but Sir grips the back of her head, gently but firmly, pushing more of himself inside. She can feel there's still so much of his manhood outside her mouth that she fears she might gag.

"Relax. Relax. Take as much of me into your mouth as you can. Show me that you don't want to be ruined by all those boys."

He thrusts himself back and forth slightly, Neve's saliva coating his manhood and her stretched lips, making this first inch or two of him easier to accept the more slick he and she become. He encourages her head to move to his rhythm, and soon she surrenders to sucking him, relaxing into it, noticing the coarse dark fuzz of his hair and his heavy, slapping balls. Sensing this moment, Sir drives a little more of himself into her mouth, holding her head steady until she grows comfortable with this next half-inch.

And so this continues: Sir's still-swelling manhood filling her mouth more and more; each time, Neve sure she can take no more; then her mouth and throat yielding to the jolts of his body and her head; her lips sliding faster; his penis sliding deeper. But now his thrusts are becoming erratic—too fast, too deep—and he pants and gasps while holding her head against him. Neve gags and tries to pull back; to break free. But he gives three... four... five final big thrusts into her mouth and lets out a cry—then she feels his manhood throbbing violently before the back of her mouth fills with his hot, sticky saltiness.

Sir strokes her head as he pulls back a little.

"Swallow me. Swallow me. Good girl."

Neve swallows, the motion causing her tongue to ripple back against his still sensitive tip. He makes a gasp and she pangs at this tiny sense of agency; of having given pleasure. Sir tugs backwards, her lips and jaw slackening as he withdraws from her sloppy, used mouth. She remains on the floor, on her knees, watching as he fastens himself away, marvelling that she took a grown man's penis so ably into her mouth. She feels proud, electrified, alive—different.

Sir finishes buckling his belt and then extends a hand to help her back onto her feet. She blinks up at him as he wipes off her wet lips, cheeks, and chin.

He tells her that she is, by nature, a slut, but that he won't stand to see her ruined by all those boys she'll be otherwise going with this coming summer. She is to report to his study for detention every Tuesday and Thursday til the end of the school year.

"You're dismissed, Neve."

She plucks her bag and jacket from the floor where they lay beside her while she knelt for him, and goes to leave.

"Oh, and Neve," he says as she touches the doorknob. "Do you touch yourself? Down... there?"

He flicks his eyes down to her crotch. Her face flushes, giving her away—perhaps giving away how her virgin pussy is a hot, slick inferno right now, too.

"You won't touch yourself again until I'm done with you," Sir commands. "You understand me, Neve?"

Neve nods and leaves—her punishment for today complete.

She lies in bed that night, tossing and turning. There are four more weeks of this school year left, and Thursday is just two days away. She rolls onto her side, hugging at her pillow and hooking her legs around her duvet. The pressure between her thighs feels so good... She rocks against it so softly and slowly, longing for that sweet release—only now knowing that there are greater pleasures than the mere strokes of her fingertips can provide.

Besides, she fears that Sir will know, *just know*, that she disobeyed him—that she is the slut he suspects her to be...

She kicks the duvet back over her body and waits for sleep to come.

***

Soon enough it is Thursday's detention, and young Neve finds herself bent over Sir's body on her hands and knees on the battered old chaise longue in his study.

He has hitched Neve's skirt up over her backside and is alternatively spanking and stroking her bottom over her cute cotton panties. He reminds her what a bad girl she is, what a little slut she is, between each stroke-spank.

Neve is fixated on the bulge in Sir's trousers—so tantalisingly close to her mouth. She wonders: will today's punishment allow her to revisit that first confusing encounter she has been thinking about almost non-stop since..?

Yes, yes! Sir frees himself from his clothing amidst his admonishments. ("See what you do to me, you little slut! I must teach you a lesson! You must be punished!") Neve gasps at the sight of his manhood. It is different somehow from this angle... Bigger, prouder, more explorable..?

Sir strokes her hair with his free hand, but, concerned he will take charge of her head, she shakes him off: she wants to savour him for herself this time.

Slowly, hesitatingly, Neve moves her mouth down towards the eye of his penis—it winks expectantly at her, while his shaft and balls twitch and writhe. Neve pokes out her tongue and traces it across the tip. Sir moans and gives her a harder whack... but then a tender and longer caress to soothe it. Neve licks and licks, pokes and circles—getting to know him with her curious tongue; on her own terms.

Sir's slaps and admonishments soften to caresses as the licks become longer and languid, relaxing into a light sucking. Soon Neve is rewarded with him skimming his fingers across her crotch. She feels her wetness saturating her panties, and those parts she alone has touched swelling with each casual graze.

The more she focuses on her own sensations, the more her mouth sinks instinctively around his manhood. How quickly Neve's head is bobbing confidently up and down in tune with the subtle motions of his hips, while her hips grind frustratedly at his whispering touches. She feels she could explode at the lightest real touch; yet it is Sir who explodes once again into the depths of her swallowing mouth.

He sends her on her way—with, again, the instruction not to touch herself 'down there'.

***

And so the next three or four detentions continue. Neve, always in the same position, suckling longingly on his penis; he, administering spanks, caresses, and verbal reprimands—now with her white cotton panties around her ankles and his light finger-grazes probing more intimately. Her legs quiver and quake as he skilfully avoids that pinnacle of pleasure of her pussy; she motions to touch it herself, such is her wild delirium. This attracts a particularly brutal array of spanks on her bare ass, causing her to gasp and gag on Sir's cock.

Suddenly, his fingers are circling the middle of her pussy. Neve knows the basics of sex—has heard the gossip about fingering and this kind of masturbation—but she still finds tampons a scary body-shock. And yet she convulses at the thought of Sir touching her in this way; a conflict that erupts within her as her mind cannot catch up with a body that is pushing back on his fingers—a naïve but alive body wanting to be felt, filled, fulfilled.

"Such a little slut, wanting me inside you."

With that, Sir plunges one finger deep inside her pussy— just as he pushes her head hard and deep onto his cock, gagging and choking her with his fat, throbbing penis.

"You think you want me inside you; a man inside a girl! You can't even take my cock fully inside your mouth. But I can feel how much you like me fucking you with my finger, you little slut. Bad girl... Suck me, suck me! And I'll fuck you with my finger, like all those boys you fantasise about."

Neve fucks back against his finger, feeling the tight stretch around it and the deep new sensations within her, as she gorges on his cock. He explodes loud and hard and endlessly into her mouth, and she swallows him deep; him stroking and clutching at her hair as she emerges gasping and rocking against his fingers.

For a moment, Sir seems to wane—his digit not returning her insistent thrusts. And here is Neve so close to something spectacular; sensations so new and inevitable.

Sir beholds this sight, of such a beautiful young thing fucking against his soaked wet finger. He grabs her nearside hip with the hand that had been holding her head, and... drives a second finger inside her tight little cunt.

Neve cries with shock and pleasure, and eases back into this new invasion. She feels Sir press down and forwards inside her; the pressure is exquisite—him holding her hips and swirling his curl of big, strong fingers in and out of her. She rocks and rocks and rocks against him, until the moment comes—it is like something she never experienced before; nothing like her bedroom touches. Her mind and body are one giant firework of bliss and satisfaction, leaving her a gasping, shuddering wreck as the explosion subsides.

When she is finally quiet and still against his fingers, Sir withdraws them and gently pulls her panties back up from around her ankles. He motions for her to sit beside him, instructing her to redress him—which she does—and to lick his fingers, wet with her juices, clean. As she sucks away her strange sweetness she notices she still does not feel fully satiated and wishes Sir would touch her again.

Sir returns to his desk and wordlessly resumes marking workbooks. Neve is confused: how could she have displeased him?

She slips silently out the room... resisting the urge to rush to the girls' loos and touch herself until those fireworks happen a second time, instead heading home to keep her no-touching promise til next time.

*** *

Neve returns to Sir's study on Thursday filled with trepidation—and tingling from head-to-toe. Tuesday and Wednesday night were torturous, abstaining from herself. She longs for the latest escalation in her slutty lessons...

But she finds Sir at his desk in a sour mood. Barely acknowledging her, he simply indicates for her to sit opposite him where a pen and a stack of paper are already laid out on the desk.

"You will spend today's detention writing out lines, Neve," Sir says whilst still scribbling marks and comments in workbooks. "Write the message on the board, 500 times."

Neve gawks at him; not even a spanking?! She shifts in her chair, crossing and uncrossing her legs, itching with frustration; yearning for the touch she experienced just two days ago. Just to take him in her hungry mouth and vicariously experience his pleasure would suffice. Or merely to feel his eyes on her...

Sir reaches for the long wooden ruler that rests beside his blackboard and her pussy beats with hope. But he simply taps the line he has chalked on the blackboard: 'I AM A

SLUT'. Then he returns his attentions to the pile of workbooks.

Neve frowns and then, picking up pen and paper, resides herself to her fate.

I AM A SLUT.

I AM A SLUT.

I AM A SLUT...

***

Today is the Tuesday of the last week of this school year. The girls are rowdy at the prospect of summer freedom; but not young Neve. She sleepwalks through the day's lesson, and barely manages a wan smile at friends' chatter about parties and boys. She traipses off to her usual detention wondering what the consequences would even be should she skip it. She cannot bear the withdrawal of Sir's attentions.

She knocks on his door and waits to be summoned, before entering and closing the door behind her. She finds Sir sat on the chaise longue beside an older girl—Jessica— who she recognises from sixth form. Neve is taken aback by another girl's presence, but Jessica returns a blank look and sits passively beside Sir.

"Ah, yes, Neve. Come in, come in. Drop your bags down there. Your jacket, too. Take a seat in my chair, please. Yes, behind the desk, right there. There's something I want you to see."

Neve sits in his imposing leather swivel chair, feeling very small within it—and smaller still in Jessica's surprise presence.

"Each year I select a pupil in need of my special tutorage," Sir says for Neve's benefit but while appraising Jessica. "Jessica was much like you, Neve, at your age; showing all the signs of making poor choices. But she has been receptive to my lessons—she's a good girl, a very good girl. And this is her final lesson now that she's 18; she leaves school this week and will be at university soon."

Sir leans in—and tenderly kisses Jessica's lips. Neve's lips burn with envy, above and below. She wonders if they've kissed before; sensing not, from how breathless and eager Jessica seems.

"I'm so proud of you, Jessica," Sir tells her. "You've waited so long for this, haven't you?"

Jessica nods, hungry for another kiss.

"Take off your clothes, Jessica."

Jessica hesitates and glances towards Neve.

"Ignore her. Stand and remove your clothes. I wish to see you one last time."

Jessica rises from the chaise longue and slowly peels off her school uniform. She unbuttons her white blouse and shakes it off, dropping it to the floor; next, she eases down her grey skirt and pulls off her shoes and socks. She stands there in a pale bra and—Neve notes—fashionably patterned lacy knickers. Her breasts are fuller than Neve's; her hips wider, too. She looks beautiful—like a woman.

Sir nods in encouragement. Jessica unhooks her bra, baring her pert breasts and large nipples. Then she shimmies down her knickers, exposing a frizz of blondish pubic hair that's been neatly trimmed. She caresses a breast with one hand and strokes the curve of her stomach with her other.

Sir looks her over appreciatively. Then extends a hand, which she takes, pulling her onto his lap, her legs splayed above his bulging groin, her arms clasped steady behind his neck. Sir kisses her deeply, passionately, before his mouth kisses and licks and nips its way down to her breasts.

Neve watches as he suckles at Jessica's hard nipples, longing for her little titties to develop so beautifully. She writhes slightly in the chair—wet and mesmerised.

Sir teethes at Jessica's nipple while his hand squeezes her other nub. Meanwhile, his free hand snakes down her side, taking in the contours of her hip, ass cheek, and thigh. Jessica begins to rock and moan as his hand caresses her stomach and then slips down between her legs.

Neve wonders at the sight of his hand working the front of her pussy; Neve felt his big, long fingers fucking her pussy, but feels she could melt if those fingers stroked, slapped, and clutched at her clit. She watches Jessica's tanned, peachy ass clench and flinch with excitement as she grinds against his touch.

"Would you like to suck me again? One last time?"

Sir withdraws his hand and puts his juicy fingers up to Jessica's mouth to lick clean. She breaks from her near-ecstasy to slurp on him while nodding enthusiastically. Sir gives her rock-hard nipples one or two more hungry sucks as she slides down between his knees.

Jessica eagerly frees Sir from his trousers and underwear, and beholds his glorious erection. Neve can see the careful licks and kisses she lavishes it with from her vantage point; she can also glimpse Jessica's red, swollen pussy as she kneels to suck Sir's cock one last ceremonious time.

Neve envies the sophistication of Jessica's carefully trimmed hair crowning her stimulated parts—and also her more considered sucks on Sir's penis. Neve takes in a breath as Jessica ducks further down between his legs and takes one of his heavy, hairy balls into her mouth—she sucks and tugs teasingly on it while looking up into his eyes. Neve sees he doesn't control this student's head—she seems expert in her twirling tonguing and deep throating.

Sir's excitement is growing, but Jessica's 'graduation' from Sir's lessons clearly is not limited to his pleasure.

"Have you decided how you want me to take you?"

"Mmm," Jessica nods in the positive up and down his shaft. Then she pulls back, wiping her face and standing, naked, before him.

"Yes, Sir," she affirms.

Sir seems to divine what she has in mind. He breaks into a slight, uncharacteristic smile.

"You girls: always so nostalgic! Would you like me to..? As well?"

Jessica gives a nod, and then turns—and walks towards Neve at the opposite side of Sir's desk. Jessica assumes the position Neve did on the day of that first beating; her hands gripped at the edge of the desk, and her ass turned out and upwards. She and Neve are eye-to-eye. Jessica flashes Neve a strange, animalistic look of connection.

"Would you pass me that, Neve, please?"

Neve is shaken from her fixation on Jessica by Sir, now stood up from the chaise and beside the desk, gesticulating at her. She is distracted by his wet, protruding manhood, but realises he desires the long wooden ruler resting by the blackboard to her side. She grapples for it and extends it to him.

Thwack! Sir administers a first blow on Jessica's willing ass.

"One!", Jessica counts out, still maintaining strange eye contact with Neve.

Thwack! Thwack! Thwack!

"Two! Three! Four!"

Jessica's breasts sway as she rocks against the blows. Her nipples are like bullets. She closes her eyes as Sir strokes his hand across her ass. Neve imagines how red it is—how red his penis is.

Thwack! Thwack! Thwack!

"Five! Six! Seven!"

Jessica eases her feet back a bit more, steeling herself against the desk, her head and neck swaying in pleasure.

Thwack! Thwack!

"Eight! Nine!"

Then Sir is up directly behind her, the ruler discarded at their side. Neve realises that he must be about to push himself inside Jessica, who seems to be awaiting one last spank... But instead Jessica lurches forwards onto the desk, gasping in a mix of pleasure and pain, as Sir drives his ample penis inside her virgin slit.

Jessica's eyes open and widen as she processes this new —and much anticipated—sensation. She looks at and through Neve as Sir starts to probe her from behind.

"Take all of me now, Jessica. Don't resist. I am a man and you are a woman now—not a girl, hmm?"

He grips Jessica's shoulder as he nestles himself fully inside her. She writhes against him, accommodating his manhood and becoming more and more aroused. Sir fucks her, gently but determinately—Neve can hear his balls slapping against Jessica's upper thighs; she can feel their smell hanging in the air.

Neve imagines what it must feel like to be in Jessica's body; to have craved this moment for two more school years. As if manifesting Neve's fantasy, Jessica cries out and collapses forwards onto the desk, exploding with pleasure. Her arms flop forwards uselessly as she experiences wave after wave of aftershock, Sir gripping round her belly to keep her upright as he continues his rhythmic fucking.

She remains like a rag-doll until Sir reaches beneath her belly to the tip of her pussy. He starts to massage her there, making her regain her senses—as well as her grip on the desk. Her face is rosy and ruddy; her mouth making a surprised 'O' shape as Sir milks her for more pleasure than she was expecting. He reaches forwards to grasp a breast with his spare hand, rolling her hard nipple roughly through his finger tips—as if showing Neve what he is doing to that pearl between Jessica's legs...

She starts to convulse again just as Sir's thrusts become faster and more insistent. Neve knows this moment from her sucking the manhood that is now buried so deeply inside this girl's pussy. Sir's fingers dance between Jessica's quaking legs as he explodes inside her; him holding her steady around the shoulder as he rubs her to another glorious climax.

Jessica and Sir pant before Neve at the desk, a conjoined beast, with Jessica still jutting her hips back against her teacher and still grinding herself against his loosened hand on her pussy. But Sir pulls back and closes himself back up in his clothing: done.

"Come and sit down, Jessica. Rest yourself. You did very, very well for your first fuck. Such a good girl."

Jessica, stupefied, allows herself to be led back down to the chaise longue. She flops down onto it. Sir kisses her and whispers words of encouragement about how well she did. She still tingles from the touch of his hand across her thighs, hips, belly, breasts—this seems to tell Sir that Jessica has more to give.

Sir glances back at Neve and then arranges Jessica so that Neve has the perfect view. He hitches one leg atop the arm of the chaise, and splays the other widely on the floor. Neve has the perfect full view of Jessica's sodden, flaming, engorged cunt. It is still pulsating from her first but keen fucking. Sir licks two fingers and starts swirling them around Jessica's pussy for Neve to see, his delicious cum oozing from her as he dips in and out.

Neve is frozen in her seat and yet feels her pussy responding in perfect unison to all this. But there are some acts girls of her age are yet to imagine; the whispers from older girls not having reached Neve's part of the playground of what boys—men—might do with their mouths beyond kiss. And so when Sir slides down from the chaise and kneels before Jessica and begins to kiss and—and—suck and —and—and—and lick her slit with his tongue... Oh!

Neve gasps just as Jessica does. Sir bores his tongue in deep, lapping at Jessica's raw insides. Then he pauses...

"You may leave now, Neve," he says, without looking back at her.

His face hovers over Jessica's dripping cunny as Neve gathers up her things; tears of confusion and frustration in her eyes; hot juices saturating her naïve white cotton panties.

As she reaches for the doorknob, Sir plunges those two so-wanted fingers inside Jessica's pussy. She moans exhaustedly, too spent to fuck back onto them as Neve would so gladly do.

Neve exits just as Sir mashes his face back down into Jessica's neat fuzz, hearing Jessica cry with ecstasy as she shuts the door behind her.

Neve wonders how many times he will repeat that lesson today.

***

Thursday: Neve's final lesson with Sir of this school year. Friday is the start of the holidays and so Neve's friends spill out of the last class ready for summer. But not Neve. She dutifully heads to Sir's study—perplexed as to what he has in store for her.

Neve spent the past two nights in raptures about what she witnessed, so close to stroking and fingering herself to blissful relief. She has been conspiring to find a local boy at the summer park hangouts and boozy sleepovers, swearing that she will mash her enlightened little cunt down onto his sharp, bald, teenaged prick no matter...

But: Sir would know..? *Just know.* And then she'd be denied the exquisite pleasures afforded to Jessica once she'd turned 18...

As she enters Sir's study for the last time this school year, Neve realises that this is the lesson he intends to teach: she will say no to crude, indiscriminate pleasures, and save herself for him.

Inside the study, Sir removes her clothes and instructs her to lie down on the chaise—just as Jessica did. Neve contemplates that no one has seen her naked like this, keeping her legs firmly clamped together at first. Then Sir parts them as he intended; she feels truly naked now—a man, a grown man, gazing at her now not-so-innocent pussy.

Sir tells her he will teach her a lesson to make sure she behaves herself this summer... Then he slowly flutters kisses down her body... and––.

***

"Four, three, two, one! And you're back in the room!"

Not Neve, of course—no, she left hours ago! No, YOU, Dear Reader!

Yes, Dr Karoly will be most interested to know just how caught up you and I both were with Neve's favoured fantasy... Hence me writing it up here for you to experience through my far superior penmanship than as suffered by me via Neve's inarticulate, but slutty, slutty mouth.

It goes without saying that this is the fantasy of a grown, consenting adult woman, and is not to be taken literally. But it always surprises—and slightly disappoints—me just how effective such simple, predictable, misogynistic 'sexy-innocent-rape' plot-lines work betwixt my legs if not inside my brain. Such scenarios are invariably played out in porn from the male perspective, but many a woman's mind rattles with similar fap-fodder, I've found. Indeed, E L James, author of the *50 Shades* series, made a tidy sum from such inequitable, religio-virginal-teen-vampy *Twilight* sentiments. Perhaps the yardstick for achieving a truly feminist society will be fully expunging jolly good spankings from 'Sir' from our minds?

Anyway, you're wondering what the therapeutic applications of Neve's—ahem!—'lesson' could possibly be, aren't you?! Well, after bringing her up from her deep, deep state of hypnosis to a more neutral place, I simply installed 'Sir' inside her subconscious mind. The suggestion I have left her with is to apply this role-play to her current baby-making misery; to transform husband Lars's ministrations into a sexy punishment for their mutual pleasure.

I think we can agree I'm worth every penny of my fee.

***

I write this final entry into Neve's case file some 10 months after I last saw her.

All my appointment notes say of her third and fourth sessions is, respectively, 'almond croissant, warm' and 'artisanal doughnut'. Followed by: 'PREY'. So our main conclusion is that my post-hypnotic demand for Neve to bring me a better quality of forgotten snack worked a treat.

Despite my curiosity as to whether my suggestions took hold, I resisted prying into Neve and Lars's procreation attempts during these remaining sessions. To be a hypnotist of my ilk is a constant struggle to maintain professional ethics. Plus learning of their punctual inseminations, no matter the sexy-spin these would-be-breeders put on it, would just have been ick.

I seem to hazily recall spending these sessions mostly playing womb sounds, catching up on some admin, and congratulating myself on my childfree existence...

Such is the lack of closure on Neve's case, though, that I've been moved to look her up on social media. I see before me an Instagram feed awash with nauseatingly contrived and filtered photos of her 'bump' and subsequent 'bundle of joy'. Why is everything this baby possesses beige? What kind of HR professional throws a 'gender reveal' party in these modern times?! And just how long do you think this plastic-free toy aesthetic is going to last, hmm?

Enraged by the sight of a particularly expensive Jellycat plush (in cream, of all colours!), I scan Neve's feed to see if she's in any way 'credited' me for this debacle. I sigh in relief —amidst the kale smoothies, soothing candles, and Goopy post-cupping-treatment pics, I see she credits a local homeopath with her actual pregnancy. Phew!

So. Welcome to Planet Earth, Neve's Void-Filler! Your mother is your first hypnotist and everything you'll come to think you know is probably wrong... Until, that is, you have a breakdown in your mid-30s and come seek out me and my kind!

Like I said: it's all gravy to us hypnotists.

CASE #143 / KALLIA

Death be-cums her! Accidentally turning the tormenting demon of an insomniac client's bad dreams into her sexy incubus-bitch.

Cluttering up the planet with new life, in the form of Neve's void-filling baby, prompted me to suspend hypnotic investigations of a sexual nature. The titillation—sorry, erm, professional insights—from her, and Ian's, fantasies had faded from my mind and marital bed. Instead, I returned to bread-and-butter, by-the-book hypnotherapy work: comedy phobias and pain control.

But I was bored. So bored, I consented to meet that ex-colleague-frenemy for coffee. Big mistake. As I suspected, she is part of a conspiracy of former coworkers who think my career-pivot into hypnotism is some sort of joke or cry for help; that I simply must want to return to soulless corporate work; to their rat race.

But my career died a slow and painful death—along, as it turned out, with my reproductive system. Yes, early perimenopause was the hidden cause of my varying rages, brain-fuzzes, funks, fizzes, and inabilities. And there I was thinking I'd finally developed principles! Me, railing against capitalism, The Man, and the end of the world being nigh! A real vibe-killer, given my position as a senior marketing-communications green-washer and virtue-signaller for a major multinational.

My final weeks in early 2019 were spent manifesting an HR Cold War, where a regrettable internal e-newsletter I edited and sent whilst drunk was pitted against my alleged experience with a handsy managing director at Cheese & Wine Wednesday. I then called in sick with stress for sufficient weeks for The Powers That Be to give me sufficient money to fuck off. And fuck off I did. The plan was for Addy to support me while I struck out as a freelance consultant. But always-on, always-urgent corporate clients are so very trying when it feels like your womb might agonisingly burst forth from your belly, alien-style... and inflict agonising death, from across the bloodied boardroom table, upon said clients instead.

When the hair on my head started to fall out and sprout instead from my face, Addy urged me to seek medical attention. I'd hoped I'd be diagnosed as a witch. My incandescence to discover that my superfluous uterus had simply run out of oestrogen at the ripe age of 42 was complete. (To the point that I worry that I *may* have next manifested a global pandemic. Sorry about that.)

My HRT kicked in just as the UK lockdown lifted. I saw the world—and myself—so clearly then. Twenty-five years spent tracking and predicting trends told me that a mental health pandemic would follow the physical one. And what else is an egomaniacal-marcoms-witch emerging from the burning embers of her career supposed to do but capitalise on that?

So, as I sat across from my ex-colleague, I saw what small part of me that had come here seeking crumbs of contacts and contracts evaporate like the steam from my americano. Instead, I tore with gusto at my cronut while watching the corporate walking-dead of London, limping and twitching with stresses, strains, neuroses, sadness, and secret button and balloon phobias galore. I'd rather spend the rest of my working days lifting the lids of their crazed brains than write one more—albeit very lucrative—report on 'good capitalism' saving people, planet, and profits.

We parted our old coffee haunt ambiguously. She returned to the belly of that grey concrete beast that once devoured all my time, joy, and sense of purpose. I returned to the spring sunshine of my back garden, where I supped rosé and plotted in loungewear...

My ex-colleague's puzzlement at my refusal to rejoin the corporate rank, but whilst lacking the decency to just fade away as a 'kept' wife, irked me. I am A Hypnotist, not a hobbyist! It dawned on me that my hypnotherapy business needed a focus; a niche. Without one, I would forever be tempted towards forbidden brain-fruits and thus wonder if I'd need back-up work.

And: abracadabra! Within a couple of hours, I'd sent a targeted Instagram ad campaign into the ether, positioning myself as a 'corporate wellness and effectiveness' specialist!

***

That, Dear Reader, brings us to today's 11am: Kallia, a young woman working for a behemoth media group. She responded to the 'young Millennial' version of my campaign by booking up to tackle her stress and insomnia before I'd even opened the second bottle of rosé. Is there a Millennial or Gen-Z-er not suffering such afflictions these days..? Let's hope not, for I've got bills to pay—and a bread-and-butter, by-the-book, sometimes-boring-but-now-risk-free hypnotherapy business to build! Thank you, capitalism. Thank you, Kallia!

She judders up outside my front window on a bike, a bundle of oversized clothing and personable smiles and gestures. I feel more like a concierge than a Svengali as she apologetically hands me a coatigan, a leather backpack, and three full carrier bags to find homes for. She defogs her giant glasses and flicks back her mop of curly hair as she provides TMI about her abundance of apparel and luggage. She was unsure of the weather and is dashing about all day on a number of demeaning errands for her entry-level corporate media job.

Finally, we move into my treatment room and settle into our respective seats. Kallia admires the aesthetic while fussing with her iPhone—it is popping with notifications and I can sense that she's reluctant to silence it. She makes a pantomime of putting it away while she instead flicks through some key messages. In spite of this, I'm surprised how quickly I've warmed to her—she is vibrant, bouncy, kookily beautiful. I wait patiently and passively while she slides her phone into her bag and wiggles back into the recliner.

I run Kallia through her pre-session form; a standard and, for the client, reassuring part of the hypnotherapy ritual—it gives a professional, even medical, gloss to the proceedings. I usually glean clues as to the real root of the presenting problem at this point, but Kallia becomes weirdly inarticulate in describing her stress and insomnia. She fidgets in the recliner and her face becomes dour—I anticipated this session as a simple reboot of her sleeping habits and reframe of negative thinking styles, but this shift in mood is curious..?

I rattle off my pre-talk, where I (disingenuously) explain what hypnosis is and isn't, and what the client should do and expect, eager to hypnotise and unfurl this mystery...

***

"Death is coming for me!"

I've just completed counting Kallia—93, 95, 96, 98, 99, 100—down a long, winding staircase 'into' 'deep' 'hypnosis', when she suddenly sits bolt upright, eyes wide open in terror, and splurts out those words.

My instinct is to buckle up for a thrilling abreaction! But then she sighs, kicks off her shoes and tucks her legs up into a cross-legged position, and turns to face me, quite composed. And very much not hypnotised.

"I didn't know what to say, before... You'll think I'm mad!"

"I have a very high threshold for madness," I reply. "And you can be assured that anything we discuss, or which you reveal here while hypnotised, is completely confidential."

(Dear Reader: lol.)

Kallia looks down into her lap, pulls her legs tighter in, and sighs. She clearly wants to get something off her chest.

"It started a couple of years back," she begins, still focused downwards, picking distractedly at her tatty striped sock. "I get these dreams... But they're not dreams! I, I... Ugh."

"Go on," I say, encouragingly.

"I fall asleep... Or, no. I'm *falling* asleep, you know? Somewhere between the two. Not in a dream yet. I'm aware of my room, my bed, the duvet wrapped around me, but I'm about to drift off... Just like I was just then, with you. Which is why I couldn't... But, anyway, then I... I sense this, this— *presence*. This dark presence, in the corner of my room. And I'm just overcome with, with terror. Pure terror. But it's like I'm paralysed. I can't move. Then I can feel the presence moving towards me. I want to scream, to get away, but I'm completely frozen. And the presence, it's sort of, it's like it's hovering above me. And then there's this pressure on my chest, suffocating—evil—down, down on me. Killing me, coming for me. <u>Death</u>. Oh, it's just––!"

Kallia looks at me imploringly, visibly upset.

"It's okay," I say. "You're safe. Please continue."

She returns her attentions to her sock and takes a breath to speak.

"I feel like my chest will, like, cave in from the pressure. And I'm paralysed and terrified, but I'm fighting with all my will to scream and get away; like, just *willing* my body and my mouth to move. Then it's... This is almost the worst part of it... I, like, turn the light on, throw the covers up, get up, screaming the place down—but that happens two, three times. Each time I'm sort of... snatched back into paralysis, in the dark, that, that... Thing... Him. Death! Him above me, bearing down on me. Terrified. It's... terrifying!

"So, this fight to get away replays like that, like I'm trapped between these nightmare realities. Until I find myself screaming in the corner of the room, the lights all on, the duvet hurled across the floor, my housemates running in —and I'm properly awake this time. I sort of 'come to', you know. Stop screaming. Calm down. The presence is gone— that's the important thing. It's left.

"This happens every couple of weeks or so. I know it sounds crazy: 'Death is coming for me'! But, like, He... is. I, I... That's why—the insomnia. I'm scared every time I go to sleep. Shit scared. Scared to... And the tiredness is making me stressed at work, at life. It's... Uhn."

Kallia slumps forwards and rubs her temples. She looks hopeless.

"It's called sleep paralysis," I say matter-of-factly.

"Huh?"

Kallia looks up at me.

"Sleep paralysis. Your body is asleep but your brain is awake. So your body really is paralysed, and you are indeed trapped between these two realities."

Kallia's jaw gapes as I explain that feelings of fear, of a presence in the room, and the sensation of something or someone pushing down on you is common to anyone experiencing sleep paralysis. That, across ages, cultures and geographies, people have given character and life to these waking nightmares; from demons, the Devil and, indeed, Death, to the jinn, and the incubus or succubus.

Perhaps the most satisfying part of being a hypnotist is witnessing, at your doing, someone's narrative—a powerful, harmful, consuming narrative—collapsing all in one moment. But, better still, is witnessing that moment in their normal waking reality. The former is akin to telling someone an important truth when they're drunk; the latter is potent, real, lasting—but they may not thank you for it, let alone pay you for it. Hence the need for the intoxication of hypnotism.

Kallia stares into nothing, her eyes flicking back and forth as she processes this. She frowns and gives a little shake of her head. Then her face screws up into a sort of comical disgust.

"Well, I... Well, I guess I feel really stupid now! Oh, wow."

"There's no need to feel stupid," I say as I put my notebook aside, kick off my shoes, and mirror her more casual body language. "You're not. 'Death' used to come for me, too, when I was in my 20s."

"Really?! Like, seriously?!"

"Sure. I came across a news article on sleep paralysis one day, and probably felt much like you do now as I read it. It was reassuring to learn that people across time and space experience the same things; all the stories and myths. And that helped me."

"Huh. Hm. So, like, what..? You just stopped being scared when it happened? I don't... I, I'm not sure I wouldn't still find it—it's still frightening! You know?! It's still gotta be frightening when it's happening to you, right? Even if you know, rationally, before and after when you're awake. Like how a horror movie is still frightening even if you're not living it."

I give a knowing smile. "Have you heard of lucid dreaming?"

"What, like, *Inception*-type shit?"

"I guess a bit like the movie, sure," I laugh. "Lucid dreaming is where you become aware you're dreaming while you're dreaming. You can practise it, improve at it. I began by reminding myself each time before I went to bed about the facts of sleep paralysis, and reassured myself I could wake myself up and turn the lights on after the first two or

71

three 'phantom' wakings. Soon, I was aware when it was happening and kept calm while I willed myself to wake up. And the fear, insomnia, and stress went away."

Kallia nods thoughtfully.

I glance at the clock behind her while she mulls, wondering what, if any, hypnosis I can squeeze into this session. This is now just a fortuitous chat; hardly the stuff of repeat business and, in turn, catching corporate monkeys from higher up the tree. Whilst distracted, the words tumble out of my mouth...

"And then you can start to control the dream."

Kallia gives me a quizzical look. "Control it?"

"Well, yes, erm... If you're aware you're dreaming while you're dreaming, you can impose your imagination; shape and manipulate the dream. Maybe the presence is a positive one. Maybe that hovering, pressing sensation from above is relaxing... pleasurable."

Kallia shakes her head. "I don't think I could find that... No, nope. It's too--."

"But maybe there's something you've experienced where that pressure—that restriction, being overpowered—was pleasurable?"

A sensation-memory courses through my body: when now my night-time succubus visits me, he bestows ripple after ripple of pleasure down my body, pulsing in peaks at my pussy. He only leaves when I dream-cum in a shimmering, slow-motion energy wave... Mmm...

"Pleasurable like a massage... or being given a big hug!", I quickly and firmly add. (Let's keep this wholesome, Lilith!)

But I fear something about my faraway expression must have sparked Kallia's search for an appropriate sensation-memory...

"Well, I suppose there is something like that," she says, biting her lip and with a glint in her eye. "So if I connect the two, then..?" She blushes and shoots me a nervous look. "Do I have to, like, tell you about it? For the hypnotherapy to work? I'm not sure I could..."

"No, no! Not at all," comes my hasty reply. "You'd simply connect the two concepts in your mind while hypnotised and, following my prompts, prepare your mind to replace the sleep paralysis with your preferred imaginings. You wouldn't need to say anything at all."

I glance again at the clock, keen to dispense some hypnosis now we've landed on the broad solution. But Kallia rumples her brow and pulls at her further tattering sock.

"But that's... that's not how fantasies work, is it? You have to tell yourself the story, don't you? The whole story, you know? Experience it, like you would a story? At least that's what I... I can't just, like, remember that fear from the dream, all those dreams, and then—what?—replace it with... pleasure. I..?"

I give a silent sigh, defeated by Kallia's innate knowledge of how her mind works.

She suddenly perks up. "But I could... tell you while I'm hypnotised! Can't I? Because I won't, like, remember it—and then be embarrassed about it? Because that's what hypnosis does, right? You forget, but it works. Yeah? Yeah!"

Touché, Kallia. "Well, if that is your expectation and desire, then, yes, you will neither remember nor be embarrassed. And you will automatically replace your fear with the pleasure."

"Okay... Okay, perfect! Let's do it!"

Kallia squishes back into the recliner as I clear my throat to begin the induction.

Dear Reader: you can't deny that I tried!

I'll leave you with Kallia's words for now...

***

I've just turned 20 and am back home after finishing my second year of uni. My hometown's a shit-hole. And I'm stuck here with my mum, stepdad, and younger brother all break, topping up my student loan with crappy waitressing work. I have serious FOMO—my uni mates are travelling and partying, thanks to their loaded parents. It sucks.

So, two weeks in, I'm mostly holed up in my old bedroom, hate-scrolling Instagram. I'm so miserable I'm tempted to reach out to my ex-townie mates that I've all but forgotten—they barely scraped an A-Level while I made it to Cambridge. I browse a couple of profiles—one old girlfriend is a pregnant hairdresser, and the school's rapey alpha-male bully is now a cop. Fuck this!

I promise myself this is my last summer here—I'll get a big-city internship lined up straight after finishing my degree and finally start my life. I will work and study til term-time, and suffer this summer of zero fun and zero friends knowing it's my last.

My waitressing job is at a gastro pub in a nearby village. I'm behind the bar, on my hands and knees, trying to grapple a new jar of fancy olives out from the back of a cupboard, when I hear someone calling my name. I get up, giant jar of olives swilling in my arms, and turn to see a guy smiling at me from over the bar. He looks familiar but I'm drawing a blank.

"Kallia, right? It's... I'm Dee. Er, Dean Tempest. We used to go to school together? I was a couple of years above you..?"

I vaguely realise: oh, yeah. Dean Temple—Tempest...? Nerd. A bit spotty. Hair full of gel. I think we were in a school play together..? But otherwise: Dean Tempest—forgettable and forgotten.

But then I look at the guy smiling across the bar from me. Taller, muscular, chiselled, confident—HOT. You should know never to write off the nerds, Kally—you're one of them!

I blush, flattered. "Oh, yeah—Dean. Okay, yeah. Hi."

But then I recall the hands-and-knees position I was just in on the floor when he 'recognised' 'me'. "Well, hey, yeah. I'm glad I have such a recognisable... arse."

"No, no, I—."

I move to the service end of the bar and start stroppily spooning out olives. Dee follows me, pint in hand.

"I saw you earlier. I just thought I'd say 'hi' and..."

Dee's confidence seems to dissipate, like I've brought him back to the boy he was at school. I feel kinda bad, but my manager is giving me evils from across the restaurant. I pick up my tray of olives and go to walk away.

"And, well, yeah, you do also have a very recognisable arse, actually. It was on maybe my Top 10—no, 20?—Best Arses back in the day..? Hm. But, anyways, just wanted to say 'hi'."

I glance back at him, embarrassed yet amused. He gives me a cheeky look up from my bum, and waves me off with a smile.

He sups a pint while reading a book at a table in the bar area while I work the restaurant. I occasionally look over, expecting him to be eyeing me. But he's not. What is he reading?! Is that Dostoevsky?! Great. I've just been a bitch to the only hot man in this town who actually reads books. Nice one, Kally.

I finish up my lunchtime shift and find myself in the staff loo slapping on the lip-balm and scrunching up my hair. I strategically exit via the bar area—a totally pointless route towards the village bus stop—and see Dee's table is empty. Oh, well.

I wander out via the beer garden, squinting in the afternoon sunlight as I head up to the gate to leave. Then I hear my name.

Dee is stationed at a shady table beneath a tree, finishing up his pint. He waves enthusiastically to me, indicating for me to come. I head over, trying to look cool.

He rattles his empty glass at me while gulping down his last mouthful. Oh, so he just wants fucking service.

"I'm not working anymore and it's bar service anyway, so you'll have to get it yourself," I say, turning to go.

"No! No. God, this is... I was gonna ask if you wanted a drink. With me. If you... Look, I heard you're at Cambridge, right?"

"Yeah. So?"

"I'm at Durham, doing my Master's. And I'm here for the summer and I just thought... I mean, it's pretty much you, me, a few—what?—sports science students..?"

I break out into a grin, and can't help but join in at hating on our former townie classmates. "A couple of leisure-and-tourism kids... Um, does beauty school count?"

***

We spent the rest of the afternoon getting pissed under that tree, talking about our studies and futures and shitty hometown. And we hung out over the next few weeks, too. Just as mates. I mean, I guess we found each other attractive, but we were still tethered to our awkward school days, you know? But then things changed.

Dee's friend Ewan was down visiting for a couple of weeks. They were at Durham together and Ewan was fed up with the damp summer of Scotland, where he hailed from, so decided to soak up the Southeast rays in our depressed coastal town.

Ewan was a rugby lad. Posh. Too posh for my liking. Brown eyes, foppish, reddish hair. That endlessly teasing sense of humour of private school boys. But he was fun and silly—and: HOT.

We started hanging out as a trio and, one evening, we decided to do a film night round my house. Mum and my stepdad were away for the weekend, and my brother was round a friend's, so we had the place to ourselves. We set up in my room—I had a double bed and a telly—so we could smoke weed without stinking the place out. It was a hot, sweaty night—all of us in shorts and t-shirts—with just a cheap fan blowing to keep us cool and, worse, I got stuck in the middle between them. We chatted and joked over a shitty horror movie; scantily clad girls getting stabbed—that sort of thing.

We were stoned and drunk. I provided a sarcastic feminist critique, which Dee chuckled at while Ewan watched us interact. Ewan had been flirting with me, but I guess he also saw the attraction—the tension—between me and Dee... I don't remember how it happened exactly—it's hazy. But Ewan started making comments; about me, my cleverness... my appearance, my body.

I felt awkward... but kind of flattered. Dee tried to fend him off, but that teasing dynamic kicked in—Ewan knew Dee's weakness was his school-days-self. He gloated about how Dee was still the "nerd" around women—that he could never "close the deal". Dee told him to fuck off, trying but failing to pretend he was sharing the joke. I sort of batted at each of their chests with my arms.

"Let's watch the film," I insisted.

Ewan gripped my arm still on his chest, while Dee sort of gently caressed my other arm. It was a weird feeling being trapped between them.

We concentrated, bleary eyed, on the TV—only to realise a sex scene was in progress. Awkward!

Ewan sat upright, decisive, still gripping my hand. He looked down at me and Dee, slouched further horizontally on the bed. We looked up to him, frowning.

"You two should make out."

"What? Fuck off, mate," Dee fired back.

"No, I'm serious. You two should make out. Right now. I'm doing both of you a favour. You're both clearly useless. I insist."

Ewan had that public schoolboy bravado. That white male privilege could be grimly charming—and convincing—

those few years back! And I must admit I was kinda turned on; by Dee; by both of them...

"Admit it, Nix." (Ewan had christened me with a public-school-style nickname, based on my surname.) "You like Tempo, don't you?"

"Leave her alone, mate." Dee turned back to the telly. My arm was still draped across his chest, and his hand stroked down into the palm of mine. His sweetness juxtaposed with Ewan's insistent grip on my arm—and the on-screen fucking Dee was pretending to concertedly watch. I let out a burst of laughter at the ridiculous, hot, sweet, domineering awkwardness of it all.

"I do like you."

Dee looked back at me.

"Kiss her, for fuck's sake!"

I gave his hand a squeeze. He leaned across and kissed me softly on the lips. It was a slow, brief kiss; his tongue shyly exploring mine. He went to pull back, but I felt suddenly bold and hungry for him. I kissed back at him, our lips and tongues building a bit more passion. I motioned to move the arm held by Ewan to Dee's body, but Ewan held it: not captive—if I'd have pulled it free, I don't doubt that he would have released me—but there was some sense that... that he was a part of this.

The actress in the film faked a loud orgasm on screen, which only seemed to add to the sense of electricity and possibility in the room. Dee let go of my hand to run his through my hair and I felt my body yearning to press against him. The actor faked his loud orgasm—but then came a shrill scream. Another grisly murder ensued. We broke off, giggling, trying to dispel how truly turned on we were.

Ewan let out a satisfied laugh, too, and lit up another joint. We passed it between us, both guys snuggled up to me, letting the film wash over us. I put an arm around each of them, bringing us into a hot, sweaty embrace. Ewan brought the joint to and from my lips, then passed it to Dee before resting his hand on my belly. I felt floaty and so fucking turned on. And I could see that they both had hard-ons.

Dee placed the near-dead joint in my mouth for me to take a couple more puffs. Ewan took it to finish it before nuzzling up to my neck. Dee kissed me—slow, soft, gentle again. His hand joined Ewan's on my stomach, higher up. That feeling of two different hands on me... it was... Dee broke off his kiss on my lips and worked his way down my neck. I gave a slight moan and arched my back. Suddenly, Ewan's face was looking down at me and Dee. We both looked up—I guess he was asking permission. I can't believe I did this! But I nodded whilst giving Dee's neck an encouraging caress—I didn't want him to stop.

Ewan's lips were on mine. His kiss was harder, faster, sucking in my lips, his tongue fat and deep in my mouth, swirling my tongue. Dee's hand crept up towards my bra whilst Ewan's grasped at my hips. I was aware I was starting to pant and moan—there was no brushing this off now. I wanted to surrender to this—whatever 'this' was... and would be.

Ewan pulled back from his kiss and I leaned to kiss Dee again. We took turns, three, four times. But they seemed hesitant to touch my body—I longed for Dee to knead at my tits and Ewan to slide his hand down my shorts. Before I knew it, I'd wrangled my arms free and was pulling off my t-shirt and bra. I flopped back on the bed, my arms splayed above my head, in drunk-stoned shock at what I'd done.

Dee and Ewan looked at my naked upper body, shining with sweat, my nipples hard. Dee's hand slid back and forth across my midriff.

"You're sure?", Dee asked.

"Yes. Yes," I replied.

"Yes?", Ewan added.

"Yes."

Dee kissed me, our warm and wet mouths clashing passionately together, as his hand cupped my breast. I closed my eyes, writhing as he gently squeezed my nipple between two fingers. I felt the weight of Ewan move on the mattress as he pulled off his t-shirt and shorts, glimpsing that he'd kept his boxers on. His body was muscular and tanned. The outline of his hard cock made my cunt even wetter with excitement. It was Dee I liked and wanted, but this felt natural and irresistible.

Dee kissed down my neck to my other breast. I felt his breath on my nipple; it seemed to be a moment of reverence for him—about to lick and suck on the titties of his school-time crush. I looked down to watch him tenderly taking my hard nub between his lips, and circle it with his tongue, before enveloping it with his mouth. Then, Ewan was next to me again, his bare torso against my bare skin. He rested an arm over my arms, still laying above my head on the bed, effectively trapping them there but lightly so.

"You two look so good together," he whispered, before planting a heavy kiss on my mouth.

His hand rested on the waist of my shorts, caressing me lightly through the fabric... tugging the waistband up ever so slightly so that I could feel the pressure against my clit. I lay there, feeling Ewan's tongue in my mouth and Dee's on my breast. Ewan started toying with the buttons to my shorts, popping one, two...

"No." I broke off from the kiss. "Dee. I want..."

Dee suckled on the tip of my nipple while he glanced at where Ewan's hand was heading. Ewan's hand obediently retreated and was immediately replaced by Dee's. He stroked across my lower belly while still suckling on my breast.

Ewan shrugged it off with a grin and looked at me: what now?

I arched my back and poked my bare breast upwards at him slightly.

"Yeah?"

I nodded and closed my eyes. Now I had a mouth on each breast. Ewan was rougher—he sucked hard and gave small bites. His stubble scratched against my skin. His arms held me down harder, because of the angle. I liked it.

Dee pulled away from my breast and got up from the bed. We stared into each other's eyes as he pulled off his t-shirt. His body was lithe and beautiful—I noticed the details in ways I had not cared about with Ewan: a mole, a scar, the pattern of his hair. He unzipped his shorts, dropped them, and climbed out of them. I could see the hardness in his underwear and the wet patch of his pre-cum. I wanted to reach out and touch him, feel him, and motioned to move my arm. For the first time, Ewan consciously restrained me. I liked it.

Dee moved to the foot of the bed as Ewan kissed back up to my face.

"You want him to eat your pussy, huh?"

"Mmm," was all I could respond before his lips were back on mine.

I felt Dee's fingers pry open my last button and slide my shorts down my legs and off. Then he pulled my sopping wet knickers down and off. I was naked with these two men. I writhed my closed legs, waiting for Dee's next move. I suddenly panicked about condoms. Would either of them film or photograph me? Ewan must have felt my distraction, kissing and gripping down harder on me.

Dee's hands were on my ankles, spreading my legs. He parted them wider than I was expecting, but I let him position me; expose me. I imagined him there, reverently gazing at my glistening cunt. His hands slid up my calves and inner thighs as he positioned himself kneeling between my wide-open legs. Then his breath was on me, then his lips, his tongue, his whole mouth. Two tongues between lips—mouth and pussy—was already close to making me cum.

Dee teased me, kissing around my pussy when I ground too insistently against his mouth. Why Ewan claimed he struggled with women, I couldn't figure! Ewan was the one struggling; thrusting and rubbing his hard-on against my thigh.

He broke off from kissing me. "I so want to fuck you."

At that moment, Dee slid two fingers inside me, fucking them slowly in and out. I let out a loud moan of pleasure. I looked down to see Dee kneeled upright in front of my open legs, concentrating on my throbbing pussy and his handiwork.

"What would you like, Kal?", Dee asked without looking up. At the same time, he thrust his fingers deeper inside me, twisting them as they sunk into my wet slit. I cried out, so ready to cum.

The words just came out my mouth: "I... I want him to fuck me. Then I want you."

I meant that: I want you. I wanted Dee in the way you want a lover—to know and feel him better. But I wanted

Ewan to fuck me; right then, in this moment. He was foreplay; our sex toy.

Ewan needed no more encouragement than that. He pounced off the bed and dug out the condoms I directed him to in my bedside drawer.

Meanwhile, Dee came and lay by my side. I felt his cock, still concealed in his underwear, hard against the thigh of my still wide-open legs. I realised I hadn't seen or felt Ewan's cock—the first I'd experience would be him pushing himself inside me. My body shuddered with anticipation as Dee gazed at me.

"You're so beautiful."

"Will you hold me down? And kiss me?"

Dee propped a pillow beneath my hips so that he could kiss and gently restrain me while I was being fucked by his friend. I closed my eyes, kissed Dee's lips, and squeezed his hand as I felt Ewan's weight on the mattress as he got between my legs.

Next came the sensation of an unfamiliar cock rubbing into my wetness, pressing at my slit. I gasped against Dee's mouth as I felt this firm, wide dick pushing partway inside me. Ewan thrusted against me, in and out, driving himself deeper, deeper. I could tell through his boxers that he was hung, but this was the biggest cock I'd ever had. He grasped at my hips as he fucked deep into me, hitting my cervix in a pleasurable pain. But he was just fucking my cunt—he wasn't pressed against my clit and so I couldn't cum. Oh, it was torture! And so I was writing hard against Dee, trying to pull my arm free so I could touch my clit.

"You want to cum?", Dee asked between my frustrated kisses.

I nodded deliriously.

Dee slid one hand down my body and planted two fingers each side of my clit. He rocked my swollen part between his fingers as Ewan fucked me harder, faster, deeper. I cried and moaned and groaned as I came; Dee's fingers still either side of my clit; Ewan's cock filling me up. My pleasure tipped Ewan over the edge, with him climaxing inside my tight pussy in mighty throbs.

Ewan pulled out of me, and Dee and I immediately curled into an embrace. I pressed myself against his underwear, desperate to have him next, pulling at his waistband, wanting to know what's inside.

Ewan, cleaned up, handed Dee a condom and lay down the other side of me to watch. Dee eased his underwear down to reveal a juicy, perfectly proportioned cock. I pulled the cushion out from beneath my hips as he put the condom on. Then I pulled him on top of me, wrapping my arms and legs around him. We fucked and kissed surprisingly gently while Ewan watched. Dee's dick a perfect fit for my pussy; our bodies the perfect fit together. We moved together til we both came hard at the same time.

Soon we were all asleep in a naked tangle. I woke to find Ewan nuzzling against my back and neck, his erect cock pressing into the small of my back. Dee roused and I kissed him as Ewan slid a condom on and fucked me from behind, Dee and I masturbating each other to climax. Later, in the early hours as the sun was rising, I straddled Ewan's cock, taking in its whole depth and breadth while Dee stood to the side of the bed watching, me sucking his cock and only cumming when he shot his load into my gasping mouth.

***

Kallia shudders in the recliner, lost in the memory. She is lost so long I wonder if she's done the work to override the terrors of sleep paralysis and should start to bring her back out. But, eventually, she breaks back into her narrative.

"I met up with Dee and Ewan a couple of times over the next week, but I was busy working and Dee was busy showing Ewan the delights of a depressed coastal town. It all felt pretty chilled—like Dee and I were just any summer romance, and Ewan was just his visiting mate. I couldn't wait to be with Dee again and made myself cum every night thinking of how we would wile the rest of the summer away... But I couldn't get that sensation of Ewan holding me down while Dee ate my pussy out of my mind—it had been ecstasy..."

She breaks back out, her lighter tone marking an aside to me.

"Okay, so the next thing happened but didn't happen—you'll know what I mean."

Then, she continues.

"The next stop on Ewan's summer tour was Kent, starting with what he promised would be an epic house party at one of his rich friend's parents' house on the Friday. So we all caught the train and would be crashing on a sofa or floor as best we could before Dee and I headed back home on Saturday. We'd had a few too many train beers by the time we arrived at this crazy, fancy mansion out in the middle of nowhere. It was a 21st birthday celebration for some public school friend of Ewan's and it was, indeed, epic: pool, bouncy castle, hog roast, DJ, endless drinks. I'd never been to a house—mansion!—like that before or since. Just... epic!

"We were pretty fucked up—beer, wine, weed, some coke. You know when you're just getting together with someone and you've got this, like, magnetic draw together? Playful touching and hugs, then tentative kisses that get real fiery? Well, it was like that with Dee—building through the evening. But there were moments like that with Ewan, too. He'd joke about, and grip me in a big embrace. I was in my bikini and him in his swimming shorts, so: his skin on mine. Then we kissed while Dee was off getting more drinks. And by the time we were all doing coke together, we were just sort of taking it in turns again. I was so turned on—I wanted them both one last time.

"It was the early hours by now and Ewan seemed to sense the time was right if something was going to happen. He made a big deal of us needing to scout out somewhere to crash and said he had somewhere in mind. We grabbed our bags and weaved our way through this labyrinthine house. Ewan explained he'd spent a couple of weeks here every summer since he was 11 and so knew the house like the back of his hand. He was sure he could "bags" us a room that "gen pop" would never find. I mean, we were literally in another wing from the main house—apparently, his friend had his own wing?! It was ker-razy. But he was right; just off possibly the seventh sitting room I'd seen was a small snug surrounded by bookcases with a large sofa-daybed-thing inside. Ewan shut the door behind us, casting us into a semi-darkness lit only by the moon through the skylight, and gave a satisfied grin.

"The charade over, we dumped our bags and immediately became a tangle of hungry, horny bodies. Four hands pulled off my kaftan and bikini while we kissed and the boys shed their clothes. I took a hard cock in each hand and tugged at their different shapes while hands roved my breasts, clit, and slit.

"Somehow I found myself lying face up on the sofa-thing, with Dee between my legs, lapping gently at my cunt. I was trying to suck Ewan's cock from the side, but the height wasn't working and so I pulled him across me—him straddling me; 'kinging' me. My hands were trapped beneath him, leaving them free only to caress his tight ass. He teased me with his balls—I took them in my mouth, sucking them gently in and out. He started to tease me with the tip of his dick, letting me lick the taut line of skin below his cum-hole. I made my tongue into a hard point, and ran it up and down. Soon he was filling my mouth with the head of his wideness and I was yearning for Dee to fuck me so that I could have both their cocks inside me, filling me, at the same time."

Here, Kallia shifts tone again—what's known as a 'code-switch', for those of you still reading for purely educational purposes—to signal to me the transition to the aforementioned fantasy within this reality.

"In my fantasy version, though, it's not Dee who fucks me—instead, someone enters the room and interrupts us. All I can see from the corner of my eye is a silhouette male figure in the light of the ajar door. 'Oh,' they exclaim, and motion to leave. But Ewan seems unaware of the stranger and just rams his cock deeper into my mouth. My eyes close as I focus on deep-throating him, us both entranced.

"But what keeps the dark stranger there is Dee. Dee pulls back from my pussy, giving the stranger a full view of my swollen, wet cunt shining in the moonlight. I realise I could shut my legs to indicate my non-consent, but instead I open them wider.

"He says to the dark stranger: 'Isn't she beautiful?' And this seems to beckon the stranger into the room. The door closes behind him, and I hear creaks on the floorboards as the stranger kneels beside Dee. They are both looking at me, really looking. I can feel my pussy pulsing with shy wonder while Ewan's cock slowly thrusts between the lips of my mouth, the weight of him—the pressure of him—bearing down on my chest; restraining me.

"Dee's voice says: 'You can touch her.'

"And then I feel strange, rough, large hands caressing up my thighs and then tickling through the hairs framing my cunt. A large finger slides inside me, then two, hooking up at my g-spot. I give a gurgling gasp around Ewan's cock. Dee's familiar fingers rest either side of my clit, applying pressure but no motion—he doesn't want me to cum... yet.

"Dee again: 'Would you like to fuck her?'

"I hear the stranger stand and unshackle a belt buckle and buttons; clothing dropping to the floor; a condom wrapper crackling open and a sheath being slid on. Dee moves aside and the stranger takes his position kneeling upright between my legs, his rough hands raising up my legs so he can really see and get inside this mysterious pussy he's about to fuck.

"I feel the pressure of his penis against my opening; I wonder how big he will be. He pierces me quickly and fully—he is all the way deep inside of me, my pussy struggling to mould around his length and girth. I cry out as best I can with Ewan inside my mouth. He fills my mouth deeper with himself, staying still in there, as if pacifying me, his full pressure on my chest.

"The stranger fucks me roughly and selfishly, but slowly and deeply. Each time his groin hits my clit and upper pelvis, I thrust back against him and I feel myself closer to cumming. I suck eagerly on Ewan's cock, causing him to start face-fucking me again. The three of us are in sync, Dee watching, the release nearing. I feel the stranger's pushes becoming faster; as he cums he presses against me fully and so I am finally released with the hardest, longest orgasm. My stifled moans, rocking body, and whirling tongue trigger Ewan to explode deep into my mouth. And, oh!"

***

Kallia experiences some sort of full-body, no-contact orgasm while recounting the crescendo of her story-cum-fantasy. Once the convulsions through her body subside, she lays floppily on my recliner, a soft, relaxed smile on her face.

I note that my panties are slick with wetness and that I'm longing for the same release as she. But I maintain my professionalism, giving Kallia the suggestions that she desired—that she has complete amnesia for regaling me with this account, but that she will remember to run this fantasy every time she experiences sleep paralysis.

I have to confess that the pressure of someone straddling your chest, filling your mouth with their cock, while a 'phantom stranger' fucks you to orgasm is an excellent reframing of the otherwise night-time terror of sleep paralysis. So much so, that my incubus will be supplied with the same fantasy next time he visits me...

Kallia leaves woozily happy and relaxed. The moment her bike wobbles out of sight, I throw myself down upon the recliner. Dear Reader, I'm sorry to say that my professionalism lapsed—as did my hand, right down inside my panties, where I stroked myself to orgasm.

I lay there, panting for a moment, before letting out a blast of laughter. I could have simply instructed Kallia to stop sleeping on her back—which is also known to trigger sleep paralysis.

But I think you'll agree that the insomnia cure that I so innocently sleepwalked into is the better of the two solutions.

***

Kallia calls me a fortnight later to cancel the follow-up appointment she'd made as she's most satisfied with her adventures in lucid dreaming. I don't even charge her my late-cancellation fee; she has Dee, Ewan, her phantom stranger—and my incubus—to thank for that.

CASE #151 / MARCUS

Running with it! My foray into the alien world of sports performance hypnosis sees a client 'milked' into achieving his new personal best.

Ugh, I've been dreading my 3.30 appointment today. So much so that I must confess to having drunk half a bottle of a very nice Chablis with my lunchtime omelette to brace myself for this session.

Marcus. *Marcus*. You just know he's going to be ghastly, don't you? Not only is this confirmed by the client intake form he's filled in, but also by how Marcus comes to me: via my Cash Cow.

The Cash Cow is a comfortably well-off woman in her late 50s who counts fortnightly sessions with me amongst her merry-go-round of 'professional wife' and charitable-board-member duties and diversions. I feature alongside spa days, coffee mornings, tweakments, gala fundraisings, and new-fangled workouts, and so on and so forth. I can't even recall what her presenting problem was, to be honest..? My role since she first started patronising me is to provide faux-friendship and positive suggestions while she bathes in what she believes to be a healing 'trance'. It's easy, regular money and I would not butcher my relationship with the Cash Cow for the world.

Cash Cow met Marcus at one of her charity's gala dinners, where the rich network in the name of vol au vents, Veuve, and poverty. He's a banker (told you he'd be ghastly, didn't I?) in his late 40s who's plateaued at marathon running and wants to progress to things called 'ultramarathons' and 'triathlons'. And so this is how I find myself stiffed with my first 'sports performance' client.

I loathe competitive sports. I cannot imagine anything more pointless and soulless than aiding this Marcus man in running, biking, and swimming the farthest and fastest. Sports and physical performance feats pitting people against one another are predicated on masculinity, and male strengths and traits, and so I object to being inveigled into such pissing contests... But then I remember the Cash Cow and think about how much I'd like that new car. Hence pouring lashings of lunchtime wine over my noble feminist objections.

A red Tesla slides into the driveway outside my annex and a tall, well-built, suave man in a suit emerges. Marcus strides into my lobby waiting area as if he owns it, barking greetings at me. He drops his jacket and bag on a chair, and pretends to admire an abstract painting I bought from a local artist that I'm rather fond of, but which he is clearly unimpressed (and perplexed) by. I hang his coat and store his bag, my anger flaring at being forced into this subservient position. It is important for the efficacy of my treatments that this be my space—my power—but Marcus is stomping all over that dynamic with his bespoke leather brogues and white male privilege.

Marcus blares on as I invite him into the treatment room, seeking common conversational ground between me, A Woman, and his wife's acquaintance with the Cash Cow. I learn that he and his wife have spawned three children, and die a bit inside. I wish I'd drunk more wine... He comments on the handsome appearance of the house and this annex, revealing Addy's career as an architect who designed and built our abode. Marcus wonders if he knows Addy's firm and asks if he might get a business card? Then he deigns to ask me how I got into hypnotherapy and how long I've been practising. I briefly respond but can tell he's not really listening, and so I encourage him into the recliner with my hand as I wrap up this tedious interaction.

"Yeah, my wife doesn't work either," he concludes as he settles back into the seat.

I suspect Mrs Marcus would not concur that raising this man's offspring constitutes not working. I wonder if I can upsell him on hypnotherapy for her..? I reckon I could have her serving him divorce papers within just five—no, four— sessions. Something to remember to weave into my post-hypnotic suggestions...

"You might wish to remove your tie," comes my cool reply.

(So that I might strangle you with it.)

Marcus wrangles off his tie and unbuttons the top of his shirt. Finally he seems ready to commence.

And so I start by reiterating my understanding of the reason Marcus is here, as detailed in his pre-form, and pretend to give a shit about his sporting aspirations. Next, I reel off my pre-talk.

Marcus struggles to listen, presumably because of my gender and the meaningless stakes of spending £1,200 on 90 minutes of my time. (The wealthier you are, the higher it goes.) He decides his cufflinks must also come off, and sets about rolling up his sleeves and generally faffing with his crisp, white shirt. Finally, he settles down, smushing his back against the recliner with violence.

"And so if you'd like to––."

"I'm sorry. Sorry. I just don't think this, this... mumbo-jumbo... is going to work on me. I know some top athletes swear by it... hypnosis. But I'm very strong-willed, you see, Lillian? It is 'Lillian', isn't it? I mean, maybe I need someone who those guys use... Someone who's used to getting into a head like mine. But this... mumbo-jumbo. No offence. I'll still pay you."

"Lilith."

"What?"

"Lilith. My name is Lilith."

"Oh."

I smile to myself, performatively and genuinely: I had been expecting this reaction. Marcus does not *believe* he can be hypnotised; and he's particularly affronted by the notion that a woman could hypnotise him. I could, of course, take his money and never see him again. But this would disappoint the Cash Cow—and not lead to me lucratively counselling Marcus's wife through their impending separation and messy divorce.

"You're quite right, of course, Marcus. Hypnosis is 'mumbo-jumbo'—if you believe it to be so."

"Well, yeah. Exactly."

"And if you believe that only a certain person, or type of person, can hypnotise you, then that, too, might come to pass."

Marcus gives a shruggy nod.

"But you're also here because you know that we have within our individual power the ability to manipulate our beliefs, yes? The sportsmen you admire, they singularly believe that they will win—be the best, fastest, most enduring—often in the face of clear adversity and failure. Yes?"

"Right, yes, that's exactly what I want—to be able to push myself that extra mile, you know?"

"Mm, yes. I see and understand completely."

I get up abruptly from my chair and flick my metronome to a fast pace. I then walk quickly over to my bookcase and pluck a vintage tome from my top shelf, flicking through it. Marcus looks quizzically at me. I ponder over the book and then give a decisive nod. Then open and close a window—

my goal is to confuse and unnerve him. Finally, he finds me standing behind him. He strains to look over his shoulders at me.

"You know, since you're a man so in tune with physicality —with physical performance—you might benefit from a more... physical induction into hypnosis."

"Oh?"

"Yes. There's been some fascinating scientific studies. Are you familiar with 'waking alert hypnosis'? People are put into hypnosis while riding an exercise bike—nothing 'mumbo-jumbo' about that, I'm sure you'll agree?"

"Well, yes, that sounds..."

"But you didn't come here to get all hot and sweaty in your suit, did you? So what I have in mind is an 'active alert' hypnosis induction bespoke to you. It will simply involve some light touches to your arms, shoulders, and head. Would that be acceptable?"

I can see that Marcus is flattered and pleased to be getting more for his buck than the average pleb he imagines I serve.

"Yeah. Yes. Okay, we can try that."

"Good. Very good. Then we shall begin."

I wait. Finally, Marcus realises I'm waiting for him to turn his head away from me and settle back down. He does so.

I take an audible breath in for no reason whatsoever, which I'm pleased to note he copies, and then touch his upper arms with my hands before removing them.

"Raise your arms out to your sides, strong and stiff, please."

He does so, flexing his muscles to their fullest—an unsustainable level of exertion that will further work to my advantage.

"Keep your arms out to your sides, strong and stiff, while placing all your concentration upon the metronome. It is set to the pace of a heart at moderate exercising rate. Think of it as your heart rate—something you wish to mindfully observe. Soon you will note your real heart rate is perfectly in tune with it. You may wish to close your eyes to help you better connect with the sound and your body, but it's up to you—you may remain awake and alert if you prefer."

I start to administer moderate to lighter taps and touches up and down Marcus's arms and across his shoulders. He glances back, eyes still open. I tap him hard to draw attention to the slight relaxation in his arm caused by the distraction.

"These physical sensations you will feel less and less the more you focus on your stiff, strong arms, and the metronome syncing with your heart and body. These sensations are the leg cramps a champion runner learns to ignore; the blows a boxer does not feel. You are pace, muscle, and will—nothing more."

Marcus has obeyed my instructions; his head is facing forwards and nodding down as he concentrates on the metronome and the zoning out of my taps and touches. I continue my random motions—sometimes hard; sometimes barely noticeable—and now up over his neck and head as well as arms and shoulders, all while deploying yet more motivational suggestions. I almost convince myself that I've invented an excellent method to sell to sporting knuckle-heads! But I have something more basic in mind...

Marcus's right arm, his dominant one, starts to fatigue and quiver. I press and squeeze firmly on this arm, with Marcus—predictably—putting all his effort into bolstering its strong stiffness. This distracts Marcus entirely from the light taps and touches of my left-hand fingers—two of which now press into the side of his neck... and onto his carotid artery... thus cutting off the oxygen to his brain... and causing him to pass out. Marcus's arms flop to his sides and his head lolls forwards, truly 'entranced'.

This secret of old-school stage hypnotists takes just seconds to work and, while there is a chance of causing death or brain damage (don't try it at home, kids!), it is a trusty method of 'inducing' instant 'hypnosis' in the most obstinate of subjects, of which Marcus counts as one. I calculate that I'm one of the few female hypnotists to utilise this method, past or present, and... and... I probably shouldn't drink at lunchtime because, oh fuck, is he still breathing?!

Yes! Marcus is alive and rousing, and so I rush back to my seat in front of him and flick the metronome to a slow pace. The illusion I'm creating as Marcus regains consciousness is that he's already in a deep state of hypnosis and has experienced amnesia for the rest of the process and the time that's passed.

"...91, there, deep, in your place of power; 93, deeper and deeper into hypnosis; 94, 95, pace, muscle and will—nothing more."

Marcus's eyes roll and flicker slightly open. He becomes aware that his mouth is gaping slightly, and so closes it, coming round.

"Eyes firmly shut, body fully and completely relaxed."

Marcus obeys in body and behaviour—I have won this battle of wills.

I continue: "97, 99, 100. Pace, muscle, will—nothing more... *aside from awaiting what I, your hypnotist, next suggest.*"

I pause, observing Marcus's heavy breathing and apparently—hopefully?!—hypnotised state. The momentary loss of consciousness certainly convinced him hypnosis was afoot. But will the illusion last? I reach out to check he's truly under my spell, raising his wrist between my fingers before letting his arm drop heavily back by his side. No response. Satisfied with this dramatic new twist in my hypnotic prowess, I grab a cold tin of G&T from the back of my kitchenette fridge and knock it back in celebration... and to calm my nerves at almost killing a client.

I sit there, supping on my beverage, mulling what to do with him... What, I wonder, might motivate a man such as Marcus to run faster, harder, and better..?

Perhaps as if his life depended upon it..?

***

You, Marcus, are out for a run late at night. Your feet pound a narrow but straight country road surrounded by hedgerows and billowing fields of wheat and other crops. A full moon hangs in the sky, illuminating you and your path, and stars twinkle all around. The distance is dotted with a few still lit-up houses, but you are otherwise alone. It is peaceful. You can focus completely on your pace, muscle, and will—one foot after the other, breathing evenly, your body and mind in sync.

But you are, as you've been for a while now, dissatisfied with your performance. You feel—you know—you are not hitting your peak. You exert all your will on your body to do better—you force a harder pace, an increased stride... but your breathing becomes laboured and ragged, and your feet and arms lose their elegant coordination. You slow to a stop, panting, massaging the twinge of a stitch in your side, listening to the beat of your heart. Dejected but not defeated.

You stand there in the quiet moonlight, only the rustle of wind and wildlife to be heard against the heavings of your breath and the beatings of your heart. You scan the horizon for some landmark to make your next goal—a side-turning or large tree to sprint hard towards in your quest to attain the very best performance you so desire and demand of yourself.

A strange light catches the corner of your eye..? You turn your head and see a blueish-white light dart and blink downwards from the sky—fast, momentary. 'Must be an aircraft,' you think to yourself as you lean down to tighten the laces of your running shoes. But then the light glints again to your other side, then in front of you, behind you, all around. You turn, trying to make sense of these confusing darts of strange lights..?

The lights grow closer, more intense, gaining both purple and golden-yellow hues, but they are intermittent still. You squint, trying to adjust between the light and the dark. You listen out—perhaps it is an out-of-control vehicle and you need to get off the road? You realise that the world is eerily quiet; there is a void of noise even though you can see spooked birds flapping a hasty retreat from the hedgerow.

Suddenly, the lights emanate all around and above you, and you begin to sense a low rumble in the beams. You start to panic—what is this?! Perhaps you should run..? But your eyes are drawn to the intensity of the blue-golden light up above in the centre of the rays surrounding you—you gaze up into it, mesmerised. Then sonic ripples beat down around you—you feel your body succumbing to these gently powerful pulses. You feel your legs give way and your eyes roll back closed as you start to sink down to the ground...

But, instead, you feel the sensation of weightlessly, comfortably, dreamily floating up, up into the air—and towards the centre of the mysterious lights.

***

You awaken woozily to pure, brilliant whiteness. For this long moment, you are solely your consciousness—you cannot make sense of this blankness before you. Perhaps you have died and this is the after-life..?

It is only once you become aware of the blinking of your eyes, and explore your space and your body with your hands that you reconnect with who you are. You realise you're lying inside some sort of cocoon; you feel warm, safe, comfortable, and disinclined to move in spite of a rational, primal terror that irks you like a fruit fly in the back of your mind.

You realise that you are naked. And that you can't tell whether you're lying vertically, horizontally or at some other angle, which is a most peculiar feeling. You see that key points across your body are flashing with data of a language or characters you cannot recognise affixed to transparent monitors that seem like a second-skin. Finally, you realise your groin is completely bald of hair—but a puff of air hits your face before you can process this.

And then all is black again.

***

You are brought back to consciousness in what seems to be a pristine, sterile, futuristic medical room. You are propped up in a recliner ergonomically perfect for your naked and exposed body. You note with strange acceptance that your arms are restrained by your sides and that your legs are in stirrups, your ankles fastened securely at the bottom of the chair.

You see your flaccid manhood lying atop your bald testicles, wondering again at your hairless appearance. You sense that your ass—your asshole—so widely exposed by your position in the stirrups—is also completely removed of hair. There is that fruit fly of terror irritating the back of your mind again... Monitors over your heart and wrist pulse-points blink, triggering a small puff of air from a device to the side of your head, perfectly timed to deploy as you inhale. You lie back, relaxed and accepting.

You are not surprised when three alien beings glide into the room and surround you. Yes, you knew, deep down, what this was the moment you could no longer dismiss the strange lights as an aircraft. An alien abduction. But you continue to believe in your ability to disbelieve—perhaps you were hit by a vehicle and are now hallucinating whilst in a coma..? Perhaps..? Perhaps..? You find these explanations comforting as the beings speechlessly communicate over your bare, helpless body.

The beings are tall and sleek, with bulbous heads and large black eyes. The surfaces of their bodies seem to pulsate and ripple with energies, colours, and textures—like an electric octopus might. They pay no heed to your confused, imploring looks or futile attempts to conjure words. They simply go about their work—measuring and scanning your body, working as if as one.

A device is placed over your head by one of the beings. It affixes pads over each of your temples and a white circle like the lens of a pair of glasses is flipped down over one of your eyes. You note the being's three-fingered appendage—hand —and the plush pads that pulse with lights at the top of each long, slender 'fingertip' as it sets up the head device. That is all you can really process in your woozy state—these alien hands inspecting you, scanning you, touching you.

Suddenly you feel the strangest sensation against your manhood—you look down and see an alien hand pulling your penis and testicles up and back. A device held by another hand runs up and down your perineum—the area between your testicles and anus. The pressure feels pleasant and novel; you have always prized your physique and sporting performance over simple bodily pleasures. A 3D hologram of what you presume is your prostate emits from the scanning device, which the alien beings scrutinise and seem to telepathically confer upon.

The hands and devices retreat from your body. Another *pfft* of tranquillising air prevents you from concerning yourself with the next part of their procedures. But you feel the stirrups being further raised and spread apart; and a cool spritz of something onto your anus. You do not feel or care beyond this because, now, the headset has been activated. You know that you are still present in the room— you can still see the beings conducting their tests. But you find yourself simultaneously plunged into an immersive, full-sensory pleasure experience. It is as if the aliens have extracted and condensed the ultimate of human sexual pleasure and injected you with it. Jarring images flash upon the lens above your eye, too brief for you to consciously process, but somehow overloading your brain with every erotic visual you could knowingly and unknowingly conceive of. Your ears are filled with abstract, incidental sounds of sex—the motions of bodies moving, of masturbation, of skin against skin. Smells and tastes flood your senses, too—sweat, dirty sheets, the sweetness of cunt, the saltiness of semen... Your whole body quakes with the sensations of both touching and being touched. You are the most turned on you've ever been in your life, and feel on the edge of some ecstatic release that you cannot fathom.

And, then, just like that, your head device deactivates. The stimulation of your senses dissipates. You pant and writhe for a moment, and then look down—your penis is standing proud and pinkly swollen in desperate arousal, buoyed by your nude, twitching, bursting balls. Just as you process this reaction, a being approaches with a tubular device open at the front and with a cupping section affixed to the bottom of its rear. One of the beings places your testicles comfily into the cup and positions the tube against your pole-like penis. Then, with a swish of the being's illuminated digits, the tube closes tightly around your cock.

You gasp in fear as well as in purely physical reaction to these alien sensations. Your dissonance as to whether you're to be castrated whilst experiencing a suspension in a pre-orgasmic state causes your heart to race. The *pfft* of air comes again and you sink back into the recliner, subdued. You note that you feel cool and light inside—a feeling not dissimilar to the colonic irrigations you have sometimes sought in the pursuit of your health and fitness goals: you realise that your bowels have been emptied.

An alien summons a dish from the side counter, it floating into the crux of his trio of digits. You glimpse a small, sleek, black shape inside. It morphs into different shapes—from slug-like, to bulbous, to a thin, twirling cord, to a fat ripple of curves, and back to an inert, thin cord. Is it alive?! Your panic results in another whiff of anaesthetising air. You resolve to control your heart rate from now on; to keep your wits about you. But, for now, you are docile as the black Thing is removed from the tray with forceps... and the forceps disappear between your legs.

You barely feel the Thing sliding into your anus; it has made itself so thin and gentle, plus your asshole must have been anaesthetised and lubricated for the cleansing of your colon. You lay there, wondering, hoping, if this is perhaps some new scan. But then you start to feel the Thing—moving, exploring, expanding, and contracting. You feel the sensations and pressure against your prostate; it is as if the Thing is familiarising itself with your gland—mapping it, testing it, agitating it. It dances, twirls, and pulses inside of you; long, short, fat, thin. It is like nothing you've ever felt before.

Your body begins to rock softy as it reacts to the pressure building. The sensation is confusing; somewhere between cumming and peeing. You want to moan and cry in pleasure but are embarrassed and angered by these alien beings triggering—tricking—your sexual response. The Thing seems to sense your resistance; it flattens itself back from your prostate and then slowly, slowly grows in length and girth. You can't help but let out a cry as it begins to feel like your ass is full of what feels like a penis—five inches, six, seven... getting fatter each time. Your mind flashes with rememberings of easing your own hardened cock inside the asses of the women you've been with; the bodily and verbal feedback they gave you whilst you were caught up in your own pleasures suddenly makes sense. You feel full, stretched, flustered, flushed, rushed, invaded—and oddly emotional.

The morphed cock Thing sends pulsating ripples through itself as it starts to thrust back and forth—it is fucking you hard and deep now—and yet all the while concealed, hidden within your body; kept secret inside the tender folds of your rectum. It starts to send out a hump of shape to hit your prostate as it moves. These feelings are all so new and intense, and soon you are surrendering to them in spite of your previously perceived aversion to such an act on you, a man. Your eyes are closed and you are unashamedly moaning and writhing now, indifferent to the gazes, checks, and adjustments of the beings. The hump continues to balloon and press against your prostate as the deep, filling thrusts work you closer to orgasm.

Finally, a buzzing squeeze is added to the stirring inside you. You feel the pressure explode up from your bowels through your balls and up, up through your tightly encased shaft. Your orgasm is hard, long, and plentiful. An alien clicks the top of the cock-cylinder off—it must have collected your cum..? The pod is inserted into a machine that renders some kind of reading. You wonder what that might mean..? You sink back exhausted, sensing the Thing slowly deflating and making itself unobtrusive inside your anus—but not leaving it. A strong puff of the air hits your lungs and oblivion takes you over before you can wonder about that.

***

Next: it's like that no-man's-land between dreaming and waking. Your eyes are still closed and you expect to open them to find yourself in your bed; to confirm that this was all a dream. But then, just as your eyelids start to flicker, you feel this roving, pulsating movement inside of you; a thud against your prostate, as if that Thing were trying deliberately to wake you. You remember that the intoxicating air will subdue you or send you back to oblivion if you start to panic. And so you take a moment to calm yourself and your heart rate, and to check in with your body.

You figure out that you are suspended in a harness supporting your legs, upper body, and forehead. A soft gag is stuffed in your mouth that prevents you from biting. It feels like your cock and balls are still imprisoned in the tubular device. And, yes, the Thing is working your prostate, the pressure—and pleasure—building.

You decide to venture opening your eyes. Keep calm. Find a weapon. Try to escape. But—oh!—the panic and the horror when you do open them! You are naked and impossibly immobilised within this harness, suspended as you are in a crouching position angled slightly downwards. You give some useless tugs at your wrists and ankles, but then force yourself to breathe and be calm—the air-dispenser is indeed positioned to the side of your face.

The creeping feeling comes over you that yours is not the only horror unfolding. You realise you're in a large white atrium packed as far as your eyes can see with men similarly held around, below, and above you. Unlike you, they are unconscious. But their bodies rock and their mouths moan, automatically and involuntarily, as yours did on the inspection chair and as it is doing now despite your better wishes. They have Things inside them, too, you realise—massaging their prostates; pumping them to almighty assgasms.

You notice the man hanging next to you starting to violently convulse. He cums powerfully but with a soft murmur, his milky load shooting into a clear cap at the top of his cock-cylinder where the test pod previously was. You watch as his spunk slides down a tube into a centralised tank at the bottom of the room. The Thing twirls and whirls exquisitely against your p-spot as you see man after man squeezed dry of their semen. It hits you: 'They're milking us! Milking us!'. 'Yes!', the Thing seems to respond, working at you harder and faster! 'Yes! Yes!'

A man in the opposite row rouses from his air-induced slumber post-assgasm and makes blearily-terrified eye contact with you. 'They're milking us!', you scream to one another with your eyes from across the abyss. The man is wafted with air and his head drops down, unconscious. His face reminds you of a man running beside you on a treadmill in a hotel gym on a business trip, who you saw once—or maybe every time you took such a trip. He outperformed you, you think..? Instantly, his body begins to jerk and moan, the whole nightmare process starting again.

Your heart is undeniably racing now. The Thing buzzes and balloons against your prostate in a desperate climactical frenzy for your seed. The air is dispensed with a *pfft* as pleasure and terror collide. You unwillingly cum on the cusp of consciousness; your creamy white vital fluid sliding down that tube and into the tank is the last thing you see before all is nothing again.

***

You are standing back at the side of the lonely country road, Marcus, precisely as you last were. The night is dark, still, and unspectacular. The moon and the stars are just as you remember them; you check your Apple watch and find the time, and your stats and vitals just as you last glanced them. You have the strangest feeling that..? Memories of..? No. Just one of those momentary flickers of nonsense thought. A fruit fly in the back of your mind to swat away. Your will prevails.

A peculiar tingle in your bowels suggests you may need to return home sooner than planned to relieve yourself. You turn and reset your watch to record your run back. A sudden movement in the hedgerow and the flicker of what must be airplane lights in the distant sky spook you. You run full pelt back home.

You have never run harder, faster or better. It is a new personal best. This is your peak.

***

Marcus calls me sheepishly a couple of weeks after our, ahem, probing first appointment. He'd been sceptical, but he's broken his running plateau and is progressing his training. He'd like to schedule monthly motivational sessions until his first ultra-marathon, six months from now. I graciously diarise him while fantasising how to spend his fees...

Oh, and could he please make an appointment for his wife, too?

And so Marcus and his wife become Cash Cows, too. He, being sexually tortured at the freaky hands of an increasingly inventive bunch of aliens piloted by a drunk hypnotist. She, working her perimenopausal rage out on a husband who's developed new bedroom kinks she's sadistically glad to fulfil. I've particularly left Mrs Marcus with the post-hypnotic suggestion that the strap-on dildos her husband keeps buying seem simply too puny and small, and that they must progress to bigger, girthier, beastlier models. Alas, divorce no longer seems on the cards now that things have gotten so much more interesting betwixt these two. But, in happier news, they've racked up so much of my therapy time that the soft-top option on my new car is looking increasingly feasible.

The Cash Cow is happy, too, and keen to farm out further recommendations. But I make sure to steer her off sporting men in future during our next session of hypnosis.

There are only so many Cash Cow clients one hypnotist can milk.

CASE #172 / JENNIFER

A 'future-life progression' leads a mature client into an imaginary sex shop, where she's helped with a very happy hypnotic shopping trip.

I find myself scrolling LinkedIn—that ghastly pit of workplace lies—in the seven minutes before my 3pm appointment. I like to present an air of cool, calm productivity upon a client's arrival; as if I'm engrossed in their notes or my hectic schedule. I sip coffee, look studious, pass the time.

'Productifying' every spare minute of one's life is a pernicious myth of this self-help industry of which I now find myself a part. I keep up appearances, of course—it's important that clients and prospects believe I've cracked such habits. But, in reality, I, too, fritter away plenty of my time doom-scrolling social media to kill otherwise vacant minutes.

I'm ostensibly here on the hunt for the 'corporate wellness and effectiveness' clients I'm supposedly catering to in my ongoing efforts to phase out anything sexual. But stalking people and their posts for common work mental health gripes leads to me imaging myself in their professional skins: getting that promotion; giving that talk; giving a 'brand-ambassador' shit.

Becoming a hypnotist does, indeed, seem to have brought all my strengths, skills, experiences, and ego full circle. But we invest so much identity and purpose into our work. I felt powerful and proud to wield my suggestions amongst global change-makers, no matter my subsequent disillusionment at contributing only to the status quo. I was 'The Great and Powerful Oz'! Only for the perimenopause to pull back the curtain...

As a mistress of changing minds, I cannot help but lament the loss of a larger stage and audience. That perimenopause strikes just as you feel at your most driven, and dangerous, is a cruel twist of fate that I, for one, didn't see coming (or, least, coming so soon). I suppose these scribblings serve to remind me that I am only temporarily diminished—great magicians rise again! That the life I look back on is in black-and-white; the present, technicolour—not vice-versa.

My cursor hovers over 'liking' a post by a grey suit concerning leadership, mentorship, and mental health. I am forever conflicted over maintaining useful connections and curating activity aligned to my services... versus beaming revenge-curses through the inter-web into the profile pictures of The Patriarchy (and anyone working in HR).

Mercifully, I am saved by the sound of a black cab juddering to a halt outside my window. Jennifer, 57, spills out the taxi—a curvy, coiffured woman who still doesn't seem to have conquered the art of walking in heels despite her years of practice. She totters to the cabbie's window and passes him a 20-pound-note with nude-manicured fingers, not stopping for change. Her arms are festooned with shopping bags and a heavy, earthy toned poncho that she's carrying. She struggles to unfurl the locks of long, bouncy hair caught in her worn leather bucket bag. She practically staggers to my door, laden, yet proud, like a refugee of privilege.

Jennifer's entrance ends my malevolent beamings into a former manager's portrait pic and her bullshit post about diversity, inclusion, and equality goals. I stand to accept the two air kisses Jennifer instigated last session that is clearly now A Thing. She greets me as a friend and confidante, fussing through her bags for an artisanal aromatherapy candle she's picked up that I simply must smell. She gives up, dumping her cargo behind my desk as the emboldened client she's become, and speculating that my reception area would really benefit from some incense.

I've no desire to turn my hypnosis playground into a spa, but I've got a soft spot for Jennifer and so humour her interior design tips. She, too, is a woman diminished: by marital betrayal; by redundancy as a mother to distant adult children; by Father Time. Her need for a new identity and purpose is hindered by her idolatry of her youth and her past. Jennifer is just the kind of post-menopausal woman who becomes an endearing yet comedic 'ghost', haunting her perceived 20-something 'prime' years, bewailing unfinished business that barely started.

This is Jennifer's fifth visit. So far, she's dodged hypnosis and instead regaled me with the tragicomedy of her life. She's charming, articulate, fragile, and scattered. Painful recollections of her ex or children are batted away with youthful, beautiful, sexy triumphs. She sneakily seeks validation, making quips about her 'tweakments', HRT, wardrobe investments, and sexual frustrations. She speculates what kind of man she might snare next, as if a lover were a choice of sandwich filling rather than a complex, sentient being.

Her constant subtext is: "I've still got it, right? Right. Right? Right!"

I'm a hypnotist—not a 'talk therapist', who seeks to capitalise on, and thus perpetuate, the narrative loops we all are prone to get stuck on from time-to-traumatic-time. But I've permitted Jennifer to tell me her story; someone so committed to the superficial and the feminine is rarely truly listened to, after all. She came to me whilst 'shopping' the internet for that new sense of identity, purpose, and oomph she so needs—unfavourably comparing herself to her ex's young replacement model has left her itching to spend that divorce settlement. She calls it serendipity that she found my over-50s 'reboot' package. I call it targeted Facebook advertising.

***

Jennifer's sense of providence and ease in my presence has, however, lulled her into a perfect state of false security. I cautioned her at the close of our last session that this visit would mark the next phase of my work with her—and would include hypnosis. But, as predicted, she has arrived as if ready to share a bottle or three of rosé in the sunshine—rather than to change her life.

"So, are you ready? To experience hypnosis?", I ask as I usher her into my treatment room.

"Oh, yeah, yep, yes!", she exclaims, knocking back a long, hot-ironed curl that's tangled with the silk neck scarf she's peeling off. I wonder how many humans her hair has been harvested from while she chatters; it is simply too abundant to be all her own...

"It's been on my mind all week. I mean..." She pauses to put her hand to her mouth, pensive, and makes a comedy grimace. "I did worry it was a bit weird. Wacky, you know? Bit scary, maybe. You must get that all the time, though. And I just get verbal diarrhoea... when I'm nervous! You must have had it up to here with me, me, me! All my sob stories. Can't stop myself! My ex always said I get verbal diarrhoea when I'm... Ugh, there I go again! Sorry!"

She mimes zipping her mouth closed and clowns self-depreciatingly.

"There's nothing to apologise for," I reassure her as I close the door behind her. "You clearly needed to tell you story. To get it out of your system."

"Yes, yes, right!", Jennifer chimes in. "That's it. This is like a... a juice fast for my brain! Time to move back onto solid foods though! So. No more sob stories, promise. You know, I was chatting to my hairdresser Saturday about this session and he swears by hypnosis. Lost 50 pounds years back with a 'hypnotic gastric band'. Do you do those? He's kept the weight off, too. If he even sees a piece of chocolate cake, he just thinks of, you know, doo-doo. Not for me, that one. But still—amazing. Then he got his dog phobia sorted. Oh, and he did some business coaching thing—neuro-mind-something with that hypnotist off the telly. Has five salons now, so: must have worked. And he's still using self-hypnosis all the time—to manifest."

I resist the urge to roll my eyes and motion instead for Jennifer to settle into the recliner. She tugs off her tan heeled boots, revealing greying childish socks. Despite her best efforts to present the mirage of a sophisticated, monied adult woman to the world, she's also got a 15-year-old trapped in that body alongside the fantasy of her 20-something 'prime' self. Quite the crowd.

I decide to turn the hairdresser's spurious sharings about hypnotism against Jennifer to aid today's objective. Jennifer has, thanks to her credulous and superstitious coiffeur, had her negative perceptions transformed into positive expectations. Now all I need do is hijack her rudimentary beliefs.

"How interesting," I say as I settle beside her into my seat. "Do you know what method he uses to induce self-hypnosis? A lot of people struggle with it, so it's always useful to hear what works for some."

"Oh, yes!", Jennifer scooches back into the recliner, enthused by her apparent insights. "He showed me. He has a crystal-healing pendant he wears around his neck. It's stunning. Green. He said it was for luck, for manifesting... Can't remember..?"

"Aventurine. For prosperity and wealth. Known as the luckiest of all crystals. By those who believe in such things."

"Yes, that's it. Aventurine. He holds it in front of his eyes, focuses on it as it swings back and forth, and he goes into a trance. Then he does his mantras."

Jennifer mimes holding the pendulum in front of her gaze with one hand while subconsciously clutching at a necklace faintly visible beneath her cashmere dress with the other. I've suspected since day one that she's wearing her wedding ring beneath the soft funnels of her signature knitwear. It's peculiar when the superstitious and spiritually inclined create such counteractive charms and spells.

"I didn't think you'd approve of that sort of thing," Jennifer says, fiddling with her bad juju.

"Just doing my job."

What sort of hypnotist would I be if I could not harness the crude magick and wonderment of these mere mortals to cure them of their mental afflictions—and justify my premium £800 fee?!

I get up and cross to my bookcase. I expected my production of a dark wooden box containing unknown secrets to get more of a reaction from Jennifer, but she seems distracted and continues to toy with her hidden necklace. I return to my seat, holding the box in my lap, and wait for her to return her attentions to me.

I open the box with majesty. Inside are a number of crystal pendants neatly displayed in the box. Some are legit and for which I know their type and apparent meanings. Others are simply interesting pieces of coloured glass or polished stone for those seekers in need of something more exotic onto which they can project their spiritual wants and needs. Their differing shapes and varieties, together with the aged mahogany box, create the impression that this is some old, precious artefact. But it was, in fact, quickly curated from Etsy last year when I first encountered a client who associated crystal nonsense with hypnosis.

"Ooh! Gorgeous." Jennifer leans in to peruse the pendants. I enjoy the waft of her expensive perfume that comes with her movement.

"Perhaps you could select the one you feel most drawn to? The one you feel is sure to guide you into hypnosis?"

Jennifer scans her hand across the contents of the box, as if to allow only her fingers to decide her hypnotic conduit. But I've already noted her eyes focusing on the pink crystal captured in an ornate gold fixing—and, indeed, her fingers pause above it.

"Rose quartz. For love," I say with a wise smile. I pluck the pendant out the box and dangle it in my fingers in front of Jennifer's eager eyes.

"Really? Love? I just felt so drawn to its energy, its beauty, its purity. I had no idea."

I don't believe for one moment that a woman of Jennifer's years and inclinations has missed the memo that rose quartz is associated with amore. But I'm grateful for the speedy, predictable decision—the inclusion of the custom creations in my box of tricks is testament to the ego-maniacal soul-searching the selection of a gemstone has sometimes triggered. One particularly difficult subject was won over only by a piece of translucent polymer clay that they imbued with great personal meaning and ancient wisdom.

I trickle Jennifer's chosen stone into her waiting upturned palms before snapping the box shut and slipping it beneath my chair so that no further existential searching takes place. She dandles the crystal and its chain through her fingers. But she bites her lip, as if still hesitant. My bet is she has some jewellery related lament to share, probably about that hex around her neck, before she'll try to laugh it off with a *Pretty Woman* anecdote from her heyday. I decide to press on.

Jennifer listens to my pre-talk and obeys my instructions to relax into position and prepare for hypnosis. She gets as far as swaying the pendant gently back and forth in front of her eyes, and even fluttering her eyelids as if close to closing. But then she snatches the pendant into her fist and blurts out what's on her mind.

"Past-life regression!"

"No, Jennifer."

"No, please, Lilith. Hear me out. Just hear me out. Because Ferdinando—that's my hairdresser, right—he also saw this medium-hypnotist-lady who absolutely changed his life. Truly. She regressed him back to a little boy—turned out a dog bit him when he was just a toddler. He had no memory of it whatsoever, but that's where his fear started. Said it really helped him see how understanding these scars, the ones we don't consciously know about, could help him heal. So he kept seeing her and they went right back to his birth! His birth! I mean, he experienced *being born*, Lilith! Remembered his mother saying something to a nurse that he swears—<u>swears</u>—she never told him before. But his mum said that's what happened; she'd worried to the nurse about swaddling him too tight. He described the fear of the birth, the coldness outside his mother's body, but then the love and the warmth. Anyway, next they went back to his conception and then to before that. And that's when they started the past life stuff. He was a poor little Indian boy in the early days of the Raj whose daddy beat him for not working hard enough and then pushed him down a well to die. And then he was a Suffragette. And something else that I forget...

"Anyway. The hypnotist-lady told him it was clear that his reincarnation cycle was to suffer at the hands of men—but to endure and prevail until the cycle ended. He's got one more life to live, apparently. After this one. It really, really helped him make sense of what was going on with his boyfriend at the time. Been married to his husband three years now. So I just thought..."

"No."

Jennifer shoots me a flirty, sulky pout. I can see she's determined. I don't believe we have literal past lives and avoid this folly of a 'therapy' because so few people are able to contextualise these imaginings, co-created between the subject and the hypnotist, as metaphor—and a transient and not necessarily helpful one at that. But there's no point trying to disavow Jennifer of her desires and beliefs—a more cunning strategy is needed.

"I know it's not on your list of services, but I just figured I could, you know, order 'off-menu'..?"

She bites her lip again, weighing up whether to confess more 'woo-woo' to me. She decides 'yes': "I have these recurring dreams. Had them for years..."

Yes, yes. I can imagine. You're Cleopatra. Marie Antoinette. A wrongly ravished Victorian housemaid, who subsequently hurled herself and her baby into a lake. Aren't we all, Jennifer?! Who wants to be a tosher or tanner, or a Mesopotamian shit-shoveler, though? And why do the most basic facts of even the most famous cases of hypnotic past-life regression (I'm looking at you, Bridey Murphy) never check out?!

"In this dream, I'm 17 or 18... I'm in a castle... Medieval, I think. It's cold and I'm afraid..."

"So, you're a young woman?", I interject.

"Erm, yes."

"And what do you think you can learn and gain from the past life of this... this Medieval... *princess*—I assume she is a princess?"

Jennifer blushes.

"So, what can you learn and gain from this princess that you can't from your own past? Which, Jennifer, you've covered in significant detail over our past four sessions."

"Well, there's a lot we can learn from the past... From history. Ugh, I can tell you don't believe in this stuff! But it's just, you know, exciting, interesting."

"So is a TV box-set or good book, Jennifer. Look, I'm open to persuasion as to the relevance of the story of a beautiful young women who—hmm... suffers some sort of heartbreak and thwarted love..?—whether real or imagined, if you could just..?"

"Okay, okay, you've made your point. Christ, I've been to fancy restaurants more accommodating than you! This is worse than that time in Venice when I asked for gluten-free. But, fine. Fine. What are we doing, then? I stare into this crystal and then you say nice stuff to me while I'm out of it? I just don't see how that helps me. I'd be doing therapy with Ferdinando if that was all it took—he's much nicer than you."

I can see Jennifer is truly sulking now. If she weren't so adept at making herself agreeable, she'd probably stomp out, never to return.

I give her a playful but mysterious smile. I'm not some chef she can order off-menu from—because she has no idea what I'm cooking with.

"What about... 'future-life progression'?"

Jennifer eyes light up. I can see her now, imagining her young future-self bouncing about a terraformed Mars or technotropolis utopia in a sparkly silver mini-dress and kinky-boots. (Don't think I haven't studied all the 'future-life' hypnotic experiments, too, Dear Reader—and noted the highly impractical apparel women 150 years into our apocalyptic future are apparently sporting.)

"Yes," I lean in conspiratorially. "It's not something I typically offer. But your problem, I believe, is not in your past—it's in your present and *then* your future. You're *scriptless*, Jennifer. So it doesn't matter how many times you run a story—a script—of a young, beautiful, promising woman who's been wronged. No matter the time or place, the pages will be blank beyond the precise point you're stuck at now. So I'm not talking far, distant planets and spaceships and romances on the moon."

She blushes again.

"No, I'm talking this-life, now-life, 'future-life' progression. Jennifer, in our time together, you've raised a lot of possibilities for your future, wouldn't you agree? Holidays, dating services, changing your appearance, selling up and moving areas... What you're experiencing is very understandable. We all have periods in our lives where it's as if we're stumbling around in a dark room, searching for the light. When you finally find it and flip that switch on, it all seems so obvious, doesn't it? I avoid sharing personal information with clients, but, if I may, being diagnosed with early perimenopause was that moment for me. I'd spent a couple of years before that, stumbling around in my own darkness; wondering if I should find a new job; questioning a happy marriage; doubting myself and my sanity. A diagnosis and a dose of oestrogen was my 'light switch' moment. It all made sense. It all cascaded from there.

"But I think sometimes we need to be reminded that the light switch is there. Otherwise we can spend too long in the dark. Imagine the months—years!—of time and stress I'd have wasted on, say, a job change to solve what turned out to only be a symptom of the problem. We wouldn't be sitting here together today. Dating or moving house, or whatever, before you've flipped that light switch on could be like that for you, yes? And I can only see that, for you, remaining focused on the past—yours or whoever's—is keeping you in the dark for longer."

Jennifer's hand drifts from the hidden necklace into her lap. She passes the rose quartz pendant from palm to palm.

"I suppose I'm just not sure... I don't know... what to do. Where to start. What I want." She speaks in a small, lost voice whilst gazing into nothing. I'm pleased to be in touch with that teenaged self inside her; the person she was before she was told she was beautiful and sexually desirable, and would be fulfilled by a man.

Well, I think you know precisely the remedy for that feeling," I say as I cross my arms and sit back expectantly in my chair.

Jennifer looks at me with a weak frown. "But I..?"

"Let's go shopping, Jennifer. For the future."

***

Jennifer proves a surprisingly docile hypnotic subject. Wearing her out with so many confusing, conflicting new thoughts and feelings has paid off. She came here in the manner of a woman expecting to get woozy on a bottle of wine, and I'm wryly pleased to have delivered on that vibe as she surrenders to the swinging pendulum in front of her eyes and my guiding suggestions.

"Your eyelids are becoming heavier and heavier; the soft pinks and golds of the pendulum are a safe blur; you want to surrender to that warm, safe state you sense before you—by closing your eyes and entering into hypnosis. And as I count down from five, four, three, two, and one—yes, eyes closed, body and mind relaxed, hypnotised, and ready for this special shopping experience."

Jennifer's eyes close on command and she slumps forwards, breathing deeply and evenly. I lean across to her and, firmly planting my hand on her forehead, push her back upright into the recliner. She lolls back, comfortably and unconsciously, drunk on my hypnotic brew. The arm holding the pendant sinks into her lap.

"That's right. And while you allow your mind to drift and explore during this session, your hand will remain connected to the pendant, and, in turn, you will remain connected to your body and reality—able to return when you're ready."

I remind Jennifer of the hypnotic context we've agreed: that she is going on a very special shopping trip—in search of some kind of key to open up her waiting future. I tell her that she is in control and will remember whatever she cares to about what we do here today. (A rare occasion on which I actually mean it.) I suggest that we co-create the experience up to a point, but that, when she's fully immersed, she may feel me fading into the background. But perhaps she will encounter other characters and guides who help her along the way.

"I want you to tap into all the times shopping has inspired, delighted, changed, and surprised you," I instruct. "You are here to browse, explore, try, and, perhaps, buy."

Jennifer licks her lips and I notice her fingers rub the crystal. All good signs of anticipation, but I want her deeper than this.

"When you're ready, I will deepen your hypnosis so that you are fully immersed in this experience. At present, your state of hypnosis is like when you start a good movie at home: your focus extends beyond the screen. You know, those small distractions that you're soon to forget—getting comfy, dimming the lights, adjusting the volume. But the next deepener will take you to that place where you're really immersed, really focused. You can still contextualise and comment on that focus—for instance, discussing your experience with me and knowing you're in hypnosis. But you can fully and safely surrender to the 'reality' of your hypnotic shopping for periods of time without these meta insights. Do you understand?"

Jennifer nods. I deploy the deepener, taking her into a mental void of rosy pink haze, and watch as she practically melts back into the recliner. I explain to her that I'm taking her six months into the future, where she is free from her current preoccupations with the past. She waits in this pink haze, absorbing confidence and hope for the future. Then I tell her it is time to emerge into the imaginary shopping place she's created.

***

"Where are you, Jennifer?"

"Shopping, I... I, um..."

And here's my issue with 'past-life regression', Dear Reader—leading questions are always required to extract information. And such questions and prompts lead, shape, and direct the course of the 'past life'. Fortunately, there is only so much potential for my contaminating Jennifer's mind, and destiny, thanks to our shopping set-up. I'm imagining some sort of 'self-love' epiphany; an acceptance of her age and adult womanhood; a shedding of these confections; an embracing of new, independent decision-making; and a conclusion that a lover will follow from there, rather than come first.

"Are you on a shopping street, Jennifer? Or in a mall? Or somewhere else?"

"Oh! It's a mall. A mall."

"Describe it for me, please?"

"Oh, it's huge. And so beautiful. Endless, almost. Shops for miles. I want to say... 'opulent'. Like in Dubai. But dark, golden, dreamy. So many shops. Cafes, bars, restaurants. Stalls. So much... choice."

Given the recent sexual trajectory my work has taken, I suddenly worry that Jennifer is so scriptless—and so anti her ex-husband and men—and yet so buzzing with sexual energy—that she might have the epiphany that she's a lesbian! Is she about to fall in love, and lust, with the first beautiful sales rep to flatteringly flog her the wares she imagines she needs?! I decide to keep her focus broad and superficial as to who she may encounter. This is, I calculate, an otherwise risk-free scenario.

"Who else is in the mall?"

"There are people around. But it's not too busy. Strangely... peaceful. Shoppers, people working there. Everyone looks very nice, smart, fashionable. I'm walking through the mall, and people are drinking coffees and stuff outside a bar. Lots of plants and trees and the sound of water—water features. Oh? Oh! There aren't any children? No babies or families. All adults?"

"I said you might be surprised. Tell me about the people seated drinking outside the bar."

"There's a mix. Young and older, women and men. Some people on their own, a few girlfriends drinking and sharing food. Larger groups. It's not so busy, but there's a nice atmosphere. The waiters are friendly and helpful. Everyone is smiling."

"If you wanted to stop for refreshments, perhaps there's an individual or group that you'd be drawn to sit near to? Perhaps in the hope of striking up a conversation?"

"Well, there's... Um, there's a biggish group of wo... men drinking in the corner. Yes. Men. Businessmen on a lunch. A work thing. A lot of them my age or above. There are a couple who look kind of... friendly. Nice. But handsome. Manly. Oh, he! One smiled at me! Hah."

I smile to myself. Sexuality is complicated and, for many of us, probably mutable if we're so inclined. I'd be delighted for Jennifer to explore her sexuality, but I think we can agree, Dear Reader, that in this case a White Knight of any gender or sex is counterproductive. I wonder if Jennifer will need to be tempted away from Mr Imaginary Right, but she prompts herself to continue on.

"But I want to keep walking," she announces. "I want to know what they're selling at these stalls up ahead."

I ask Jennifer to describe the shops, stalls, and attractions to me, but tell her that she won't yet venture inside any or interact with staff at stalls and so on. I let her know that she makes the rules. The trashiest fast-food outlet could be next door to an exclusive designer boutique; there could be stores housing essential or desirable services, from a health check-up to a fortune teller. There's nothing she's too rich or poor for—any place she enters is friendly, welcoming, and helpful. The only limit is her imagination.

She describes a retail cornucopia—a calm, luxurious shopping mecca of hopes, dreams, and possibilities. Jennifer's favourite stores and brands line the mall, juxtaposed to suit her tastes and whims, with store workers posted outside offering her free samples as if they're handing out the holy sacrament. Cosmetologists, confectioners, and unknown niche retailers pepper the layout—does she want a pedicure, a cupcake, or a splendid new hat from that fancy milliners..? Stalls of silk scarves, flowers, exotic foods, jewellery, and more run through the centre of the mall, catching her eye and tempting her to them. Imagine a perfect mall meeting the dream of a historic, high-end capital city department store, with the vibrancy of an Arabian bazaar. An opulent, plush, soothing but calm space—free of screaming children and fraught families.

Sounds like heaven. And Jennifer certainly seems to be in heaven; it is increasingly tricky to pry commentary from her, so enjoyable is her time in this perfect shopping mall.

I wait patiently for her to finish describing a resplendent flower archway adorning a macaron retailer that's caught her fancy. Then I interject that it is time for the next phase of her shopping trip. When I count down from five to one, not now, but soon, on the count of one she will find herself standing outside the shop or place she wants, and needs, to go inside.

"Importantly, I want you to free your mind of any preconceptions you have about what this shop or place might be. And of what might happen inside. You might be surprised. So, when I count down, on one, you will tell me where you are and will continue this level of conversation.

But after that, you will enter the shop or place in a yet deeper level of hypnosis—where you will simply report what you experience to me whilst being completely unconscious of that action. As far as you are concerned, you are simply experiencing something fully and presently. Do you understand, Jennifer?

"Yes."

"So, your mind is clear and you're ready to see the shop or place you want, and need, to enter. Counting down now from five, four, three, two—one."

Jennifer twitches slightly in the recliner, though her eyes remain comfortably closed. I wait.

"Oh. Oh! It's a... It's a sex shop!"

I massage my brow with my hand. A sex shop! I should have foreseen that Jennifer's fading sexpot façade, coupled with her girlish repression and unfulfilling marriage, might lead us here...

"A sex shop? Like an Ann Summers?", I ask in hopes we can keep this high-street clean.

"Well, yes. But no. I've been in Ann Summers. The underwear, really. I always felt so embarrassed, you know, the further back you got. But I tried to buy a few things, when my marriage was... To pep things up. I never really... But this shop is—different. Like a mix of all those places I've seen. Like the most beautiful lingerie—silk, lace, velvet; racy but really classy stuff. But then there's..."—she giggles, seeing scandalous, mysterious things. "Oh, I don't even know what..?! It's also like those shops in Soho. Where all those dirty old men in macs go. Oh, you wouldn't believe what I'm looking at! I've never seen... Gosh, oh!"

I break out into a silent chuckle, contemplating what exotic, erotic wonders Jennifer is seeing within—fisting dildos and cover-art for hardcore porn DVDs mixed with artisanal velvet whips and Chantilly lace slips. Hopefully her prudishness will keep us from yet more hypnotic sex exploits—she just needs to rehearse the courage to buy a Rampant Rabbit and, in turn, find a nice chap who'll use it on her. Right, Lilith? Right?!

"Just know that your mind has picked the shop you want, and need, to go inside, no matter how surprised you are, Jennifer. Have faith in the wisdom of your subconscious mind. And, when you're ready, go deeper into hypnosis—and go through the door."

Dear Reader, I'll leave you with Jennifer as she ventures now through it...

***

A bell sounds as I open the door to the shop. I cringe that the 'ding' has drawn attention to me. My instinct is to leave, but I see no one has noticed me—the few customers continue browsing, and the staff at the tills are busy serving. I'm curious to see what's inside, so I push the door closed and take a few steps in.

I feel kind of awed by what's around me. It's like a sensory overload. So many sensual fabrics and textures—silks, lace, satin, velvet; sheer, stretchy; criss-crosses of straps and fastenings and embellishments... It's mostly lingerie and... sexy... wear... here, as you go in. For women, but I guess stuff for men, too. Or I'm not always sure nowadays. It's like nothing I've seen before. It's not presented how I'm used to seeing fashion—collections, colours, seasons, mix-and-match. It's like different... moods. The styles don't conform—where you'd expect a pretty floral pink thing, or reds or animal prints... it's as if those standard things are missing. I run my fingers through feather boas and trims. I see latex and rubber creations further ahead.

There's a mix of people browsing the shop—women, men, all sorts, alone and together, different ages and styles. The shop assistants look nice, too. I feel okay, comfortable. I'm realising that the store is gorgeously decorated. It's sort of neutral—warm, soft lighting, plush carpet, glossy wood fittings, deep leather seating areas. I thought it would be that 'boudoir' style. Or, worse, dark and creepy. But this is like... like a five-star hotel. The air is infused with a deep, rich fragrance, and ambient music notes like nothing I've heard before play in the background. I'm pleased that the staff are leaving me to my own devices—I hate when they pester you to help as if you already know what you want, or that they'll decide it for you. I feel comfortable and excited to look around.

I go further inside the store, intricate lingerie wafting around me as I pass through the displays. Mannequins model shiny latex numbers with a thousand zips and ties, or barely there baby-dolls and harnesses. I see masks, and nipple tassels, and more varieties of lubricants than I could ever have imagined existed. I see a section for DVDs and books, just as I reach a display for, umm, spanking filled with whips, chains, paddles, and all sorts. I run my fingers through the long leather fronds of a whip—I wonder that it might feel surprisingly gentle and nice, and slosh the strands against the bare skin of my lower arm. There is so much to take in and touch—my fingers work their way across firm rubber spikes, cool chains, and swathes of buttery nubuck leather.

I move through the store, feeling bold—on a mission, almost. I now know what I want to see—and feel: the vibrators. I've been in a couple of high-street stores and I've always just bought whatever basic thing the shop assistant recommended. I hate that they pester you when you just want to figure it out for yourself. To play and think. I see a wall displaying the kinds of models I've seen before and so I go over and enjoy just looking at the different shapes, sizes, colours. Placards beneath each product give notes on their function and pleasures. I pick one up, wondering how it might feel to hold it against myself. I accidentally hit the 'on' button and it starts to buzz enthusiastically in my hands. I giggle but worry I've attracted attention—it's not quiet! No one is looking though.

I read somewhere that you can test how a vibrator might feel on your intimate parts on the tip of your nose. So I tentatively press the smooth white baton to my face and feel its vibes ripple through my nose. I giggle again: look at me, testing sex toys in the middle of this store! I feel more and more confident, picking up products, holding them, caressing them, testing their different vibration patterns, feeling the buzz on my skin—nose, fingertips, cheeks, lips... It is so nice to explore this place undisturbed. I realise that there are all sorts of weird and wonderful toys and implements around a corner from this basic selection, and that I'm free to see and explore this, too. I weave my way into the displays.

I'm standing in front of a brightly lit cabinet of... of curiosities..? It looks more like a collection of beautiful crystals, geodes, arty stuff than sex toys—they seem to be made from coloured glass, polished stone, shining chrome, and glossy ceramics. My eyes scan the shapes—I see dildos and I guess some are... butt plugs. Not that I've ever..! I don't know what..? I'm trying to imagine what they might do... Who they're for? For me, or for a man? I never had much luck with my g-spot, but the shapes and bumps on these metal ones don't make much sense... I just can't work out..?

Oh! Hmh. Ugh. I just suddenly feel so, so sad. It's overwhelming. Such sadness. I don't know what most of these things are for—don't know what most of the stuff in this shop is. I think I should leave. I want to leave! I think I'm going to cry...

Oh, no! No! No! Oh, eff... Someone's coming over. This is, this is... I don't belong here. Must be a shop assistant, coming to ask if I need help. Uhn, this is just mortifying! I need to... But they're here now, asking me how I am today and if I mind them interrupting me. I'm just on autopilot with the pleasantries, waiting to say: 'I'm just browsing, thanks!' Then I can get out of here.

Strange, though. She's carrying a clipboard and isn't dressed like the other shop assistants..? And I'm not even sure 'she's' a 'she'. I can't tell if they're a girl or a boy..? Their hair is cropped short like a boy but they're wearing fabulous makeup—the eye makeup beneath their glasses is just... wow. They're dressed in a black shirt, black trousers, those big black boots like my daughter used to wear—Doc Martens. Can't tell, from their figure... Not that it matters; not that I'm... Non-binary, or trans—I think it's..? Not that I'm... They're striking, confident, beautiful. Those nails! They're holding a clipboard. I realise I'm being rude, not listening, responding.

They're asking me if I'd be interested in taking part in some market research today? On the brand's new product lines. They gesture towards the 'staff only' area, I guess where the research is taking place, and I see a woman around my age coming from there back into the main store with another researcher carrying a clipboard. There's something about the easy confidence and straightforwardness of this person that's putting me at ease. They say they're keen to speak to women of my demographic. I crack a joke about my age. They laugh and put a hand on my upper arm, reassuring and encouraging, telling me more. I find myself nodding in agreement and following them into the back room—it's like I'm in a bit of a dream, I suppose.

***

The researcher shows me into a luxurious, softly lit room. In the centre is a table, with two chairs either side. On top of the table is a large, velvet-covered tray laid out with a variety of sex toys. I realise that this is for the market research, and am relieved that they're not quite as mystifying as the items I was just looking at! The desk and chairs seem to have been brought in specially; otherwise this room seems to be for private dressing and styling, and maybe photoshoots. There's a clutter of photography, lighting, and filming equipment in one corner. And clothes rails packed with skimpy, sensual, scary underwear and outfits near a full-length mirror. Squashy bits of modular sofa line the room, with one corner arranged into a generous chaise longue. Artistic photos of women—no, people—of all different shapes and sizes line the walls—

they're naked and it's kind of abstract so I can't tell what's going on in them, but it's... it's all very beautiful and luscious and new for me.

The researcher invites me to take a seat and asks me to fill the form waiting for me on the desk with my personal details. They offer me a glass of Prosecco—they know people participating in the research can get a little nervous, but they want me to have fun and relax. "Why not!", I say as I scribble down my details. The researcher draws back a heavy damask curtain at the back of the room and pours me a generous glass of fizz from a wine fridge just behind the partition. But in the background, I can see—oh, wow! It's like *50 Shades of Grey* in there! Bloody hell! Some sort of bench, table thing, with straps for arms and legs. All sorts of things hung behind it—whips and stuff, but a gas mask?! Oh! And a harness that you wear with an absolutely enormous plastic...

"I hope you're not going to torture me?", I blurt out—half joking, half worried what I've gotten myself into. They smile and tug the curtain closed, handing me my Prosecco. They assure me 'no', explaining with a smile that those items are just being stored there for a photoshoot, and to ignore them. I gulp some fizz and make nervous small-talk; I feel as if the alcohol has gone to my head already! I'm buzzy, curious—I went to a couple of Ann Summers parties back in the 90s, but the girls were just laughing, making fun, pissed. It was all Rampant Rabbits, chocolate willies, gossip about our husbands' prowess. But there's something about this, and the researcher, that feels so different. It's like... like I'm in sex-toy school! On a course. I get to learn. Take it seriously.

The researcher chats through what we're here to do—getting feedback on the new and improved 'beginner's' line—and tells me it should take about half an hour. I joke about being a lady of leisure, with all the time in the world, and take another swig of drink. They notice my glass is almost empty and so retrieve the bottle, filling me up again and leaving it there. I feel so easy in their company, so I surrender to this being a fun new experience.

The researcher hands me one, two, three vibrators. I quickly lose my need to chitter-chatter and make jokes; they want to know what I think of the size, shape, colour, texture, ease of use, vibration patterns. They score my thoughts on branding, packaging, price-points. It's almost like we're colleagues—they describe the features and benefits; skin-smooth silicone, a flesh-top tip, bath- and shower-proof, special-edition decoration. I find myself making all sorts of intimate comments—this pressure doesn't feel quite enough; too big, too small; 'no thanks' to it talking to my phone with that Bluetooth nonsense. I caress my nose, face, neck with the vibes with more and more confidence, reporting back on what pleasure this one or that one might give me. I'm like Goldilocks—which one will be just right?

But now I'm outside my comfort-zone again—the researcher presents me with a fuchsia pink tool I haven't seen before. It's like a vibrating dildo that's been part split down the middle—the top is forked like a lizard's tongue. I can feel myself blushing... The researcher remains coolly kind as they professionally talk me through the product, again presuming and inferring nothing. "So it goes either side of your... your clit?"—I'm nervous and sheepish again. I take the toy in my hand and insert my pinky finger between the two buzzing forks. The sensation instantly makes me wonder what it would feel like between my legs. The researcher seems to sense my perplexity and inquisitiveness; that's just one of its possible uses, they're saying. You can use it internally, or some people involve it in oral sex. They show me the product leaflet, illustrated with these possibilities. I feel quite overwhelmed—I used a vibrator to help things along with my ex, but we never... I'm mumbling my feedback on price-point and packaging and gulping fizz.

I'm about a third of the way through the bottle as we progress onto a 'his-n-hers' first butt plug gift set, special lubricants, and... anal beads. I'm giddy and something beyond embarrassed—like I'm just lost at sea in all this. The researcher passes me a small, sleek clitoral stimulator, demonstrating how the cap at the top ripples and putters over your... clit. They neutrally explain how it's aimed at solo masturbation; that it's something to take your time with. My mind spins off wondering what this would feel like—such a completely alien sensation. I realise I'm turned on, moist below. I'm surprised to feel like that without it being because of the other person; it's never not been about the man I'm with...

The researcher must see it's getting all too much, so assures me this is the last product. They pour me a penultimate glass of fizz and hand me a gift box, telling me to open it. I pull off the packaging and open what looks to be an ornate diamanté necklace and bracelet set. I'm confused why I'm being shown costume jewellery—it's the sort of thing I'd expect 20-year-olds to be into—but the researcher smiles in a sort of twinkly way and tells me to take it out. The bracelet is in fact a tiny thong and the necklace comprises strands of crystals attached to two clips that I realise are nipple clamps. I run the strands through my fingers and snap one of the clamps against my little finger. That sadness comes again. I've imagined so many new and exciting sensations so far, but I'm sad I haven't tried something so simple as this grip on my nipples. I don't know what comes over me... "Can I try it on?".

I stand in front of the full-length mirror, staring at my reflection inside the opulent gold frame. I take a breath and slowly peel off my jumper, revealing my bra. It is so strange, but I don't feel self-conscious as I reach to unhook my underwear—this room, with its costumes and hidden hardcore equipment, must have seen far more shocking things than my sagging boobs. I release them from my bra, which I drape on a clothes rail, its pretty-but-worn appearance clashing with the textures, colours, and excitements of the rest of the rail. I nestle my breasts with my hands, discretely hardening my nipples ready for the clamps. I study myself in the mirror—not too bad for two breast-fed kids.

The researcher stands waiting nearby, friendly, and neutral. I tell myself this isn't much different from a bra fitting. I extend a hand to take the chest jewellery and the researcher drapes it into my fingers. But I'm fumbling with the clips and have tangled the strands. "Would you like me to do it?" I pass the knot of diamantés back to the researcher, who expertly unfurls it. I turn slightly to them, my titties bare, my nipples standing hard and proud. I watch as the first clamp gapes open around my nub—and then snaps closed. I give a little gasp. The grasp is firmer than I expected, and the cool little teeth of the clamp dig into my pink, delicate skin. I'm just about to tune into the sensations running down my body, when the sharp bite of the second clamp engulfs my other nipple. I gasp again. Then the researcher drops the three strands of diamantés. The weight tugs at my nipples, with a pleasingly biting pressure.

"Stunning," the researcher says, gesturing me to admire myself in the mirror. I turn to do so, studying my swollen, pinched nipples and the cascades of crystals shining in rows down to my belly button. I arrange my hair around my shoulders and take myself in. I half wish to be seen by a lover, some man who'll make love to me, but I half don't. I've never worn, done, something like this just for me. I tug lightly at the strands, feeling the pull on my nipples. Then I zone back in, realising that I'm lost in this moment for what must be as mundane as a bra-fitting for this researcher. I flush and make my apologies, motioning to collect my clothes and remove the jewellery.

"Oh, please don't rush on my account!", the researcher is saying with a smile. "We've finished with the research, but please just take your time getting dressed. You haven't even finished your drink." They glance at the clock on the wall: it's just gone one. "I have to take my lunch hour anyway. So why don't you lock the door behind me so you can get dressed and then leave when you're ready? The room isn't needed til I'm back, so it's really no bother." They collect up their bag and jacket, already decided that this is the best solution to my state of undress and their diminishing lunch hour. Before I know it, they've slipped out their door with a friendly thanks and goodbye.

I stand alone in the room for a moment, then quickly move to lock the door in case someone comes in. My instinct is to dress and leave, but the last of the Prosecco is calling to me—I feel I need to calm myself! I like the feel of the nipple clamps as the strands swish against my bare skin as I move. I give a light, playful shimmy as I pour the remains of the bottle into my glass and sip it down. My eyes are drawn to the clothes rail—there can't be any harm in looking..? I've nearly a whole hour before anyone will be back...

As I child, I adored my dressing up box—sifting through these much more adult costumes and creations feels just as joyful as that. But looking turns into touching, and touching turns into holding items up against my body in the mirror. I drape a fat feather boa around my shoulders, enjoying its tickling caresses as I admire myself. Now I'm trying on a fine silk kimono—no, this sheer kaftan—wait, this bead-fringed satin dressing gown! It's all too beautiful... I play with gloves, head pieces, chokers, and glittery stick-on nipple covers. I sip from my glass as I leaf through the rail—this is like shopping, but not as I know it!

I turn back to the table, running my hands across all the toys. I really would like to find out what that fork-tongued vibe feels like... Or that fluttering, suckering of the clit-stimulator.... That chaise longue looks so comfy and inviting... But that would be crazy and wrong! I do want a peek at the *50 Shades* contraption in the next room before I go, though... Just a quick peek.

***

I duck behind the heavy curtain into the darkened room. There's a heavy, human smell—I wonder what's happened in this room before. I feel like I'm in a secret, forbidden world. I'm moving carefully, quietly, even though I'm alone. I approach the bench. I take in its workings—arm, leg, and head supports. Restraints. Different ways to adjust it and use it. Do you lie face up or down? Maybe either..? I touch the soft black leatherette covering, pull at the arm restraints —my mind is a whirr. The booze has made me bold, so now I'm leaving my glass on the sideboard and climbing onto the bench. I lay there, face up, and let out a laugh. Me: on a sex bench! I reach my hands up and stretch my feet out, wondering what it might feel like to be trapped here—at someone's mercy.

The nipple clamps pull sideways at my nipples as gravity slides my breasts flatter. I squeeze one clamp a little harder with my fingers, just to feel its teeth again, gasping, feeling the longing in my body. Whips and paddles and strange implements hang above me just in arm's reach. I slap my thighs with a heart-shaped paddle, but the thwacking feels numbed through my jeans. I try a spiked plastic beater, but the barrier over my skin is dissatisfying. Instead, I swish and thwack the soft ropes of a flogger against my belly, urging myself that it's time to get up and leave.

I get up off the bench, planning to do just that. But then I notice that the wider room has furniture and things covered up with dust sheets. I can't help my curiosity... I peel back a corner of sheeting over a big pile of something in the back. Seeing a hand makes me jump! But then I realise I'm looking at a mannequin. I throw the sheet back further, and I'm actually looking at a big heap of mannequins. Many are still partly or fully dressed in items from the store. It's a strange sight—one female figure in pretty lingerie; one broken male figure in just a gas-mask fetish thing that attaches to the... groin; another androgynous figure, laying face down, covered in harnesses. I wrestle a male figure that catches my eye from this odd knot of bodies, to take a look. His mouth is open in an 'o' and plugged with a ball gag. His chest is a criss-cross of leather harnessing. And at his pelvis is a strap-on holding... a huge—huge!—dildo.

My hand shyly slides around the dildo. I've never touched something like this... It's firm inside, but soft to the touch like flesh, with some give. I 'boiiing' the tip, watching it wobble. I don't know why, but I look at the face of the mannequin as if it sees me! Somehow that ball gag is reassuring—I finger the straps around 'his' face and smoosh the ball into his gaping mouth. I examine his rubbery manhood with no shame now—it must be nine inches and I don't know how wide. I trace the straps at his pelvis, wondering how to get this thing off, working at the fastenings, pushing plastic limbs and bits of lingerie out my way.

Frustrated, I grapple the mannequin from the pile and sling him on the sex bench. I'm worried for time, but maybe this is my only chance to try on a strap-on. I flip him onto his side and figure out the fastening system, freeing it from his hips and then sliding it down over his legs. Breathing heavily, I step into the harness, with that big dildo quivering inside it, and try to hike it up over my jeans. But their bulk and rough texture stop me getting the straps high enough. I glance at my watch—still 40 minutes! I don't know why this urge is so strong, but, as I yank down the harness, I also unbutton my jeans and pull them down with it. Kicking off my mules, I step out of the straps and my jeans and separate out the harness. What I am doing? Am I really going to do this? Here I am, in my knickers, trying on a strap-on! But that's normal in a place like this, right?

Clutching the strap-on in my hand, I take my final swig of fizz and then return to the other room. Standing in front of the mirror so I can see what I'm doing, I step inside the harness and pull it up around my hips. The fat, rubbery giant bobs at my groin as I tighten up the straps. With the harness secure, I look at myself—straight on and then in profile. I feel sort of... magnificent! So many feelings and sensations, I can't describe... A pair of long satin gloves are draped over the mirror. I pull them on and caress my faux cock through silken fingertips. I watch myself side on as my hand and fingers mimic masturbating it, this role-play feeling more and more of a turn on as I grip firmer and faster.

I realise how much I want to make myself orgasm; I figure I'll be moments, minutes... and then out of here. I snatch the clit-stimulator off the table and flop down into the chaise longue. I have a full view of myself in the mirror—the shimmering diamantés hanging between my hot pink pinched nipples; the monster faux cock, a midnight blue with glittering swirls, sat proudly at my groin amongst the tight black leather straps. I remember how to switch the stimulator on, flustered, hurrying, disbelieving of what I'm doing, but confident I can cum before the researcher is back.

The stimulator putters in my hand. I part my legs and see the wet stain in my cream panties. I'll use the toy over my knickers and rinse it in the back sink; I just want, need, to orgasm. Coy and unsure, I position the tip of the toy over my clit. I moan and gasp quietly, playing with the placing and pressure. Ripples of pleasure run over and through my clit, and I grip my strap-on cock through my gloved hands, masturbating it as if a lover. But the pleasure is building too gently and slowly; I tap for different patterns, longing to be taken over the edge, but I'm left in agony. I remember what the researcher said about taking your time with this one. The one thing I don't have! I consider stripping off my panties, grasping a vibrator against my naked, slippery wet clit; even using my fingers. But I can't, I can't! I've gotten so carried away!

I pull myself off the chaise longue and return to the back room. I rinse the stimulator off in the sink, dry it with the hand towel, and return it carefully to its place in the velvet tray. My hand strokes over the toys longingly; my body is screaming for release, but this has gone far enough—I'll buy the fork-tongued toy and maybe a couple of those vibes before I leave, and please myself appropriately at home.

I pad back into the back room and unhook the harness. I feel sad to say goodbye to such a magnificent penis; I can't imagine I'll be wearing such a thing again—what kind of lover, man, would be into that..? I redress the mannequin in the harness, carefully—almost tenderly—adjusting the straps to his fibreglass body, and nudging and nestling his deep blue cock back into its perfect place. I pick up my jeans and shoes, figuring I should dress myself before putting this room back to rights, and return to the main room. I look at myself in the mirror one last time, taking in the chest jewellery and the sight of me in my sodden panties. I look good, sexy. But it's more about what I see in my face—I am turned on. I have a physical need, a want, a desire. It is about me.

Suddenly, as if possessed, I've fetched the mannequin from the back room and laid him down flat on the chaise longue. I'm overcome by the desire to feel that huge dildo pushing inside me; to ride this 'man' purely for my own pleasure—*to make love to myself.* I take the soft, squidgy vibrator from the tray and slide my panties down my legs. I'm still not sure what I'm going to do..? Have I gone out of my mind?! I glance at the clock on the wall—20 minutes til the researcher's break is over. I press the vibrator on and flip it to the setting I liked the most; feeling it rumbling and buzzing in the clutches of my hand. Slowly, I edge it down past the strings of diamantés to my mound of hair, sensing the tension building.

The rumbling head of the vibrator meets my clit. I groan and shake, as I stand there in front of the mannequin. Maybe I'll just make myself cum like this, staring at that beast of a cock..? I press the vibe harder against myself, rocking slightly, at the thought of impaling myself on it. I can no longer resist; I kneel beside the mannequin, and then swing one leg over his hip, straddling him, my cunny poised over the giant dildo. I grip the mannequin's shoulders with one hand and stare into his blank, lifeless face and that plugged-up mouth of his. I enjoy the look and feel of the crystals dangling from my chest and the pull of the clamps from this angle. Then I slowly lower myself onto him, the tip of the dildo nuzzling inside my wet slit, whilst I hold the soft vibe against my clit. I stifle a small cry as I bear down on this never-ending shaft, its girth stretching me apart and its length grazing my cervix.

I rock my wet cunny up and down the dildo, grinding my clit against the vibrator. It is a strange thrill to only have to please myself. I realise I don't want to move as much as I would with a man—I simply want to bear as much of myself down on this dick as I can take, stretched out, and feeling that warm bruised tenderness as it knocks against my cervix. I rock it inside me, my clit feeling bloated and hot against the vibe. Building, building. And then I explode. I'm cumming, cumming! Oh... My clit twitches against the vibe and my cunny throbs around the dildo as I pant and cry to climax. I drop forward against the mannequin, spent, satisfied—wondering how many more times I could hump this life-sized sex toy to orgasm; wondering how many more pleasures I could come up with in this room.

***

But the clock is ticking! I realise I have 10 minutes til the researcher's break ends, and so I dress, clean, and put the room to rights in a blur. I lay my mannequin back on the pile of plastic bodies, fussing to match his original position. It's funny seeing his gagged face one last time as I hide him with the sheet—I haven't been with many men, but this is one 'man' I finally don't have any feelings about! I shake the sheet over the dummies and give the room a final check, straightening the whips and floggers from above the bench and remembering to pick up my empty Prosecco glass.

Back in the main room, I return my glass to the table and neaten the toys in the tray. I flush at the thought that my cunny juices were all over the squashy vibe; that the stimulator caressed my clit. I impulsively pocket the nipple clamps chain—and, sod it, the matching thong, too; who knows what that will feel like!—before collecting my bag and jacket, giving myself a final look in the long mirror. I look ruddy and happy, and too rushed to feel ashamed of what I've done. I came here to do market research and that's certainly what I've done!

I unlock the door and slip back into the shop, grateful to go unnoticed again. I cross to the display of toys, confidently browsing for the forked-tongue toy, when I see the researcher entering through the front door of the store, their lunch hour over. They approach me, with a twinkling smile, and I hope I have the air of someone who's been browsing and shopping for most of the time since they left me. They open their mouth and say...

"One, two, three, four—and five."

***

I count Jennifer back up from this deep, immersive level of hypnosis to the place of planning and 'meta-commentary' we were previously at. She fingers the rose quartz pendant in her hand, signalling her partial reconnection with physical reality. She yawns and stretches a little, too—no wonder, given she's just experienced a full-body, no-contact orgasm on my therapy couch!

Whilst she's in this light state of hypnosis, we review her imaginary shopping trip and what she's learned from it. She marvels at her inner wisdom and insights—Ferdinando was right that we have all the answers we need right there inside us! She realises her near-future-self needs to explore her womanhood, her desires, her identity—it's not about a new man, a new look, or a change of scenery, or some crisis or need her adult children might occupy her with. She only hopes all these crazy sex toys she dreamed up exist in real life!

So I guess it's a good job I didn't humour her desires for past-life regression for it's clear her needs are thoroughly modern—to the point that she plans to take this progression literally and buy up the contents of her nearest sex shop very soon.

I ask the still-hypnotised Jennifer how she'd like to remember this session—given that the sexual nature of her vision took us both by surprise, perhaps she'd like amnesia for it? Or simply for my involvement in it? We concoct a mental block that allows her to continue seeing me for hypnotherapy whilst understanding that this happened, but to view it with strange detachment in my presence—like a dream.

***

I continued to see Jennifer as an ad hoc client for the next few months. She blossomed in authentic confidence and alluded to being on the path to the satisfaction she was seeking. But her belief in her 'inner wisdom' turned her into a bit of a 'woo-woo' junkie—she ran out of crystals on which to project her fascination with her unfurling self; I ran out of excuses not to perform 'past-life regressions' to unlock the insights she was so sure existed there.

On the evening after what turned out to be our final session, I lay in the bath, sipping an ice-cold rosé, and reflected on our breakthrough appointment whilst the artisanal candle she gifted to me burned. I reached for my forked vibrator—waterproof, of course—and pressed its parted tongues between my thighs, feeling the jitters up through my body, missing Addy who is away at a conference.

The problem with this popular belief in 'inner wisdom' is that we simply don't know what we don't know. And therein lay my conundrum in hoping to avoid my latest entanglement in a client's sexual secrets. When Jennifer panicked, upset, that she was ignorant of much of the stock in the sex store, she was, back in my therapy room, experiencing an abreaction—a violent emotional reaction to what was happening in her head while in hypnosis. She was in danger of waking herself from the trance—and that's dangerous; but only because a crappy, stunted hypnotic experience isn't good for my bottom line.

I had no choice but to stage an intervention. So. The amiably neutral market researcher? Dear Reader, that was me.

Happy shopping, Jennifer!

CASE #196 / THEO

From Maria Theresia Paradis to Anna O, all great mesmerists need a muse. Here, I meet mine—and invent the therapeutic art of 'pussy gazing'.

So, one thing led to another and I invented 'pussy gazing'...

The client is Theo, a bright, fun, athletically built man in his mid-30s with an infectious smile and soulful, hazel-greenish eyes. You can probably already detect, Dear Reader, that I had been charmed by Theo from the moment he stepped through my door.

He'd been recommended to me by a professional acquaintance—a psychotherapist of the Freudian persuasion. Sigmund Freud was, of course, the father of psychoanalysis—and, it may come as a surprise to learn, a keen student of hypnosis in his early career in the 1880s. Personally, I find Mr Freud's fixation with perverted babies and fucking one's parents absurd. But his disciples' endless quest for a client's 'inciting incident'—their 'Rosebud' moment—invariably descends into frustration at the years-long dance such therapists lead. The therapist then suggests hypnotism to get that elusive breakthrough, being cute with their client on Freud's disillusionment with, and renouncement of, hypnosis. Which is fine, because he was just kind of crap at it. And thus Freudianism and hypnotism continue their incestuously lucrative arrangement.

I'm always worried, however, that someone who's been in psychoanalysis for any period of time might be beyond my help. Such introspection and concern about your mother's breastfeeding habits creates, frankly, a peculiar brand of insanity that's tricky for anyone who isn't a rich American to pull off. When I read Theo's new client form ahead of our first session—full of vague philosophising and 'woke' self-reflections—I wondered if I'd been sent another lost cause. I was minded to send a particularly unpleasant male insomniac client my Freudian friend's way... But Pippa would make such a mess 'interpreting' his meaningless dreams and quizzing him on his sexual predilections that I'd only have more work to do six months down the line. It's such a moral conundrum to only want to send pleasant clients I'd like to spend more time with to these talky-blah charlatans.

But when Theo breezed through my door, several sessions ago now, I was relieved to find him an articulate, charming young man severely lacking in the neuroticism Freudian therapy so likes to stoke—and monetise. Though he'd booked a series of three sessions on the pretence of changing an unwanted habit, he made it clear once our first session was underway that he considered this a 'trial'—regardless of what financial penalties he incurred for cancelling subsequent sessions. He wanted to be sure he could trust and confide in me, he said. I swallowed my professional pride and agreed to this shift in my usual power dynamics—partly persuaded, perhaps, by such an agreeable vista sitting before me in my recliner.

Our first session was mostly spent on hypnotic training—testing the phenomena Theo could achieve and ensuring he could at least attain a light trance. He proved a compliant if little flirty subject, with us establishing a good rapport. I have to confess that I was unnerved by Theo's playful banter, but he struck me as one of those people who just have that charm and easy confidence about them, rather than it being particularly aimed at me. As I performed arm rigidity tests and gave suggestions for raising or lowering his arm, I found myself playing the part of a slightly po-faced teacher; correcting his hypnotic misconceptions for each crack he made about me putting him in all these strange positions against his will.

The rest of this session was spent somewhat cryptically, as Theo quizzed me on my work and philosophy as a hypnotherapist. I felt strangely exposed as I trotted out my usual sales pitch, those soulful eyes seeking something in me that I could not fathom. Whilst recent events have taken a strangely erotic turn, I've yet to find a client so... intriguing. There is something about the power dynamic and vulnerability of a client I'm seeing for hypnotherapy—and, to be brutally honest, about the silliness of hypnosis (for it is, often, Dear Reader, quite silly to do, see done, and have done)—which doesn't lend itself to the frisson that I sense from Theo...

Perhaps my recently adjusted HRT isn't quite right yet, or it's that my husband has been working away from home a lot, but I felt a worrying pang where I shouldn't as Theo strode out my door after that first encounter. When he emailed a few days later to confirm he'd like to go ahead with the next appointment, I realised I was pleased and flattered and eager to see him. Being an expert hypnotist and therapist, I did my very best to crush these weak, intrusive thoughts and feelings... only for Theo to pop up in a rather x-rated dream the night before our appointment. I worked my passions out on my rather sleepy and confused Addy, and assured myself that the dream was something to do with my daddy issues. Thank you, Mr Freud.

***

Soon enough our second session came around, with the mystery of the first instantly illuminated. Theo confided he identified as bisexual, and that he thought I could help him explore something about himself that had been bothering him. He asked if I had any experience of helping people with their sexual identity. I inwardly applauded myself for not opening the Pandora's Box of my recent client exploits—nor for inappropriate imaginings I risked having of Theo's inclusive sexuality—and kept it professional with a short affirmative answer. I also threw in, given Theo's psychoanalytical experiences, that Freud himself believed humans were all inherently bisexual—a view, I added, which resonates with me, but which has become further evolved and nuanced since Freud's time.

Theo seemed impressed with the Freudian titbit. He'd sought psychoanalysis for broader issues, but apparently Pippa has spent the past few months picking at the various possible binary meanings of his sexuality, wondering what 'maternal' and 'paternal' needs and desires of his were and weren't being met. Our hapless Freudian's fixation on the binary, gendered 'choice' she saw before Theo in fact illuminated a major barrier for him in life and love.

He was soon, he explained, to reach the grand old age of 37, and was broadly happy with how he felt about himself, his fellow humans, and the world at large. He smiled and laughed self-depreciatingly about sounding 'woke' and like a 'lefty'—he knows plenty of people, as in, white guys, who know the words but not the music when it comes to values and worldviews. But he tries to be progressive, a feminist, an ally, a good person. He's done a lot of self-reflection and work these past couple of years and actually thinks maybe he's pansexual—not bi? But he was a young adult in the 'noughties' and, well, it was the best fit at the time.

His gaze drifts into the middle distance and a secret smile spreads across his face as he reflects on all the fun he's had with both boys and girls over the years. But he's started to feel like he'd like to meet someone—a life partner; someone to build and share a life with. He tells me that he doesn't care what gender or identity that person might be, truly—he's trying to free himself from his preconceptions and to see, and love, beyond all that crap. But he realised through psychoanalysis that, deep down, he does distinguish his lovers based on their gender.

He shared his early confusions at realising he was attracted to both girls and boys. Socially accepted teenaged kicks with girls turned to small resentments at what he was repressing. He was fascinated by and fearful of girls—their delicate beauty and bodily differences. Boys, meanwhile, were both taboo and familiar, and obsessing about something he felt he couldn't act on caused friendship lines to blur, and uni to become a hedonistic embrace of his queerness. In hindsight, he objectified all his lovers—man or woman—and spent his 20s and early 30s like a kid in a candy store.

Then, a couple of years ago, he met someone online through a kink site. Their initial DMs to explore a hook-up turned into a deep correspondence. Theo bared his soul over the course of seven weeks in a way he'd never done before—he finally felt truly connected to someone and he wanted to meet. But the person he was messaging remained a mystery—he'd only known their username and that they were up for meeting people of all sexualities or identities. He realises now he was clumsy in prying for information that he'd claimed hadn't mattered; Theo had been eager to meet and had presumed that his cyber-love would need reassuring about *his* bi-ness. They, in reply, said things were complicated, and that they weren't ready to meet. Theo's heavy handedness got him 'ghosted'.

And he deserved it, too, he told me. He'd wracked his brains: maybe they were trans, or transitioning; maybe they were differently abled, obese—or just a fraud. He told himself he didn't care. But the truth was he had wanted to know if they were 'a boy' or 'a girl'—which 'bi' they were in his bisexuality. He wasn't the person he claimed to be, or wanted to be. The more he wallowed about the loss of this mysterious love, the more he realised how influenced he was by gender and gender stereotypes. Meanwhile, he hooked up with men on Grindr and wondered if an open marriage with a woman would be more conducive to his desire to have kids. He was a hypocrite—and no ally at all.

"I want to be blind to gender," he announced at the end of this confessional. "I want to see people as people. Not bodies, not options, not norms and how I might bend or break them. People. Just people."

I jotted that declaration down in my notebook, closed it, and chewed on the end of my pen, truly pensive rather than just performatively so. Theo had brought me my most interesting, intellectual hypnotic challenge to-date. Which only made me like him more.

I suppose, at the heart of my hypnosis, is the question of whether humanity—myself—can be freed from the suggestions that truly bind us. To reimagine life and ourselves beyond The Patriarchy, capitalism; beyond societal, gender, sexuality, and identity constructs; beyond the Gods and monsters that still plague us. When you can release someone from their spider phobia or nail-biting habit, that power clearly goes to one's head a bit. But deconstructing reality isn't quite so simple...

"Your mother was your first hypnotist and everything you think you know is a lie," I mutter to myself as I put my notebook and pen aside.

"Sorry?", Theo asks.

"I'll need some time to think and plan our next sessions," I reply.

"But let's use the rest of today to go a little deeper into the hypnotic trance. And to see how good you are at achieving amnesia."

***

My and Theo's hypnotic experiments have proved the most interesting and rewarding of my career so far. Each week, for the past three months, I've devised a new area of exploration. For instance, we recreated a famous hypnotic experiment where Theo was hypnotised to see himself as female in the mirror. We then expanded on this, with Theo

172

seeing himself as an ambiguous gender or viewing himself as a stranger to whom he assigns various genders. I hypnotised him to speak to the imaginary person as if they were a lover or a neutral friend, switching between male, female, and non-binary, and then we played the recordings back and analysed the differences in tone, nuance, and content.

This work revealed the extent of his biases and preconceptions. I so relished having a sparring partner who spoke the language of the 'halo effect' and 'code switching'. In the mirror experiments, he was fascinated to learn that 'he' was never unattractive, no matter how he hallucinated the changes in his facial features or how dissociated from himself he became. To separate out the 'halo effect'—how we form positive perceptions of someone based on their physical attractiveness—was, we realised, an even grander challenge. Did we need to maintain focus only on possible life partners who he finds attractive or broaden his 'gender blindness' to the wider populace? Similarly, 'code switching'—the different ways we speak to, say, a mother, a judge, or a child—revealed partialities in the way he speaks to different people, further influenced by him sizing them up as a potential lover or partner, which gave us yet more food for thought.

I even broke my rule about age regression. Fortunately, Theo was smart enough to dabble in this psychonautic adventure without taking such suggestions literally. We explored his formative years; well, we explored as best we could despite the fallibilities of memory. I think he appreciated plucking, say, a faintly remembered Christmas from his early childhood recollections and trying to be objective about it. With this memory, he recalled envying the pretty dolls and clothes bestowed on his older sister. But how much of that 'memory' is real? There are photos and some old video footage. Sure, he's seen himself crying amidst the pile of gaudy presents under the tree. But he's also laughing, smiling, gorging chocolate. Was this some formative hurt, metered out to him by ignorant parents, grandparents, and times? Or a retrospective narrative he can choose to amplify and mythologise?

And so we went on over the next few weeks. We'd exchange emails with ideas for the work of the next session. Much of it, like the stuff I note above, was done in his full conscious awareness, during or after the experiment. What would be the point of such intellectual, ideological delvings if we robbed him of the opportunity to consciously process and assimilate them? But we cultivated his ability for amnesia, too. Our rudimentary thinking was gender, sexuality, identity might simply be too strongly embedded even for someone so motivated to change and grow. It is not just 'programmed' into us at an individual level—it permeates generations and societies, and transcends geographies, cultures, and histories.

Our ambition became to simply make him forgetful of gender. It would be as with a healing heart or wound—you suddenly realise that a person or pain that was ever present in your mind has been temporarily absent; and then you start to tune into the increasing durations of that absence, til, eventually, the person or pain is but a distant memory. Never wholly gone, but popping up from time-to-time like an old song—less and less relevant as the years pass.

But if we needed the content of our sessions to be conscious and recalled, then what could we relegate to amnesia..? We fooled around with post-hypnotic suggestions. Theo would find himself performing some nonsensical task in the middle of the week between our sessions—to eat his breakfast cereal with chopsticks, to forget the rules of his squash game, to read a book from last page to first. I couldn't risk Theo—or those around him—attributing these peculiarities to illness or insanity, however. So he was instructed to realise the next day that this was likely a post-hypnotic suggestion and to report back on email, allowing me to confirm his amnesia for the instruction while in hypnosis. Theo proved almost too smart for his own good, though—the foreknowledge that he would receive such suggestions quickly muddied our waters. After the first success, any unusual, erratic behaviour was suspected of being hypnosis—he misplaced his keys, raided the fridge at 3am, felt a great urge to book a week in Ibiza. Our third attempt was rejected amidst these false associations. Finally, I stopped this experiment for fear that living with the constant expectation of performing strange unconscious requests might drive him mad—and get me sued.

I suppose I shouldn't be surprised at what we eventually agreed to cover while in hypnosis but conceal from his conscious mind... It happened naturally enough. I hope I've conveyed what a happy, confident, sexual being Theo is, and that, despite his longer-term aspirations to find a partner, he is having plenty of fun in the interim. Applying the things he'd learned about his cognitive biases in real life meant he started to share personal anecdotes and insights... He was chatting to someone on a kink-site and had realised he wasn't trying to guess their gender from the details of their DMs... He was more mindful of how he related to recurring playmates and new hook-ups... Someone on the peripheries of his social circle had tentatively come out as non-binary, and he'd been shocked at the ignorance and hostility of a couple of friends...

And so when he wanted to share something more intimate, doing it under hypnosis and with amnesia struck him as the best solution. He trusted me implicitly and wanted to share what had happened, but privacy was important to him—and to his lovers—and he didn't want to betray confidences. He mused that I, of course, could not unknow what he divulged, and I reminded him that I was not professionally bound to keep what he chose to share secret; for instance, if I believed he posed a danger to himself or another, I'd have to inform the authorities. He joked that he doubted I'd gossip about his sex life, and I—you'll be amused to learn, Dear Reader—countered certainly not without changing a few things to ensure anonymity and discretion!

Our hypnosis sessions became a game of two halves, with the latter half proving an intimate portal into Theo's sex life. I've been with relatively few men and zero women—I was too busy conforming and playing my part in 'the game of life' to think outside the box on my sexuality and identity in my early adult years. While Theo has reflected on the effects of the noughties on him, I came of age in the 90s—in the time of 'ladette' culture, when kissing other girls, let alone making love to them, was just a performative act for the pleasure of a man. To glimpse into Theo's bisexual abundancy, and his desires to blend, blur, and broaden boundaries has been quite the education—and the turn on. Intellectually and instinctively, I feel that to be queer is just sane and natural. I set out to help Theo venture down the queer 'rabbit hole'—but as someone who has fought hard to be settled and fulfilled, I've no desire to be pulled down with him.

***

But that is what seems to be happening... I write these notes after our latest session where things got a little... out of hand...

I struggle to write about what happened—perhaps I shouldn't write about it at all..? Great hypnotists have often had some sort of hypnotic muse—a confounding case that they strove to crack—like Freud and his colleague Josef Breuer and 'Anna O', the apparent hysteric Breuer treated using Freud's methods. There is always a whiff of sex and scandal around these relationships, perhaps testament to the power and mystique of hypnotism.

Theo and I spent the first part of the session reflecting on our work so far, before shifting gears to our amnesia confessional. Whilst deeply hypnotised, Theo told me in unusually dreamy tones about how he'd met someone—a woman, a cis-woman—with whom he'd really connected. But she's younger than him and just embarking on her queer journey; he fears she sees him as just a bit of fun—and a broker for her desires for threesomes. Here, his tone switched from dreamy to agitated; she commanded his respect, desire, and intrigue, but also frustration, resentment, and gloom. And he could not shake the feeling that he wouldn't feel this way about a man—there was still something about women... Some power, some hold, some 'otherness' he couldn't shake.

The problem, Dear Reader, is that I've kept Theo's confessionals clean and brief. But they are anything but. He spoke of this woman's wit, drive, and allure, but also of her sensual moans, her butterfly labia lips, and her explicit dirty talk. It is hard to be impervious to such inputs whilst making the best decisions for a client such as Theo. I noticed that he was turned on, too—his crotch packed an impressive swelling that only added to my distracted state. I made a fatal suggestion, based on our past insights about 'boys' being familiar and 'girls' a tantalising unknown, that perhaps we had focused too much on making just faces gender neutral. Perhaps he needed to extend that blindness to...

Lo! Pussy-gazing was born. There is a phenomenon in hypnotism of the subject 'hypnotising' the hypnotist—that the operator slips into the 'trance' they are suggesting, or that they pick up a subject's thoughts and speech patterns. This seemed to happen to me—Theo's trance became contagious as we both realised the obvious experiment to try. To gaze at a pussy—*my pussy*—just as he had gazed at faces, and to see it as a glorious instrument of purpose and pleasure, without attributing gendered expectations to it.

A long moment passed between us. I wondered if Theo was still in hypnosis; he gave me a strangely blank yet deep stare that convinced me he was. I cannot claim to have been thinking rationally at this point—I simply slipped my knickers down from beneath my skirt and kicked them off my feet. Then I ruched my skirt up, and rested my feet against the edge of the recliner Theo was on. He directed his stare down to my lap—and then I slowly opened my legs.

I watched Theo carefully as he gazed intently at my exposed pussy. I could feel my clit and gash pulsating hopefully; could feel the ooze of my wettening slit. I imagined how pink and luscious I must look, and thought of Addy nuzzling my hairs and nibbling at my outer lips, yearning for the touch of a tongue or the probing of fingers... I wondered if my palpable arousal wasn't undoing any possible therapeutic effects of this mad experiment?! I tried to keep my mind clear... and clean.

Time shifted, the metronome ticked on, and—as I glanced up to the clock behind Theo—I realised that what I'd felt was a brief moment of madness was a full 20 minutes. We were both entranced by this experiment, but I wisely and necessarily pulled myself out from this rabbit hole before our appointment time was up.

Rousing myself, I redressed and brought Theo out of hypnosis as if nothing extraordinary had happened, being careful to reinforce his amnesia. I cannot decide if I'm being paranoid as he exchanges goodbye pleasantries, pays, and leaves..? Is there tension in the air? The waft of my wetness and pheromones?

I'm writing these notes to stop myself acting on my arousal. But it's no good. My fingers can no longer hold this pen—I want them on my pussy...

CASE #209 / ESTHER

The devil is in the detail... and in my first hypnotic 'past-life regression' client's power-hungry cunny, as I meld therapy and witchcraft!

"**M**ight as well be witchcraft."

Esther, 46, gazes at me with her wide emerald eyes, po-faced. She sits sideways on the recliner, facing me, despite my invitation to lie down and relax. She waggles her socked feet and runs a hand through her shock of fading strawberry blonde hair.

'Fading' seems a more broadly suited description for Esther; her hair, her eyes, her smile, her complexion, her clothing, her demeanour. I gaze back her at, feeling like she's a photograph that needs its lightness and brightness amplified a few notches.

This is because Esther, a new client as of this morning's appointment, is neither ill nor ailing, physically or psychically. And she knows it.

"It's always this way with me," she explains matter-of-factly. "It's like my brain and body conspire to create this... wellbeing *Catch* 22, you know? I'll get this mysterious mess of issues and symptoms. And I'm the first to wonder if it's all in my head—if it's stress, or psychosomatic, or something that will just pass in time. So I try to do all the right things—relax, eat well, sleep well, exercise; forget it. But the problems persist and so then I wind up going back and forth to doctors and specialists... 'Dr Googling' myself. Eventually there will be something; something physical, something real. A random allergy. An underlying infection. An under-active thyroid.

"But, along the way, this is what I do. In between being gaslit by doctors and consultants. Not to mention gaslighting myself! I try out alternative treatments and stuff. Put all the onus, all the blame, on myself. A few years back, I spent a fortune on supplements and life-coaching and acupuncture, and it turned out I had a serious post-op infection!

"So, yeah. So now that I'm here—for 'hypnotherapy'!—I'm realising that I'm just gaslighting myself yet again. Wondering if a more positive mindset and some cups of Peruvian herbal tea, or whatever, might fix me—rather than, you know, the medical science, to which I and all of us in this country are entitled. So, yeah. This might as well be witchcraft for all the good it will do me."

"You sound weary," I observe.

"I am weary," Esther sighs. "My husband gets angry. Says I should shout and stomp more; get the doctors to listen and investigate. But it doesn't work like that, does it? Well, certainly not without throwing money at the problem; going private. You know, I had that op in 2014. So that was more than a year of my life beating myself up about my slow—

'slow'!—recovery. Then six months of serious antibiotics before I started to actually get better. Then it was like a miracle! All the failings I'd found in myself in hopes of solving the mystery faded away: the tiredness I'd called a lack of motivation; the inflammation I'd worried was poor diet.

"And now that I'm here, with you... I thought hypnosis might help me—I'm anxious and haven't been sleeping so well... But it's like: here we go again, Esther! Trying to treat symptoms—minor, peripheral symptoms, at that—because it's such a bloody fight to figure out what's... It's probably menopause, even though the GP said my levels are normal—whatever that means. Or I had bad Covid early doors; sinus problems for months; weird skin rashes. I'm not saying it's 'long-Covid' or anything like that. But maybe it's something to do with that... Or, I suppose at my age, I've got to start pushing for ruling out cancer... Ugh, I sound like a hypochondriac! But I promise I'm not! I know my body, and I get impatient and frustrated about this bloody healthcare system not listening to people. And I'm educated, wealthy, and privileged, so I can't even imagine...

"I'm so, so sorry. I should just pay you for this session and leave. I'm ranting and... This has actually helped me a lot; realising I'm repeating past mistakes when all I need to do is just go through the medical process and..."

Esther draws her loafers, stashed beneath the recliner, to her feet with a toe, motioning to leave. I contemplate taking her fee and instead spending the morning as I please. But something about the flicker of fire in her has stoked my interest.

"So, you're weary *and* resigned to be so?", I add.

Esther pauses from sliding her second foot into her shoe.

"Well, yes, but... no. I... I wouldn't normally be... But I suppose... No, I'm..." Her face is scrunched into a frown and she rumples her hand through her hair again.

I rise from my seat and move to the bookcase, absently straightening books as if this chore now takes precedence over her in-limbo session. I contrive to make her feel disrespected, unimportant.

"You said your husband was angry. Would you like to be angry?"

I see from the corner of my eye that Esther is chewing her lip and fidgeting in the chair. She motions as if to lie back in the couch, to avail herself of the session she's paying for either way, but she's now unsure whether I'm about to boot her out.

"No. No, that's not my way," she replies. "To shout and stomp. Sure, I'm angry at the situation; at myself. But being angry at others doesn't get you anywhere. Unless you're a man."

She shrugs a resigned laugh and eyes my reaction.

I dust my shelves with my sleeve and rearrange a few tomes.

"Then what would you like?", I ask.

Esther toes her loafer back off, seemingly playing with it, but clearly wanting now to stay and talk.

"I just... I'd just like to be heard. Listened to. To be taken seriously. Sometimes I just wish people would, you know, do what I tell them to do! Like, just get me that bloody test or... give me those drugs! Without all this persuasion, and pleading, and pleasing. All that hoopla. I'd like to be..."

I feel Esther's eyes boring into the back of my head; the fire in her belly rising as I seemingly ignore her at the very moment she's articulating her desire to be heard. I can almost hear her internal monologue screaming for me to sit the fuck back down and deliver the service she's paid me for. Such fun!

"I want to be powerful."

She delivers those five words with a new conviction. Then she swings her legs up onto the recliner, turns, and lies back. She crosses her arms combatively, impatiently.

"Huh," I exclaim as I agitate the Magic 8 Ball nestled amongst my decorate artefacts. (I find the blend of childhood nostalgia with Victorian 'cabinet of curiosities' produces a potent brew for client inductions and elicitations.)

"Would you like me to sit back down? So that we can resume our session, proper?", I ask innocently. "Signs point to yes," I add, wielding the Magic 8 Ball answer-window in her direction.

Esther nods, her face flustered and ruddy, realising that I'm toying with her.

I slide back into my seat and pass the ball back and forth between my hands. I offer a smile that I intend to be reassuring but that I've been told by Addy countless times looks menacing. The more my skills and experiences develop as a hypnotist, the more I come to appreciate these happy and useful personal 'failings'.

"But you would never say such a thing, correct?", I ask. "You'd never be so direct? So commanding? Because it wouldn't be polite or appropriate?"

Esther opens her mouth to answer, but I instead flash her the Magic 8 Ball's answer: 'My sources say no'.

Esther musters a small chuckle, unsure what to make of my strange style. And I must confess, Dear Reader, that I crawled out of bed this morning somewhat jaded and disinterested in today's client woes... Addy took me out to dinner and, over a delightful bottle of Merlot and a very bloody steak, I told him about my invention of 'pussy gazing' and how—in my mind's eye, at least—a client had probed my warm, juicy cunt.

We stayed up til the early hours role-playing my fantasy: him, transfixed by my snatch, describing its delicate folds and glistening secrets, mesmerised by me... until I could stand the frustration no more and commanded him to eat me for dessert. He obeyed every detail of my instructions—every nibble, lick, kiss perfectly attuned to the rhythms and writhes of my body. After I came for the first time, I allowed Addy to masturbate onto my sodden mound, his balmy fluid bathing my clit and stirring me once more. "Lick me clean," I demanded. Then I rocked my clit hard into his obliging mouth—to orgasm—and to sleep...

***

I digress! The point is: I thought I'd be dialling it in with Esther, a woman supplementing the miserable slog towards proper medical investigation with alternative-therapy distractions. Standard stuff for my profession. But now I find myself empathising at how a woman's fiery desires to speak directly and take agency invariably get suppressed and snuffed out...

After a lifetime of masking my power even from myself, hypnotism allowed me to unearth it and wield it proper. My marriage is also a source of my power—how many women can reveal a controversial truth to their husbands *and* steer the wheel of love-making so completely, only to gain yet more of his respect, love, and belief? But can I, a 'power' hypnotist, get an asshole male GP of a certain age and arrogance to listen to me?! No, of course not. Esther's conundrum is a relatable snafu that I'm inclined to help with. Gotta chip away at The Patriarchy bit by bit, eh!

I swivel in my chair, as if waiting for Esther to say something, but actually just letting my hangover and filthy remembrances from last night subside. Just as she's about to form words, I speak.

"It is witchcraft, you know. Hypnosis."

"Sorry, I..?" She looks completely baffled. I'm going to have to shape this session into something spellbinding if I'm to avoid my first negative Yelp review...

"Do you believe in reincarnation? Past lives?"

"What? Jesus! No! Of course not! Look, I'm really thinking this isn't for m––."

I silence Esther by holding up one finger whilst searching for her intake form on the clipboard on my side table. I study it for a moment, wondering if she really will walk. But she waits.

"No. Good. I didn't think so." I skim my eyes over the form, muttering particulars of her vocation—senior public-sector finance bod; how very practical and rational—and other biographical details in a just-audible breath.

"I don't believe in past lives either," I add. "Just in case you were––."

"Oh, no, no. Of course not." Esther placates me whilst I pretend to tick some points on her form, as if assessing her suitability for something. I note that she's eyeing her handbag and coat on the chair in the corner, as if plotting a hasty getaway.

"I've never been good with numbers," I say, peering up at her with a new scrutiny. "Words are my thing. Stories. We are the stories we tell ourselves and each other."

I place the clipboard back on the table, face-down so that she can't see how she's fared in my 'assessment'.

"Would you mind if I..?" I motion for Esther to extend her wrist so that I can take her pulse. She automatically offers up her appendage before she's consciously considered what I'm up to. I press my fingers into her pulse point whilst watching the second hand of the wall clock tick around. I've no idea what I'm doing, of course, but it looks—and feels, to Esther—meaningful somehow.

"But you don't have a story for this, do you, Esther? For this *Catch 22*? You're a smart, practical, rational person. You know medical science could easily and efficiently identify and treat a real, physical problem. But, doubting yourself and the system, you want to do due diligence on psychosomatic or psychological causes first. You're savvy to the placebo effect; the mind-body connection; and the power of the mind over the body. If you could just truly and completely believe the symptoms you're experiencing are all in your head, you could conquer them, and then focus only on the real, physical problem that is—or, then, isn't—there."

I relax my fingers from her wrist and let her hand return to her lap. Then I decisively rise from my seat and cross to a cupboard. From it, I retrieve a 1960s reel-to-reel tape recorder. I do love my vintage hypnosis references—this being the traditional means of recording such an experiment as Esther and I are about to embark upon!

I set up the recorder on the side table while I speak. "It is my professional conclusion that you need to *decide*, Esther. To decide which path to prioritise and pursue. Otherwise you will continue traipsing between the two, prolonging the time you spend in these... these limbos yet again."

"I'm sorry. What are you..? Are you recording me?"

"Not yet," I say chirpily, fussing with a flapping tape reel.

"I have to say I... I feel very unclear as to where we're going with this," Esther blurts.

"Yes. Precisely. So do I."

I return to my seat and stare expectantly at Esther.

"You're going to tell me a story. A story of your past life. While you're under hypnosis. It's a completely imaginary, made-up, nonsense 'past life' of course! The only people a hypnotist can trust with such a powerfully therapeutic task are those who absolutely don't believe in reincarnation. So you're a prime candidate."

Esther ruffles her hair and looks drained, such is the intellectual and emotional rollercoaster of social- and power-dynamic awkwardness she's been riding upon.

"I just thought you'd..?"

"Yes, I know. Do some 'relaxotherapy'. Which you'd ultimately undo. Because you don't believe. Because you're *undecided*."

She glances at her phone and glasses case on her side table, mentally gathering her things.

"I can do that if you'd like though? Easier for me."

"No, um... I'm... I mean, I'm not one for telling stories, so..."

"Doesn't matter. You'll simply respond to my questions while hypnotised. And—since we're both clear that this is completely imaginary and made-up—I'll be asking lots of leading questions. Helping you. Shaping the story. Shaping the metaphor. Shaping the insights we'll be creating together for you."

"Huh. So I guess it would kind of be like... playing make-believe with my daughter when she was little..? All her teddies and dollies having a tea-party, and I just had to play along?"

I shudder at the notion of having to humour an idiot child with such a tedious scene. I'm sure my seven-old-self presided over far richer worlds and dramas than imaginary cuppas..? And my younger brother playmate was clearly a far better subordinate-co-creator than a parent anxious to get on with the hoovering. I congratulate myself once more on my life choices and shake off the intrusive image of pouring hair-of-the-dogs for me and some dead-eyed rag dolls.

"Yes, exactly that," I say with a smile.

"Okay. Okaaay," Esther mulls. "So you're going to hypnotise me and then I'll come up with this story, and then what?"

"We'll spend the rest of today's session training you into hypnosis and getting comfortable with being recorded.

Then we'll use, oh, say... three sessions on your supposed 'past-life regression'."

I relish my use of physical air-quotes and also applaud myself for upselling this otherwise one-off, uncertain client into repeat business.

"It's your choice as to when, if, and how you listen to the recordings of the session. The reason I favour this antique recording method is that it requires decisiveness and effort to share and listen to the audio. Accounts gained through hypnosis can be a little... How should I put this..? Hesitant, fitful. Arduous. Perhaps you'll prefer me to digest the recordings into a story for you to reflect upon. And then it will be very much like the meaning and metaphor you derive from any story. Think of your daughter's childhood favourite?"

"Christ, I must have read her *Charlotte's Web* a million times."

"Right. A story of friendship, loyalty, loss. And I'm sure there are a million more meanings, lessons, inferences, and themes you, or she, could find in that tale. People who believe in 'past lives' find solace and inspiration in them, because they become the hero of a story in which they gain the things they need for their 'current' life. We know you want to be powerful. But you don't feel powerful, truly, inside yourself. And nor do you want to ape that power, as your husband urges; you don't want to pretend."

Esther nods thoughtfully. "It's like 'being' powerful is just a fantasy. Like, I'll rehearse what I want to say to a doctor in my head. In my head, I'm asking for what I want and need. But there's a disconnect between the 'being' it and..."

"Becoming it," I add.

"Yes, yes. That's it."

"There's no need to occupy your mind with these thoughts til our next session," I say as I reach to click on the recorder. Its wheels begin their soft, rhythmic whirr as I sink back in my chair, ready to induce Esther into hypnosis.

"Shall we begin the witchcraft now?", I ask. "I mean 'hypnosis', of course! I'm just joking!"

Esther nods wearily, resignedly—an ideal state for a subject to be in. Too weary and resigned to make the usual tedious protests about the hypnotic process, even.

Since she's now so acquiescent to our hypnotist-subject role-play, I reach for the antique gold fob watch I keep in the dish atop my side table. What better 'time-travelling' suggestion than the swinging timepiece associated with the all-powerful hypnotists of yesteryear! I hold it up in front of Esther's gaze, and it automatically starts to slowly sway back and forth. Her eyes begin darting back and forth in time with the watch; I decide to remain wordless as I observe her lids growing heavier with each swing of the watch. As the momentum builds and builds, I can see her pupils shrinking to pin-points; her consciousness shrinking back inside.

"And sleep. Sleep now. Sleeeeeep."

As you know full well, Dear Reader, I, as a rule, pride myself on informing and educating clients. But sometimes a bout of good old-fashioned, wordless 'power hypnotism', Svengali-style, is worth the punt. Esther's head lols and her breathing relaxes as she sinks deeper and deeper into my command.

People who believe they are smart, practical, and rational —but who are also secretly rather superstitious—make superb hypnotic subjects.

***

Esther proved a surprisingly free-thinking playmate and, over the next three sessions, she told me the story of her 'past life'. I was rather pleased with the meanings, lessons, inferences, and themes woven through its telling; presented here for your reading pleasure.

Of course, I had to steer things in a somewhat salacious direction to keep myself amused—and awake. A hypnotic regression, is—I reluctantly imagine—not dissimilar to playing make-believe with a child. An adult's utterances may be more articulate, and delivered in a less irritating pitch of voice, but they, too, are rarely linear or consistent—and are often quite, quite dull.

And so, when I played Esther a snippet of her dreamy, long-winded mutterings after our first regression session, she wisely plumped for me to echo it back to her as a proper story. You will sense, as you read of her 'past life', that it was important for Esther to cast herself into a full and coherent backstory, in order for the crucial parts to be applied to her life in the here and now.

I must admit that I've enjoyed transcribing her raw imaginings and structuring them into a therapeutic parable! Plus the additional time required has proven most lucrative... Perhaps I shall bend my rules on hypnotic past-life regression for future clients—especially if their imaginings prove such devilishly good fun as this one!

***

My name is Agnes Brigge, and I was born in the year of 1572 in the Fens of East England. This midsummer I shall turn three-and-twenty—a veritable old maid!—the year now being 1595.

'Brigge' is my married name. I was born Agnes Sole, daughter to Robin and Charlotte Sole. My Father was an apothecary; a wise and learned man who would nightly scribe his findings on the science of nature in his parchments. My elder brother, William, was apprenticed to Father, but Mother was also sage to the ways of nature, cultivating and collecting the flora and funga on which Father's trade relied.

Mother had lost three babes, stillborn, as well as my little sister, Eleanor, who had died of ague at eight years, and our first-born brother, Henry, who passed of the pox. Father and Mother took Henry's death awful hard. Henry was a fine apprentice, with a keen mind and wit; an honourable, handsome boy, betrothed to a wool trader's daughter not days before pox struck. But Bill, said Father, was a clod. Kindly, but a clod, who couldn't tell his catnip from his catmint.

Mine had been a happy girlhood, helping Mother tend to our home and land. I was muchly bewitched by the bees we kept, making a study of the nectar they collected and wondering if their honey and wax might possess the same healing powers as the blossoms they visited. I shewed Father my girlish scribings, but he dismissed them—a torpor had sunk over him at Henry's death and he worried for our family's future.

Then Death, cruel Death, came for Mother. Our village had suffered a wet, grey growing season followed by a hard winter. Crops failed and livestock died. Some farmers blamed Sibyl Barnabus, the old hag who dwelled across the marsh and who, it was said, practised witchcraft. Old Barnabus was caught filching apples from the parish orchard and, some said, had cursed the Reverend when he chided her and asked them back. Not long after, all the apples rotted to the ground full of maggots and the

Reverend broke out into pustules. Then came the rains and greyness. Before the year was out, Mother was in fever.

I tended to Mother while Father and Bill worked. It was hard toil for a girl of 13, but I did my best to manage our meagre supplies, and to keep the animals fed and well. Dear Mother did not care a fig for the village gossip about Barnabus, saying that she was just a poor old lady in need of sustenance and Christian charity. She continued my instruction on flora, fauna, and funga curatives from her sickbed—those final days before my Mother's mind was addled by the fever were filled with wisdom and wonder. While I washed and scrubbed, cooked and cleaned, she told me stories of her girlhood—of the lessons passed from her Mother, and her Mother before her, and all the women elders of the Fens. She whispered secrets to me between sips of broth.

Father returned home and found her speaking to me so; he scolded her for filling my girlish mind with such sorcery—such talk was doubly dangerous amidst the local fear-mongering about old Barnabus's curse. Mother laughed—cackled, howled—at him, as we'd never seen so before. Father gave her new tinctures and wraps, but the fever wracked her mind and body more and more from that night.

She faded away with the winter's snow—as did my girlhood. I set about as the woman of the house, toiling day and night to keep up with my and Mother's chores. Even Bill seemed to sprout out of his youth, keeping the books and making up what he lacked in knowledge and precision as an apprentice apothecary with his charm. Indeed, as spring returned to the Fens, so villagers returned to Bill for remedies against the last vestiges of Barnabus's curse. He still didn't know his catnip from his catmint, of course! But Bill's smiles and assurances seemed just the balsam for a people recovering from a winter of despair.

Father, though, had sunk further into his torpor, turning to the drink and becoming an angry, bitter man. Bill and I tried to soothe his worries and woes with hard work and good care, but it was to no avail. One morning, whilst pinning the laundry out to dry, I saw a stranger arrive at Father's apothecary on horse and trap. He was a portly, ruddy-faced fellow with a displeasing face who treated his steed most poorly. I later pressed Bill on who this stranger was; Bill said he was a prosperous farmer from across the Fens who sought Father's expertise for his ailing wife. Bill, too, had decided the stranger a slippery old toad, but he and Father had become thick friends. Soon the pair were supping ales and meads at the village inn, twice, thrice a week, carousing and conspiring.

One night, the innkeep's son, Little Jim, came a-calling at ours to fetch Father home as he'd fallen in a drunken stupor. Bill and the stranger staggered Father across the village green back home to his bed, where Bill dispensed a tincture to ease Father's sore head on the morrow. I was left alone with the stranger, who we now knew as Robert. Robert leered and slathered as he sized me and our home up, calling me 'a comely wench' and 'a fruit just ripe for the picking'. I called him a filthy swill-belly who should go home to his poor wife, and shooed him out the house. I prayed that night to Lord God not to see Robert again—why do crones like Barnabus get blamed for nature's calamities, when men like he are the real curse upon us?

Robert did return, but something between Father and he had shifted after that drunken night. Bill observed Robert buying his provisions from Father as usual, but, beneath their convivial chatter, there were harsh, whispered words. Threats..? Bill saw Father slip Robert a bottled preparation as he packed up his trap; a bottle not in the ledger. Then, one foggy dusk, as I led the cow into the stable, I saw Father gathering botanicals near a thicket where hemlock grows. I'd swear on the bible that I saw its creamy white spray of flowers in the moonlight—I had always feared poison hemlock's powers since Mother warned me of it when I was but a child.

Bill was then sent on a fool's errand to the city of Norwich to purchase wares we had no need for—all so that Father could work in solitude, drying, grinding, and mixing ingredients for a tincture. I was busy arranging beeswax soaps when Robert visited the apothecary for the last time, and saw with my own eyes Father slip something into Robert's knapsack after he'd made his purchases. The old toad gave me a strange look as he bade Father goodbye.

***

Some three weeks later, Father received a letter at the apothecary and, Bill later told me, promptly went to the inn to drink himself stupid. Bill and I waited at home, fearing that perhaps the Bailiff was a-coming—Father had sunk so much of our income into The Three Magpies of late that Bill was becoming worried for the future. At gone midnight Father stumbled in and sat silently while he ate the stew I'd kept warm for him. Eventually he pulled the crumpled letter from his jacket breast pocket, and spoke over the candlelight without looking at us—without looking at me.

"Robert's wife has passed. Consumption, it was."

"What a terrible blow, Father," says Bill.

"Indeed, indeed. Though it seems he has inherited her family farm. He is become a man of some means. Some 10 acres, has he."

Father chewed at a piece of gristle. Bill glanced at me, but I remained wide-eyed, ignorant of what was to come.

"He'll be wanting a wife, of course."

Father pulled the gristle from his mouth and slurped the meat and fat from it with his lips.

"You shall marry him, Agnes."

I felt, in that moment, as if the sky had fallen in. I gasped, and cried, and wailed. I implored Father not to send me away; to keep me to tend to the home and land, as Mother had done. To care for him and Bill til their dying day.

"Bill is promised to the wool man's daughter, in Henry's stead," Father said, without emotion.

Bill frowned, confused—both our fates being revealed to us for the first time. But his by no means as ghastly as mine.

"Please, Father!", I implored.

I protested my true love for the Blacksmith's boy, whom I'd barely blushed at, and my disgust for such a slippery old toad of more than three score years as Robert. I beat my breast and tore at my hair, begging for a different fate.

"You're to marry Robert, and that's an end to it. Bill's wife will tend the house and land, and continue the Sole line. You shall be 14 this summer, Agnes—a woman—and I can no longer keep you. You will belong to Robert and bear him the children, the son, his departed wife could not. He is a man of means now, so you will be happy and prosperous and fat. And that's an end to it."

With that, Father dragged the last scrap of fat from the gristle and plopped the inedible remains on the table.

And that is how I became Mrs Robert Brigge.

***

Nearly nine years have passed since that foul, fateful night. Now I wail and scream silently inside myself, resignedly, for who is there to listen to a forgotten, fading farmer's wife? I am fortunate to have a roof over my head, and food in my belly—as well as a busy and oft absent husband.

Indeed, Robert's greed and scheming mind means he is drawn to trading with other merchants and fellows across the Fenlands. After his first wife's untimely demise, he kept on the humble servants who worked the land and tended to the livestock, but is hated by all for his tyrannical, cruel demands. Work here is hard and relentless when Robert is present, as he seeks to squeeze every last penny from Mother Nature's bounties. I keep house and manage the workers and books with all the fairness and kindness that I can afford them—Robert has spies amongst them, though, and forbids me friendships.

Though Robert demands his conjugal rights nightly when he is a-home, I have denied him the children—the son —he so desires. This is why I am so watched and resented, by both him and his spies. Robert's tuppings, always unpleasant and painful, became yet more violent and hateful as the years wore on. He calls me a barren old hag; the runt of the Sole litter, whom my Father wittingly sold to him as a dud; a whore for any man but her husband, and thusly too sullied to grow his rightful seed.

Each night when he is a-home, after he has supped and drank a pitcher of ale, I go to our sleeping room and remove all my garments. As is the custom he has decided upon, I kneel, naked in the moonlight, on the edge of the bed. I spit on my palm and rub the wetness into my cunny, readying for my tupping. I hear his heavy, unsteady footsteps on the floorboards as he follows me in. I close my eyes tight as I hear him unbuckle his belt and unsheathe himself from his trousers. With a grunt, I feel him prodding his manhood inside of me—blessedly, it is but a small burden to bear. (I have spent enough time on farms to know that new life is oft created with larger implements than my husband possesses, including finding plenty of farmhands rolling in the hay!) Robert reminds me that I must be tupped in the fashion of livestock, from behind, if I am to be seeded as one. I silently count the number of thrusts and moans and spasms he makes until he shoots his rotten seed inside of me, this mental tally of the longest and shortest of these midnight tuppings setting my mood for the next morning.

***

What my husband does not know—but which he is wily enough to suspect—is that I am no dud; I wantonly deny him children. Not long after I became his, I found myself much afeared of—and haunted by—his first wife, Grace. As I lay in the bed in which she perished, wracked with terror as he had his way with me, again and again, I felt her presence; her spectre. I dreamed that it was me, not Father, walking among the poison hemlock; I dreamed of gathering those ghostly flowers; of my imagined picture of Grace—for I know not what she looked like—screaming in anger at me as I stuffed her mouth with those fatal blossoms.

Fearing I should go mad with fear and grief, I sought to make my peace with Grace, and to beg her forgiveness for what part my Father—and, unwittingly, I—played in her departure from our mortal coil. While Robert was away trading, I journeyed to the churchyard and sought out Grace's resting place. Finally, in a sad, shady corner, amidst a neglected tangle of brambles, and besides many a pauper's grave, I found her headstone. It was a piteous sight and only strengthened my fears—why would old Robert lay his wife to rest in such a place if he weren't glad to be rid of her? I wept as I lay a posy of daisies I'd picked along the way upon her grave, and spoke soft, imploring words to her. I brushed down her headstone with my sleeve, and pulled at the thorns and weeds intruding her resting bed, pledging to visit her as oft as I could if she spared me her anger, and instead came to know me as a friend and fellow victim in Robert's dreadful scheme.

I truly felt that she let out a great sigh of relief and peace in that moment, for a gust of breeze aided me in my efforts to clear the headstone of overgrowth and cleared the clouds from in front of the sun. I touched Grace's carved name on the stone to seal our pact, but then was startled. Sensing movement, I peered above the headstone—only to see a greyish figure watching me from betwixt the trees. I knew no one in my new home town at this time; spooked, I resolved to hurry home. But I was also spooked in the truer sense—wondering if this was the apparition of Grace come to visit me. I found myself rooted to the spot in awed fear as the figure started to move slowly towards me. As it emerged from the dappled light of the trees, I saw it was an older woman, of flesh and bone, wrapped in a tattered shawl and dress. She walked with a lame leg and hunched back, but I saw that her face—while gnarled by the years—bore me no harm.

***

Her name was Nanny Molland, and she was a wise woman who lived out past the marshes and scratched a living from her land and knowledge. She had known Grace a little and had heard that Robert Brigge had taken a new, young wife in me. She had come to lay a charm on Grace's grave in aid of us both, but had found me there instead.

Nan had made an oath to help and protect girls trapped by cruel and dangerous husbands. Some unspeakable tragedy had struck her beloved twin sister during the birth of a babe her body was too young to bear. Nan's kindness softened me to confide in her, and she became my secret friend and advisor. It was she who taught me of the potent blend of herbs and plants to brew into a tea to keep my body inhospitable to the offspring I had no desire to bring to this world as slaves to Robert. It was she who taught me how to fashion a laving device, hidden beneath a floorboard in our kitchen, from a hollowed out gourd and dried pig's intestine to wash away my husband's seed with vinegar.

If it weren't for Nan, and the spirit of Grace watching over me, I would have died long ago—of despair if not in childbirth. But since last summer I have become afeared Robert will soon kill me in punishment for not bearing his heirs. He has taken to whipping me with his belt or beating me with his bare hands after our fruitless couplings. The stable boy, who I am sure spies upon me, now makes little pretence when following me on my rare journeys into town for provision. I awaken screaming and sweating from visions of choking on some noxious liquor; or of Robert's hands around my neck.

I rarely see my dear Nan in person; instead, we leave messages for one another in common spots we can visit. I sketch a chalk symbol on a fence post on the outskirts of the farm to say I must meet with her urgently on the morrow. Robert is away and, despite the risk from his spies, I slip out on the pretence of picking the juiciest blackberries for preserving. Nan is waiting for me in a secluded clearing, and I sob as I tell her of my visions and fears.

She tells me that I'm still young and fertile; that I must cease my preventions and give Robert the children he craves to preserve my own life. She begs me to give in. But I am defiant—surprisingly so—imploring her that she would not commit her female offspring to her sister's fate in my shoes, nor see male heirs follow in Robert's cruel footsteps. I do not wish to die, I tell her, but I would sooner join Grace and Our Lord in Heaven than give in to Robert so completely. I rave about running away, but Nan becomes quiet and circumspect.

Nan looks me hard in the eyes and asks if I am quite made up in my mind—resolved to a childless life? And wish be free of my wretched husband—no matter the cost?

"That I am," I say.

Words so sure have never spilled so freely and firmly from my mouth. Gone are my girlish sobs and pleas. I fancy that I feel Grace's comforting hand on my shoulder—it is as if she knows I am not much longer to be separated from her in my refusal to bear Robert's children. Nan touches a grand old oak tree with her gnarled hands and seems to consult with the wind whispering through its leaves.

"Perchance there is another way," she mutters.

She begs of me not to run away—not yet. She tells me to come here, to this very place, in the darkness of the next waxing crescent moon. Someone will be waiting here for me —someone who can help me. Thinking that they will help me escape, I ask if I must bring them money; money I do not have. Nan says I must bring offerings of another sort—things of Robert's person; his body, his breath, his blood. Confused, I fret that I do not understand. Nan soothes me that I shall know what to bring.

She kisses my forehead and smoothes my hair and clothes, telling me I ought to return to the homestead or else the stable boy will be tattling. I bid her farewell and make my way towards the field. I turn back to see Nan making a sacred ritual or oath of some sort amongst the woodland floor—she kisses the earth and whispers to the sky, before binding strands of her wiry grey hair to a twig that she buries beneath the oak tree. Sensing she's being watched, Nan looks up at me and shoos me to continue my way home. I give her a grateful wave.

I'm momentarily struck with the strange sense that this will be the last time I see Nan... But then, before me, I see a bounteous blackberry bush sparkling with fat, juicy berries. I pick them by the handful, filling my basket to the brim so as not to rouse the suspicions of the workers. I find myself strangely hungry, and so gorge on their ripe sweetness, savouring their soft flesh as it slips down my throat.

I arrive home as if having been in a dream. I pass the stable boy brushing down our finest filly, my red-stained hands and apron testament to the truth of my errand.

***

Some nights later, under the dim silver light of the waxing crescent moon, I make my way back to the small clearing beyond the fields. I am bruised and sore from Robert's beating, but he is blind drunk in our bed and so I am emboldened as I make my flight.

Nan was right; I knew what to bring of Robert's person and I carry these offerings in my knapsack. For his 'body', I have the odious clippings from his fingers and toes that he instructed me to burn upon the fire. For his 'breath', I have filched the dirtied kerchief into which he coughs and snorts. For his 'blood', I have the vinegary swillings from washing his poking out of my cunny—the closest that oaf will get to having his own 'blood'.

I hasten through the darkness, stopping briefly to feast on the ripe berries nearby to the woodland, strangely hungry and reckless. I stumble down into the clearing as if intoxicated by their sweetness.

At first I think I am seeing Nan, but it is not the Nan I know. This old woman is clad in darker clothe—a black cape billows at her shoulders and long, wiry hair flutters out from beneath a dark brimmed hat. I strain my eyes to see her better—her body is less wizened by age; she neither hunches her back nor limps on her leg. Her face, though, seems both familiarly Nan's, yet more grotesque in years and in disfigurement.

I realise that I had wrongly believed Nan's twin sister dead at the hands of a bad husband and an ill-fated birth. But there was no doubt—before me stood the twin of Nanny Molland; estranged not through death, but, it struck me, through her surrender into witchcraft.

As if attuned to my innermost revelations, the witch looked up at me. One eye was of a piercing blue pricked with a black iris; the other pure black like the glassy, knowing orb of a crow. She gave a toothy smile and extended her arm out from beneath her long cape, her palm upturned expectantly. I realised she wanted the offerings I had been instructed to bring. I fetched them from my knapsack and dropped the bundle of 'Robert' into her mottled hands. She prodded at them with long, bony fingers, then gave a satisfied grin and nod, and shut them up inside her grasp. With that, she turned and disappeared into the darkness of the trees.

I stood there, blinking in the silvery light. My heart sank— all my life I had heard the stories of witches and their covens and their wicked ways and, just as I'd made my mind up to run away into one, I'd simply been taken for a fool by a grotesque old crone.

Perhaps Nan wanted to teach me a lesson; to see that to bear a child into this ghastly life was the best way? I wend my way back home, wondering how to resign myself to this fate.

***

Over the coming nights, I leave messages for Nan in our usual places, desirous to meet with her. I cannot tell if I want to shout at her in anger, sob into her arms, make a new plan for escape, or seek her wisdom on quickly bearing a son in hopes of being left well alone. But she does not come and does not leave me any signs in return. My sadness is complete as I find myself, naked, on hands and knees, waiting for my husband to take me...

All of a sudden, I am seized by a powerful, all-consuming vision! I am in this very position, but back in the clearing. This time, I am not alone. Amongst the trees, nude women—witches—move and dance in the warm light of a circle of bonfires. They hum and cry out in a haunting harmony of noises. Some carry baskets of plump, oozing berries and fruits, feeding them to one another. Their bodies—soft, plentiful, differing bodies, young and old, ugly and beautiful —are adorned with wreaths and garlands hewn from nature.

One witch, silhouetted by the flames, stops in front of me and feeds me blackberries, barberries, sloes, and apple. Their sweet tastes mingle in my mouth, and their juices dribble down my chin. I am hungry for more and so motion with my mouth for the witch to fill me up—she pushes a soft sloe against my lips, mushing her thumb inside my mouth as she feeds the fruit into me.

What is happening to me? Is this real..? I feel intoxicated. The witch speaks to another figure standing behind her and soon a cup is being proffered to my lips. Unseen hands pull back my head with my hair, raising me to drink the mysterious liquid. I gulp it down—the taste is confusingly familiar. It is bitter and cloying, and runs thickly down my throat. I sway gently back and forth on my hands and knees as the potion takes effect. I am so used to keeping my mind and body so very separate when I assume this position, readying for my husband to have his way with me. But now they seem to be uniting; I am alive to all the smells, sights, and sounds surrounding me. My body sways to the rhythm of the witches' music, and I feel warm and safe in the circle of fire. I thought I knew of nature's secrets, but I know of no apothecary that can provide such soothing joys.

Nan's twin approaches, grinding something in a large bowl with a pestle stone. Witches gather around her and scoop the soft, wet mixture into their hands. I feel them caressing the salve into my cuts and bruises. I have not felt tender touch since my Mother cared for me when I was young, and seem to lose my own body amongst all these hands; only the sensation of a cool-then-warm liquid dripping from the salve down my thighs, down my breasts, and between my buttocks brings me back to my own bodily sensations.

"For the pain," Nan's twin says as the last of the balsam is stroked into my body. I rock and groan at the relief.

"My sister did not understand," the twin witch continues. "He will not come unless thou desirest it. Does thou? Desirest Him?"

I look at the buxom witch before me who bears the delicious fruits. She proffers me a rosy red apple. I lick my lips longingly and she brings it to my lips. I take a bite, my teeth penetrating its firm skin as my lips draw in its crisp, sour flesh. I relish every sensation, desirous of everything and anything in this moment. I collapse down into an ecstasy of pleasure and hope, my bare breasts and belly pressed into the cool earth of the woodland floor.

I become aware that the witches have retreated from around me and are circled around the outskirts of the clearing. They hum and hold hands, their collective sounds rousing and expectant. Clouds pass over the slither of moon and a cool wind rushes over us. The fires are blown asunder, leaving only the glowing embers. I look about me, wondering if I, too, should retreat.

But then I hear it—Him.

First, it is the beastly snarl of His breath that I hear behind me. Distant but growing closer; snarling, snorting, panting—savouring what's in the air. Next, the rustle of dead leaves beneath heavy feet—His heavy gait striking the ground, each thud bringing Him closer to my resting place. Then, I feel the air around me grow cooler as His giant form moves in front of the dying fire. I motion to look behind me; to behold what approaches me in the last of the bonfire light. But a loud, fearsome roar makes me avert my eyes, my gaze instead resting on the old oak tree that Nan blessed.

The witches' chants enclosing us reach new frenzy as the beast behind me makes some sort of display—I hear and feel the flapping of huge wings, their power whipping up the detritus of the woodland floor around my bare body. I feel awed rather than afeared at what I can only wonder is the swish of a tail grazing my ankle. And when I feel the thud of heavy knees hitting the floor behind me, my heart—indeed, my whole body—pounds in time, too.

Hot, steamy breath moves up the length of my legs to my thighs to atop my buttocks, the beast savouring the offering being made by me between satisfied growls. I feel a new tingling betwixt my legs and an ooze not only from the salve the witches applied.

The coven of witches begin to recite unknown, unholy words, and to move in a thrum around us. A large, rough, leathery hand grabs at my buttock, and I gasp as claws dig into my quivering flesh. I yield to the heavy paw pushing my rear upright, raising myself onto my knees, my breasts still part-buried in the earth, my cunny fully seen by Him now. The other hand grasps the cheek of my other buttock, and I feel Him mawing at me, pulling my thighs aside to gaze at my slit. A claw that could split me asunder, end me, tenderly scrapes down the curve of my buttock and upper thigh. Coarse hair grazes me as He turns His digit to the side, entwining with the hair on my exposed mound, as if to feel as many of my textures with as many of His. He pushes my haunches higher up still, His beastly nature reminding me of the many males of the species I have seen manoeuvring their chattel into position for a rutting.

I braced to be taken, as I have been taken many times before. But instead I felt that hot, steaming breath yet closer to my most secret parts. He sniffed and savoured me—explored me up close. I flinched as I felt sizzling fronds of air emit from His nostrils and meet with the wispy hairs framing my cunny. He sniffed me in again, gripping at my thighs with His powerful paws, his muzzle so close to the crevice between my buttocks that I could feel the humidity and heat on my hole. I edged forwards in response, this so unfamiliar a feeling, to have someone—some beast—nuzzle me as if we're animals. But He gripped hard into me and rubbed His leathery face against the inside of my thigh.

I realised that His cheek was mushing into a wetness that I could not understand. Sensations coursed through my body—I was both repelled and willing Him to rub closer into me. And then I felt something slithering across my cunny—a long, slick, warm tongue. I let out a yelp as the tongue flicked across the skin of my innermost thigh and around my mound. No mortal man's tongue could be so long, making me sure I was giving myself to a true beast. I felt this fleshy pad lap against my lower lips, me writhing against such a terrible pleasure, He slathering and snarling as He licked at this carnal feast. Then a new sensation gripped at the tip of my secret parts; I felt a forked end—like the tongue of an adder—flickering at either side of my most sensitive part. His claws dug into me as I thrashed back into Him, moaning hard at such a curious tickling as this; desirous to be satisfied in some new, unknown way.

The witches fell silent, and the tongue and claws pulled away. I rocked in frustration, animal-like myself now.

"Dost thou want thine rightful share of mine power?" The voice was low and otherworldly, and the words came in a snarl.

I drew breath and the words came clear and resolute.

"Aye. I do, I do."

With that, I felt the head of His beastly phallus press against my wet, eager slit. His shaft was cold and hard—as cold and hard and unyielding as a stone. I submitted back against Him, my soft, tight cunt swallowing His cool, hard tip. His body fell forward over my mine as He drove himself a little deeper inside me. I gasped at the power of His arms; their ruddy-brown flesh, the coarse hair, the bulging muscles, the deadly talons at His fingertips. This glimpse of His form distracted me from the fullness at my slit—He stretched and filled me as I never knew possible, and yet still He was only part way inside me. His claws sunk into the soil as He ploughed further inside. I bucked back into Him, willing my body to yield to Him; to have all of Him, fully, inside of me, deeply and completely. My body was gripped with the desire to grind back and forth against His cold rock, my slippery wetness and relaxing cunt allowing Him to penetrate me fully. His torso bore down heavily over me as He thrust hard down inside me, my tiny body quaking and squirming beneath Him as He panted fearsomely beside my face.

The witches renewed their chants as my cries and moans joined their first crescendo. Tension and pressure built and built in my body, my cunny an inferno that I willed to erupt. He gripped a clawed hand into my shoulder and let His hard, cool phallus rest still, unmoving, deep, deep inside me as I shook and gasped—and exploded into pleasure. I panted into the ground, weak and sunken, as the witches wailed into a new phase of song. I felt the beast rise up onto His knees, bringing me with Him, He still inside of me, gripped in His strong embrace, me surrendered to Him.

My white thighs splayed either side of His thick, hairy flanks, and I looked down to see my sodden mound engorged around His beasthood. His paws mawed at my breasts as He began thrusting inside of me again, my body rising and falling with His motions, fully suspended atop His body as His rock pounded into my tender flesh. He groped frenziedly at my breasts and down my belly before He pressed His fat digits against the tip of my cunny.

As I cried out, the fires burst back into flames, and the witches began to whirl and whoop in an ecstatic motion. I saw, in the shadow cast by the fire, our two forms joined as one—and the giant, curled horns of The Beast—Beelzebub Himself—jutting out from our merged head. I felt myself so completely yield into Him, as if we truly had become one. He snarled and huffed beside my neck and face, Him nuzzling me almost as if we were lovers while I rode His stone phallus. His fat digit ground itself around and around my sensitive tip as He thrust faster, harder, and deeper.

I cried out as the pressure built to another explosion—it lasted long and slow, and I felt bathed in a bright, white fire as He, too, exploded into me. The witches threw themselves to the ground in convulsions of ecstasy, moaning and howling, as I felt His power pump and course into me, through me, beyond me.

I glimpsed the witch—twin Nan—naked and shining with a new ethereal beauty. She threw Robert's gatherings onto the fire... before I collapsed forwards onto my hands and knees.

***

And here I find myself, awaiting Robert, shook from this all-encompassing vision.

Coming to my senses, I spit on my palm and reach back between my legs to moisten myself. Robert was in a foul mind all day today, and boldly and gleefully told me of his plan to replace me with a new wife if I could not, would not, breed. But, despite my disgust for him, I find myself dripping with hot, sticky wetness. My cunny—and my sensitive tip— throb with the memory of that unholy dream. Is this the way the witches have fooled me? Am I cursed to now want my husband's stumpy little pecker betwixt my legs? To bear him his rotten apples?

Hearing his clomping steps on the floorboards, I brace for him—and for the beating that will follow. But instead he staggers into the room and falls down beside me on the bed, declaring himself unwell. Soon he is snoring, and so I slip away into the next room.

I stand at the window staring at the full moon floating above the fields. My finger presses against my wet, voracious tip and I rock myself to an echo of the pleasure I felt with Him—or dreamed I felt with Him.

***

I am a widow come the waning crescent of the moon.

Robert died while away in the city of Ely, in the company of a botanist he'd befriended. Witnesses—including the botanist's comely young daughter of but 12 years—said he whipped his horse for naught good reason, only for the tired old filly to rear up at him. Robert fell back and smashed his head against the stone water trough, dying painfully and deliriously some hours later.

I buried the old toad next to Grace with, I believe, her blessing, so that she could haunt and taunt him for all his damned eternity. I made little show of being the sad widow amongst the farmhands, and instead we became a merry if somewhat unproductive and unprofitable band of workers through til the first bite of winter. As for the stable-boy spy, when he proposed to kill Robert's filly for her meat due to her dangerous change in temperament, he was told to pack his things and leave the farm lest I turn him to sausages instead.

Just as old Samuel, the ploughman, was imploring me to make better plans and provisions for the coming hard winter months, there came a knock at the door. It was my brother Bill! He and his family—his wife, the miller's daughter, and their three jolly children—had come a-callin' on the way to seek greener pastures in a nearby parish. Father, it seemed, had succumbed to jaundice, but not before running the apothecary to the ground. All was not lost as Bill's wife's father had gifted them a little money to begin a new life. Besides, Bill could not mourn much—he had never much liked his trade as an apothecary, preferring his boyish days of tending to the animals and lands. Seeing that Samuel was an old farming man, he enquired as to anywhere needing such help as theirs? Sam chuckled at me and said he wondered if I'd done a deal with the Devil, such was my good fortune of late. And so Bill and his family became the steady stewards of the farm, while I rekindled my interests in nature and healing.

Indeed, I did seem to be living a blessed life, for not long after Bill and his kin took good charge of the farm, I found peace and contentment progressing Father's work. His journals and what was left of the apothecary were brought to the farm and I set up a-studying in an old barn. I resolved to live out my days a happy widow—Bill's rambunctious children were all the legacy I needed, and his wife more than pleased to let me play mother when the mood struck us all.

I set to work seeking the elixirs of that bewitching night— though certain in my mind that it was a dream, my heart was still unable to shake its reality. Amongst Father's journals, I found some of Mother's long-forgotten notes of ancient and folk wisdoms. I began to brew a potion supposed to bring the imbiber their heart's desire—I did not believe such heresy, of course, but it pleased me to make my young Mother's concoctions for real.

As I sipped on the brewed tincture, I could not help but think of twin Nan's words to me: "He will not come unless thou desirest it."

He did not come. But I must have had desire in my heart, in spite of all my wretched years as Robert's wife. Perhaps that night—that dream—was simply hope reawakening in me..? I know not, but what the fates did have in store for me was a good and handsome man.

Peter was a vagabond of seven-and-twenty years come to our town in search of work, which he found helping drain part of the marshland that was to be turned to farmland. He came to our stead while making his enquiries and Bill found him odd jobs when he wasn't working the marshes. I was like a moth to a flame for him—perhaps Mother's potion did work! All my girlish silliness and flushes that I'd not had chance to give to the blacksmith's boy all those years back and had died with my betrothal to Robert got buttered on

Pete. Bill and his wife, and the children, found it devilish funny to watch me flirt and gush so, and for Pete to so dote upon me. Mercifully Bill and his wife said we'd make a fine match, and gave me their blessing.

Alas, something held me back... And that something was my freedom. I was now a woman of means—a landowner—and a person who could protect and keep my brother and his kin, as well as the labourers who had served Grace and her family so loyally and well. For me to marry, especially in haste, could spell the end of my good fortune.

***

And yet my heart—my body—my soul—yearned for Pete. Come the Candlemas celebrations, as the town gathered together to celebrate the arrival of spring, I felt my heart would burst wanting to be with him. Dizzy on ale and the feasting and revelries, Pete and I danced and touched as if we were man and wife. I felt that the town's people were as glad to be rid of Robert as I, and thus that, with Bill's manly presence, I would escape the accusations of sinning, or of witchcraft, that had befallen other lone women of my country. As sunlight faded to moonlight, Pete stole a kiss while the young maidens danced about the maypole and the men made merry with their lutes, and horns, and pipes.

We confessed our love—and longing—for one another. But I told him I would not wed him. He told me he preferred the old pagan ways anyway, where people made their bonds and pledges to one another with only nature as their witness. Overcome by passion for him—for him not wanting to own me; to possess me—I asked that we might do it now, tonight? He kissed me hard and hot, his tongue and my tongue hungry for so much more, before pulling me by the hand away from the townspeople and merriment, and into the trees in the yonder. We tore through the darkness of the forest, hearing naught but the rustle of leaves beneath our feet, the snaps of twigs as we made our hasty path through, and the retreat of unseen startled birds and animals.

Soon, panting, we broke into a clearing in the trees. Pete gripped his hands to his knees, catching his breath, while I smoothed out my dress, brushing away the leaves and moss about my bosom and hair. The circular clearing was bathed in moonlight, and eerily silent and still. Ancient stones lay about the place in an arrangement I could not make sense of, with a large table-like slab in the centre. Remnants of fires dotted the grass. Pete grabbed me to him, kissing my neck and running his hands across my chest and waist. He murmured that, as folklore had it, our elders used to worship here—what better place to become man and wife according to nature's laws? I felt as wild as nature for him as his nuzzling edged down my neck towards my bosom. We moved as one, kissing, caressing, sighing, to the slab in the centre.

I motioned for Pete to seat himself on the stone, for him to watch while I removed my dress and undergarments. I wanted to show myself to him; to not rush in and out of this clothing, but to slowly shed my cocoon and emerge as something—someone—new. And so I unlaced the strings of my bodice, shook off my gown and petticoats, stepped out of my boots, and unfurled my hair. I stood afore Pete as naked as the day I was born, ready, and truly willing, for the first time in my life, to be as one with a man—this man.

He gestured for me to go to him, and I did; him running his hands across my milky thighs and buttocks, kissing my belly and hips. Then he stood to show himself to me— removing his shirt and unfastening breeches, my eyes drinking in his tanned skin and lithe muscles, and drawn down, down, down to the bulge at his groin. I gasped as he freed his manhood—he was quite the bull! He gave me a knowing smile as I looked up at him, drawing me into his embrace as we kissed, our flesh pressed firmly against one another. I had never felt pleasure in my breasts before, but they pulsed and tingled against his torso, making me push myself ever closer to him, wanting to feel his warm, throbbing member press back against the top of my groin, but it just a little distance from my aching body. All I knew was that I wanted to be united with him, and to feel some semblance of what I had felt that night, that dream, with... Him.

I lead Pete to the stone slab by the hand and guide us down onto it, me reclining on my back and he kneeling to my side. I pull him closer down to me to kiss me, his tongue exploring my eager mouth, his hands fondling my breasts as I stroke and tug at his arms and torso. I rest fully back, eyes closed so as to focus only on us, and I let my legs splay apart, inviting him inside of me, while our lips stay hotly locked and our arms hook around one another. He moves over me, kneeling betwixt my gaping legs, me smoothing my hands over his broad, honed back as I wait for the moment he will plough himself inside of me. Just then I have the strangest felt-memory shoot through my hands—it is as if his back were of the rough, leathery, beastly texture of He who took me the night that my fate changed..?

I gasp as I feel that, yes, his skin feels different and hot to the touch? Then his tongue seems to probe and stretch deeper inside my mouth, two forks of its snaking tip curling around mine. My eyes flicker open to, surely, confirm that my senses are deceiving me. To my relief, I see the face of my love, Pete, smiling down at me, about to enter me. But then he speaks, and yet in a voice not his own.

"I cannot give thou thine rightful share of mine power," comes *that* voice—His voice. "Thou must take it for thine own."

Pete's face contorts into a rich grin and his eyes flicker a fiery red. He seems to have grown in size and balk, but I cannot cower and take fright—I am still so desirous of him—

of Him?—so confused; so torn. My hips buck up, straining to meet His manhood—or beasthood. Whatever awaits me, I want it. I run my hands down the length of His arms, knowing that this darkened, furred, throbbing form is not what I laid my hands and eyes on moments ago.

A peculiar hum begins to build around us, emerging from the blackness of the trees. I glance around, seeking the source of the growing noise. The sooted pits around the clearing leap into flames, turning the silvery grey-blue of the clearing into a warm orange. In this light, the nude forms of a hundred or more women—witches, a coven—creep from the darkness. Their harmoniously hideous voices rise and fall as one, as they close in around us in a ritualistic procession.

I look back at Pete—at Him—in a tangle of desire and dread. The last vestiges of Pete were transforming into the beast as I realised I had merely tasted pleasure and power the night the beast and witches took me. Now I was to take Him, and complete the ritual. I found myself strangely calm as I beheld the face of the Devil incarnate. He looked upon me with eyes of burning red, pitted with bottomless black pupils. His skin was deeply grooved as an animal's, centred with a hot, shining snout through which He breathed steamy, hungry breaths upon me. Ram-like horns jutted from His head as He knelt back and upwards for me to fully behold Him, two great bat-like wings beating behind Him, and with Him rested on great hairy haunches finished with cloven hooves.

"Thou must take me, for thine self, in mine true form. As my true wife."

The witches fell silent and still with these words, and covered their eyes with their hands. Then He folded His wings back up, and moved to my side, never breaking His gaze into my eyes, and lay down beside me. I pushed myself upright to look upon Him—to see Him as the witches did not. He lay there as a giant, snorting and snarling in this submissive expectation, twice the size of a mortal man; infinite the power; offering unimaginable power to me—and unimaginable pleasure..? I put my hand to His chest and lay it where a heart would be—I felt no familiar drum beat, but watched my hand rise and fall with His beastly breath; me wanting to rock on top of that heaving torso while impaled upon His rod. And then I remembered the beastly form I'd seen and the cold, hard stone I'd felt from that night—I looked down and saw a long, thick, creamy white pole projecting out from betwixt His legs. It was a magnificent phallus, framed by a wilderness of coarse hair and hung with the heavy, swollen sacks of a bull stud at mating season. I looked back up into His endless eyes and knew He saw into my soul; my mind made up.

I clambered astride the beast's body, resting my tiny hands against that rising and falling torso, gripping my fingers into the wiry hairs and leathered skin. Then I raised my hips up and positioned myself—my slippery, delicate slit —above that giant otherworldly shaft. I quivered there for a moment, staring into the face of mine true husband. I wanted power and pleasure for mine self. And so I plunged myself down, down onto His stone-cold phallus. I felt myself seared with bright, brilliant white light as I brought Him fully inside myself, shrieking in what I could not deduce as pleasure or pain—just as if I were pure feelings and sensations. I thrust myself back and forth into His lap in time with His thunderous breathing, feeling that pressure building inside of me even more so than the first time. He gripped at my thighs as I ground my straining cunny against Him, His claws digging into my flesh and drawing a little blood. I reached up with one hand and cradled my breast, tweaking my nipple, and tracing the pink nubbled circle around it, moaning at these new gratifications.

All the while, I stared into the face of Satan; His slathering lips and snorting snout. I felt no fear nor disgust —instead I wanted to share in every sensation with Him. I strained forward to push my lips to His mouth and to kiss. His snake-like tongue returned the gesture and He gnawed my plush, rosy lips and flushed cheeks with His sharpened teeth. Laying forward like this meant that I was riding the rise and fall of His chest, with that hot sensitive tip of my cunny pressed hard against His furry nether regions. I gripped tight into the beast—*my beast*—as I felt the ecstasy rising inside of me, moaning and crying into His pointed ears as I reached my moment. I released with a scream, rising back up and arching my back, facing upwards, howling out my pleasure. The coven released in harmony with me, crying and yowling in such joys, the fires burning harder and brighter, the bodies pulsing and convulsing in solitary and collective tangles, standing, crawling, lying in the circle around us.

My pleasure seemed unending as the beast continued pumping His cool, lengthy pole inside me. I looked down into the burning embers of His eyes as His breathing grew deeper and louder. I moved in time with Him as His thrusts came harder and faster, all around us a frenzy of ecstasy from the coven. He climaxed with a roar, His claws gripping into me, puncturing my skin. I felt a flash of bright white light shoot up and through me, like lightening, ripping from Him through my body and up through my head, skywards. I seemed to feel His pleasure—some divine and total pleasure —through and beyond me, for it was not what I had felt before. I vibrated as one with the world, feeling pure pleasure—and power. I fell forward onto my beast and showered His face with tender, thankful kisses, my body still reeling from its sensations. As I breathed and nuzzled into His hot, earthy pelt, I glimpsed that the witches were writhing towards and around our stone bed—our altar—in final humming revelries.

The last thing I remember seeing before I fell into a deep, deep slumber was their swollen, distended bellies—all heavily with-child.

***

I emailed Esther a (password-protected!) document containing the above account to conclude our past-life regression work.

She wrote a short reply in thanks, but I don't know what inferences and conclusions she drew from our co-created parable because she didn't return for further hypnotherapy. I'm pleased. She indicated she would do so if she decided her symptoms were solely in her head; instead, she has decided to pursue a medical path, free of blaming and doubting herself for months and years prior to investigation and diagnosis.

You'll be proud to learn, Dear Reader, that I dabbled with her imaginings only a bit; the themes of dismissal, oppression, power, and rebirth came purely from her. Should she choose to someday listen to the tapes that I mailed to her—and my hope is that I made the first few story extractions sufficiently dull and stilted to dissuade her from doing so—then she'll find it's about 80% her. But, yes, I may have amplified the pleasure parts of the story a tad...

Such interventions were justified. Consider the denouement of Agnes gaining her witchy powers. Esther is a woman still seeking approval and permission from The Patriarchy. So I'll be damned if I'm going to lie here frigging myself to her longed-for power being simply fucked into her by The Devil incarnate.

Power is never given. It can only be taken.

And so, take it she did. Even from Him.

CASE #213 / ALICE

Using a powerful hypnotic phenomenon—and a thoroughly modern threesome—to fulfil a client's fantasy... for a therapeutic amount of cash!

Dear Reader: I knew I was going to fall... I've chased my client Theo down the proverbial rabbit hole into some—ahem—'hypnotic field-work'. And so I now find myself, from my vantage point beside this queen-sized bed, watching a curious woman called Alice amidst a press of flesh. The lyrics of the Jefferson Airplane song 'White Rabbit' play in my head:

'One pill makes you larger /

'And one pill makes you small /

'And the ones that mother gives you /

'Don't do anything at all /

'Go ask Alice...'

Logic and proportion have, it seems, indeed fallen sloppy dead when it comes to maintaining my professional boundaries. Can I still convince myself—convince you—that I am the detached narrator of these hypnotic, erotic confessions, rather than a fellow player on this increasingly surrealistic chessboard?

***

You'll remember Theo, of course—the client for whom I'd invented 'pussy-gazing'? More importantly, you'll recall the post-session debrief I did with my beloved husband Addy, where we reenacted my new innovation in hypnotherapy—to our mutual orgasmic satisfaction.

But there were consequences beyond our happy role-play... While Addy and I share fantasies, secrets, and memories of past liaisons, we don't desire to open up our marriage to other lovers. But in baring myself to Theo, I had blurred the line between fantasy and reality, and shocked Addy and I both with what I might spontaneously—recklessly—act upon.

There's no jealousy, insecurity, distrust or doubt in our marriage. But, after taking a long, hard look at my pussy, my husband took a long, hard look at my professional insurance policy. What if Theo remembers what passed between us? What if he objects to his forgotten consent?

Thankfully, hypnosis—and particularly the 'hypnoanalysis' talk-therapy popularised by Freud that Theo came to me for—became notorious for fostering false memories in people in the 1980s. So my hope was that Theo would doubt himself should any glimmer of what happened remain in his mind. A person of his sexual appetites and experiences would likely fantasise about those with whom he shared a little frisson, myself included. My pussy shall be as a fleeting x-rated vision in his mind as I maintain the professional illusion that we don't all harbour such filthy thoughts about most 'Toms, Dicks, and Harriets' we cross paths with.

Our upcoming session was left unscheduled while he took a week's vacation (Ibiza, of course) and then prioritised some work stuff. So I was surprised when he called me sooner than expected. I adopted a cool and breezy tone that I hoped would embarrass away any 'impure thoughts' he'd been having about me, and instantly squash any back-of-mind pondering about their possible reality.

I'm buoyed up by the hint of hesitation—the uncharacteristic shyness, even?—in Theo's voice. But I wonder where his awkward flatteries about me being "trusted" and "open-minded" and "professional" are heading... He clears his throat...

"I'm not sure how to ask this, Lilith. Or even if I should... ask," comes his honeyed voice over the phone. "And I'll understand if you say no. And there's no need for me to continue with our, er, work if this... if it... makes you uncomfortable. But I, we, I... I was wondering if you'd offer a, um, special appointment? Special, umm, unusual... Something quite... For a price, of course."

I pause to contemplate how much more "special" and "unusual" my hypnotic capers can get?!

"I won't be offended by you asking," I reassure him.

"Well, a friend of mine—playmate—one of my playmates, you know?—Alice, um. So I mentioned to Alice I was seeing a hypnotherapist; seeing you. Not the—not what we're actually working on! Nah. Stupid really, but we were just chatting about that Dracula movie and how vampires can hypnotise their victims—'glamour' them. Anyway, doesn't matter. We got to chatting about hypnosis and what it's doing for me—she thinks you're treating me for a fear of flying, by the way—and she said she wished she could be hypnotised. To... fulfil a fantasy."

I rub my head with my spare hand while staring despairingly into my iPhone held in the other. I'm braced for some unimaginative, misogynistic, vampire-themed hypnotised-victim sex pitch that they want me to facilitate. Has all my work with Theo on breaking down gender and identity roles and norms been for naught?! He continues chattering nervously.

"Seeing as you're helping me with something... sexual... I, we, I wondered if... if you were open to... Hmm, you see, it wouldn't be therapy, so much. You know, in your office. It would be more... in the field."

"In the field?", I echo, intrigued in spite of what cliched neck-biting fantasy likely awaits me.

"Yeah. Yep. Specifically: in the bedroom."

My mind whirrs with what sort of eye-watering sum I can demand for a remote, out-of-hours, special-unusual sexy hypnosis session...

"I was saying to Alice how weird it is that I can't remember most of what happens in our sessions," Theo continues, emboldened by my lack of reaction so far. "Like, it's weird, remembering arriving and leaving, and the bits we say will stay in my mind. But then there are these blanks. But it's cool. I'm cool, chill about them. Because I know that's what's right for me, for our process.

"Anyway. She was real impressed by that. Real interested. And it made her wonder whether hypnosis might help her— help her to forget or 'blank', or whatever—to help her fulfil her fantasy. Um, should I go on?"

"Sure," I reply, wondering what sort of consent I'd need to garner if Alice's fantasy is to be ravished by Dracula in the virginal hypnotic slumber favoured by the genre. Yawn.

"See, Alice's fantasy is... to be... watched. Watched—while she fucks. She's, er, she's very adventurous, kinda wild, confident, gorgeous. You're probably thinking this isn't a difficult fantasy for a girl like her to fulfil, right?! But she's filmed herself... a lot. Just for herself to see at first. But it didn't... it wasn't... She tried hiding the camera, so she'd forget it was there, in the room, filming her. Even put on a mask so she could share the footage anonymously on porn sites, to see if that worked for her. But she says she just can't get out of her head. There's always an awareness of the camera; that she's playing up to it. When she watches herself, she can see it in the way she moves and sounds, and... cums. And so other people watching that does nothing for her.

"Same happens if someone watches her, in person. She knows they're there, that they're present, even when she's set it up so that only the person, people, she's fucking interacts with them. She knows they have their own thoughts and feelings—maybe they want to join in or, you know, get themselves off to it. It's not about her; not about capturing the moment, objectively.

"She's always been a hedonist, but she even got big into ketamine—chasing out-of-body experiences. But that's not what she wants. She wants... authenticity. Realness. Not to create content—content for consumption. She wants to be the watched; not the watcher. She wants to be *observed*. I dunno. I just thought that maybe you could, help, maybes..?"

I bite my lip, mulling what to do. Logic and proportion tell me to decline, hang up, and cease my hypnotic liaisons with the lovely Theo. But—but—but! But yet again Theo has brought me a truly fascinating case; not to mention one which proffers the opportunity to use a true hypnotic 'super-power'... While I achieved it during my scant training period—much to the shock and awe of my fellow students, as well as the 'teacher'—and have tried it on good subjects at a couple of social occasions, it is a difficult phenomenon to weave into therapy. But it is, undeniably, a super power that I long to wield.

"Yes, yes," I purr through the phone. "I can help, Theo. For a price."

"Oh, wow! Really? That's, um, wow, brilliant. She'll be so... Thanks, Lilith."

Theo starts spit-balling about logistics—time, place, how comfortable I'll be watching him and Alice, and perhaps another playmate, as well as my methods. In assuring me that Alice will be down with any evidences of consent that I require, filmed or written, he reveals that she makes a serious crust as an online influencer. Which prompts me to further inflate the four figures I had in my head. He doesn't flinch at the sum and says he'll confirm it with Alice so we can seal the deal.

"Oh, and I'll need to send her some training materials," I add. "Some audio files for her to listen to in advance. I don't want or need to meet beforehand; why put a face to the 'Invisible Woman'? But this way she'll be trained to go into deep hypnosis for me before you, ah..."

"So it will be like with me, she'll forget you're there or something?", Theo muses.

Oh, bless! He's labouring under the illusion that I'll be using a simple amnesia to fulfil Alice's erotic wishes... But I didn't call my hypnotic power 'super' for nothing.

"No," I reply. "I shall be invisible to her."

***

My black taxi shudders to a halt alongside a smart street of terraced Georgian houses in the heart of Islington. I ask the cabbie to keep the clock running while I wait a few minutes. I check Theo's last text confirming all the arrangements for this evening, and see the house number shining in brass from the glossy black door across the street, and an intercom for the flat I'm soon to enter.

As agreed, I ping Theo a text announcing my arrival. He fires back a simple "yep", which tells me that Alice, he, and another playmate, who remains something of a mystery, are ready. I don't want to be competing with a Deliveroo driver or confused visitor to a neighbouring flat once I press that intercom—and remotely induce Alice into hypnosis.

I retrieve a couple of notes from my handbag to pay the cabbie, refusing the change he cursorily motions to get. I pause for a moment to breathe—am I really going to do this?! I exit the cab into the strangely humid air, taking in the suburban sounds and smells. The cabbie flips his 'for hire' sign back on and I watch its amber glow disappear into the darkening evening. I've purposefully deleted the Uber app from my phone to prevent me from chickening out—I have consent videos from Theo, Alice, and the third playmate, plus Addy knows full well where I am tonight and will pick me up when my work here is done, so all is set.

Yes, Dear Reader, of course I discussed this new frontier in my hypno-sex-therapy with my husband! While Alice has been busy training herself into hypnosis with my series of audio recordings, Addy and I have been busy watching threesomes on PornHub while convincing ourselves that *observing* a person in such an act is an isolated perk of my job. Since I'm not partaking in tonight's pleasures, we agreed this is on a par with listening—and fucking—along with some particularly vocal hotel-room neighbours a few years back. Or when it was novel to share details of past love-affairs for each other's gratification. Suffice to say, he was thrilled that Theo was lascivious rather than litigious, and is waiting patiently at home til he can fetch me back, and to bed, to hear about the whole thrilling escapade.

I walk across the street towards the grand house before me. I feel nervier than I anticipated—than I want to be. I've spent longer wondering what to wear for this evening than I have since I was a teenager. How does one strike the balance between being an impartial observer who isn't tempted, or tempting, to get involved, versus being a mood killer dressed for puritan comfort?! I opted for an oatmeal pussy-bow silk blouse paired with flowing black culottes, along with stylish trainers and a messy-haired updo in a business/pleasure, daytime/evening mash up that I hope strikes this new 'trail-blazing hypnotist me' tone.

I draw a breath as I step up onto the pavement, about to head up the steps. Then I blurt out a laugh as a black cat darts across my path! How perfectly apt and ironic. I'm not prone to superstition, so won't be taking this as a sign of bad luck. But hypnotism <u>is</u> the original witchcraft, and so no wonder it feels so wickedly exhilarating to be colouring outside the box of boring, safe therapising. The cat slinks off into a side alley; the perfect metaphor for the creature of the night that I am becoming.

Boosted by the presence of the traditional witch's familiar, I mount the stone grey steps up to the front door and search for the buzzer noted in Theo's penultimate text. It doesn't bear Theo's or Alice's name or initials, and so I'm left curiouser still about the third playmate I'm about to meet... They identify as non-binary and it took much negotiating to create a mutually agreeable advanced video giving their informed consent. Quite understandably, they wished to preserve their anonymity despite wanting to partake in Alice's fantasy. So all I have seen of them, know of them, is their lips and voice speaking beneath a dark masquerade mask—and the ornate, spectacular butterfly tattoo etched across their chest, which we agreed is my means to identify I have the consent of the person with whom I'm about to meet.

"Yes," comes the crackled voice from the intercom. It must be their voice because I don't recognise it as Theo's. I recite a string of five randomly chosen words clearly across the intercom. These 'magic words' command Alice to go deep into a hypnotic slumber, which has been carefully and repeatedly 'programmed' into her during the past month of hypnotic audio training. This is a make-or-break moment and few hypnotists would have the balls to take such a risk.

Yet I'm confident that Alice, and Theo, are highly invested—plus Theo, 'they', and me add to the social pressure for Alice to perform her role. I've no guarantee yet on her ability to experience a negative hallucination, in not seeing me, of course. But I'd have heard during the month of training if she weren't succeeding with the self-hypnotism, and wasn't accepting of my voice, authority, and suggestions.

A few moments later, I hear a commotion from behind the door—Theo opens it. He looks, frankly, delicious in a loose top, tight jeans, and sliders, but he's also a little flustered. He flashes me a smile, and automatically looks me over approvingly, in the way I imagine he welcomes all his hook-ups, then makes a quick, more neutral nod. I sense he subconsciously considered shaking my hand for a split-second, before dismissing the idea. I'm glad I have the power to give him amnesia as there is going to be some social awkwardness along the way.

***

"It worked," he says as we cross a black-and-white checkerboard-tiled hallway and wend our way up the sweeping staircase to the second floor flat. He ushers me through the ajar door into an airy and stylish flat. I take in the large living, dining, and kitchen open-space; all airy white and sensitively renovated, adorned with abstract pictures and artefacts, and shelves of books. A bulbous glass light fixture drips down from the ceiling above a coffee table and plush velvet sofas. Beside the seating area, a slick modern electric fire burns with a warm glow. Beyond, past a dining table littered with a laptop and life-min, French doors, left open, lead to a balcony where I glimpse an uncorked bottle of wine and half-drunk glasses. A plume of smoke from a vape floats in from the outside—I remind myself not to be quite so intrigued by Theo's aloof third playmate; it is Alice I'm here to serve.

She is stood in profile to me, still like a statue, eyes closed, around from the entry way where she heard me utter my secret hypnotic command. She is impervious to my or Theo's presence, frozen in time and space until I weave the next part of the spell. Nevertheless, Theo moves cautiously towards her, afraid he'll awaken her, unsure what comes next, and, I'm sure, unmoored from his usual charming, confident, pre-fuck role.

I expected Alice to be beautiful and she is. Dirty blonde hair falls at her shoulders and her pert breasts rise gently up and down in motion with her relaxed breathing. She wears a semi-opaque midi dress that sweeps down her perfect figure, showing off her shapely hips, firm backside, and flat tummy as it falls into flowing ruches mid-calves. Her toned, tanned limbs are a feast of tattoos, rings, and bangles. I wonder if she leaves them on to fuck..? How she styles her cunt hair..? What she smells and sounds like..?

I came of age in the 90s and spent my 20s in the noughties, so I've kissed a few girls but mostly missed any superficial, for-show, 'lipstick lesbian' experimentation that my naïve younger self saw then as about as sexually adventurous as life got. In these confessions I write for you, I hope you see before you a white, heterosexual, monogamous woman who's doing her best not to fall any further down this mid-life rabbit hole I see opening up before me. But still, as I watch Alice, and contemplate watching her in the hours to come, I sense that I don't desire a woman. But I do desire to watch her—to observe, to see, to *consume* her. I think I begin to comprehend why male and other hungry observers, real, virtual, paying, and ultimately always watched back by her, did not fulfil her fantasy—her need.

Theo and I are lingering in the entry way, me staring at Alice and Theo staring at me. The front door is still ajar and so I push it closed. I feel lost for having no coat or bag to hang, adding to the lack of social script that Theo is palpably struggling with. Instead, I flash Theo my phone and switch it off, placing it on the hallway table as pre-agreed, so that the playmates can be assured I'm neither covertly recording them—nor failing to give Alice the full attention she has paid handsomely for. We move farther into the room so that I am face-to-face with Alice. Her kohl smudged eyes are gently closed, as I'd instructed in my audio, and her bee-stung lips gently parted as she breathes serenely.

I prepare to deliver my final set of suggestions, but am interrupted by the third playmate wafting inside from the cloud of smoke at the balcony. I see their mysterious face shrouded beneath the dark mask I saw in the video. The video was brief, badly framed, and poor quality, but now I see the brilliance of their icy blue eyes staring at me. The blue of their eyes is mirrored in the large butterfly tattoo that spreads across their chest, the wings spanning their shoulders and featuring four sapphire human eyes in place of camouflage eyes. The base of the butterfly's abdomen disappears beneath their top down to their sternum, and intricate flowers frame the design. They are dressed in a tubular stretch top, skinny jeans, and a voluminous kimono, and give me a hand wave that I can't distinguish as being awkward or dismissive as they flop back into the sofa. They suck on the vape and I feel those glacial eyes penetrating me behind the mist of fragranced smoke. I'm reminded of the hookah-smoking caterpillar from *Alice in Wonderland*, so mysterious and exotic—and seemingly impolite. And so I will call them 'C' from now on.

I turn my attentions to Alice, reciting the carefully prepared script I've created. I am 'The Person Who Isn't Here'; an invisible presence who will satisfy her fantasy—her need—to be watched, really, truly watched—but she will neither see nor sense me. I also break the spell of the five magic words that I used to induce her into hypnosis over the intercom—they are known to Theo and C now, so this otherwise permanent and potent post-hypnotic suggestion must be removed.

While I'm speaking, however, my mind is half on C, vaping beside the fire, watching me watching Alice. Personally I do not concern myself with the content of other people's pants, as seems to trouble a disappointing yet minuscule faction of the Gen-X sisterhood these days. But it occurs to me that I do not know C's biology..? Theo told me they, C, identified as non-binary, which I thought little to nothing of given the broader unusualness of our arrangements. My paid role is to watch Alice; not mull my personal fancies and curiosities were I to place myself in her shoes (as pornography invites us to). I realise that the video bedazzled me with the femininity of the baroque mask, and that I made assumptions about a peek of a flat, androgynous chest versus the beauty and gendered-associations of that butterfly tattoo. I confess I had mentally prepared myself for seeing a threesome featuring two biological females, irrespective of gender identity. Upon arrival, I had seen C and seen a body I couldn't easily ascribe to a binary biology—*and C had seen me see that*.

I often preach to clients that 'the map is not the territory', and now, here I am, a white, het, cis-gendered, middle-class, unwitting, and rampantly inexperienced social-construct-of-a-woman—aka person—being gratefully reminded by this hookah-smoking caterpillar of just that. I relish the 'through the looking glass' moment and silently congratulate Theo on his intuition and insight for finding me and understanding the true meaning of the term 'open minded' better than I. What a privilege to be here—to watch Alice, but to be respectful of, deferential to, Theo's and C's presence; to afford them the invisibility that Alice is soon to afford me.

Finally fully at ease, I reach for a pot of pills stashed in my pocket, ready to dispense the final suggestion. Theo divulged that Alice had experimented with ketamine for out-of-body experiences, and also that he and his playmates regularly swallowed, sniffed, and smoked psychoactives and psychotropics as accoutrements to their intimacies. I hand Theo the pot and have him inspect them; they're empty capsules—pure placebo. Popping a pill is part of the ritual for Alice, Theo, and C; a prelude to heightened mental and physical pleasures—and a strongly held belief which I can ride as I guide Alice back up to a very lightly hypnotised state. Here, she will experience everything as waking reality —the only difference being a strange sense of a welcome presence watching her, but which she can neither see nor perceive. And when she senses that the presence is gone, or certainly when she leaves this flat (either way, meaning I will have left), all will be as it was and no one will be able to induce her into hypnosis or recreate this effect without her explicit permission. I leave her with the choice as to whether she remembers the reality of our arrangements—that she really was watched by The Person Who Isn't Here—or if she had an interesting experience with self-hypnosis that created an authentic experience of being watched. But, either way, that she would find her fantasy fully satisfied.

Satisfied also that the pills are inert, Theo hands them back to me. I place a pill in Alice's hand and then, with a shrug, dispense one each to me and Theo, before tossing the bottle to C.

C studies the blank pill bottle.

"So these... don't do anything... at all?", they frown.

I knock back my pill and then instruct Alice to do likewise. She gulps it down—and then opens her eyes. She instantly fills in the 'reality gap', as I like to term it, between now and when she was last in waking reality—when the intercom buzzed—precisely as my preparatory audios instructed her to do.

"Ugh, people were forever doing that at my old apartment building at the weekends. Just buzzing up any and all apartments til they get let in. Deliveroo drivers are the worst for it. The. Worst..."

She chatters relaxedly to Theo and C, wandering off to the balcony to retrieve her wine—passing me as she goes. Theo and C look agog as they see I'm invisible to Alice; they've been instructed to ignore me as well as any urge to comment on their and Alice's very different realities. But it's a struggle for them to reengage with Alice and the pre-play chatter.

I take a moment to enjoy being invisible: to enjoy my super power. The hypnotic phenomena of negative hallucination is mostly the prevail of gaudy stage hypnosis shows, where desperate showmen taunt their subjects with 'floating' objects or ghostly touches. They're quick to claim victory, and to suggest its end for fear of the subject undoing the magic. But me, I get to truly experience what this super power feels like for the evening—to bask in the flames conjured by a true sorcerer rather than the fizzle of sparks achieved by frauds and pretenders.

Alice potters back in from the balcony and asks Theo a highly personal question I shan't divulge here, but which certainly convinced him that Alice wasn't shamming my absence. I smile and walk across Alice's path towards the next room—the bedroom. I see her react to a slight movement in the air as I pass her, but then shrug it off. As I turn back to push the bedroom door almost shut behind me, I see Theo and C eagerly swallow down their placebo pills.

***

Here I sit on the grey stone steps outside the door to the flats some hours later. I suck uncertainly on a cigarette that I pinched and lit before sneaking out the scene of our hypnotic experiment. I haven't smoked since my 20s, and never concertedly anyway, but I felt the need for some kind of stimulant and activity. A green blip on my phone screen shows me Addy hastening towards me on the map.

The still of the London night and the scorch of the smoke in my lungs bring me back to my 20s. How long has it been since I waited amongst this city's rats and distant drunks for a 3am ride home? Yes, I must admit, Dear Reader, that seeing supple, youthful flesh—writhing, pleasing, playing, cumming—these past four hours has made me reflective; but not nostalgic. I would not trade my life, my love, my wisdom, my mistakes for the hedonistic thrills I was witness to this night—I want to progress as a person; not to fall into a fantasy of regression as seems the pitfall of many a middle-aged person.

'Middle-aged'! I don't much care for generalisations and labels, but there is nothing quite like perimenopause and the death of your former career to make you feel like there is some truth in the 'invisible 40-plus woman' trope... And yet I have just revelled in my invisibility—used it to my advantage —done something with it that apparent masters of hypnosis have neither conceived nor dared. C's butterfly tattoo seems to stare at me from my mind's eye. I worked hard to focus solely on Alice, but those four blazing blue eyes gazed at, and into, me... I thought I had emerged triumphant from the miserable cocoon I was in a couple of years back. But C makes me wonder if I am still emerging..? Still *becoming..?*

Still escaping the bored, tired scripts women like me are prescribed and so often doomed to follow.

I hear, and then see, Addy's car rolling around the corner into the road. I snub the half-smoked cigarette out on the iron railing and huff out the last breath of smoke I'll be troubling my lungs with for the foreseeable future. I hope— given Addy's aspirations for how we'll be spending the next few hours together during our debrief—that he'll find my smoky breath a heady reminder of the youth we did not misspend together.

As I approach the car, I recall my shift from wanting to *consume* Alice—and wanting to later share all the heady details with Addy for our mutual delectation—to becoming an incidental part of something private and sacred to fulfil her fantasy of being *observed*. I realise that even to try to share some poor, patchy facsimile of what happened would be to diminish the magick. I brighten at the fact that my husband—my soulmate—will be far more fascinated and aroused by my cigarette tainted mouth and shaken perspective than he would by titbits from relative youngsters' bedrooms.

I shall have to leave you, too, Dear Reader, to conjure what passed between Alice, Theo, and C in your imagination only. To imagine what it is to truly yet invisibly see someone in carnal pleasure. To see them stare hard and deep at, into, and through you as they moan, and pant, and cum as though they're looking at, into, and through a looking glass. And, all the while, to sense you're being watched, observed, and wondered about by someone else.

'Remember what the dormouse said /

'Feed your head /

'Feed your head...'

CASE #215 / JAZ

A woman with imposter syndrome imaginatively imposes herself upon—and inside—a male colleague in self-directed hypnosis gone awry!

Jaz's lips oscillate between self-deprecating smiles, angry, cruel curls, and emotional quivers as she completes her overview of the office politics that have been plaguing her. Her bright, dark eyes shrink from vulnerable to guarded as she flits her stare from her raggeding manicure, up briefly to me, and then to the bookshelves behind me.

I imagine Jaz is inwardly berating herself for not being more succinct and salient in reporting the facts of her situation. She has been on the recliner in my consulting room for 20 minutes already, wasting time describing what she ostensibly already booked in with via my client intake form: imposter syndrome.

"You should have stopped me."

Her tone is assertive, aggressive. Ah, yes, I well know women like Jaz. Jeez, I wasted the first decade of my career striving to *be* women like Jaz—a dedicated, demanding, impenetrable, professional <u>bitch</u>... but sugared by agreeable displays of 'empathy', 'kindness', and various other bullshit traits that keep women and minorities in their place, of course.

"I could have stopped you," I reply evenly. "But," I add with a pause, "sometimes you just gotta let people run their motors."

Jaz bristles. I can sense her wrangling with our power dynamics. Yes, I'm a 'service provider' and, thus, in her worldview, her subordinate. Add to that the privilege she oozes relative to me in education, wealth, and prospects—I saw her slight sneer at the reproduction antiques, and 80s and 90s childhood 'junk' dotted about my bookshelves. But the only power Jaz—any client—has in my hypnosis lair is to leave.

She doesn't. Instead she makes a drama of getting comfy and neat on the recliner, as if I'm conducting my business from an aged park bench rather than a £2.5k homage to Freud's favoured piece of therapeutic furniture.

I observe as she tugs at her bangs and jacket. I marvel at this 32-year-old corporate climber's toned calves; at the hint of hard abs beneath her black shift dress. I used to envy those women who could run, gym, and rush so hard to maintain that honed boardroom physique. Looking like you might physically beat your competition—rather than just beat them in revenues and performance—is an insidious 'boss-bitch' trend I'm glad to have limped away from.

But Jaz didn't beat her latest competition, alas. According to her tedious, petty diatribe, she lost out on a promotion into project management to a peer. She'd previously been on good, friendly, equitable terms with this colleague, but now he—yes, *he*—was her superior.

Her work has suffered in the three months since. And, worse, the workplace thought-police are concerned that she isn't living up to the company mission and values. But, thanks to an anodyne team-building workshop, the company is a-buzzing about 'imposter syndrome', which Jaz's line manager and mentor seized upon as the cause for her protege's decline. Urged by said boss to utilise her annual mental health allowance, Jaz booked up an appointment with yours truly.

Now, I suspect, Dear Reader, that something more primal is at the heart of Jaz's clearly uncharacteristic lurch into self-help. I decide to riff off that most ambiguous and perilous of corporate power dynamics that Jaz currently values—the woman manager-mentor who sees herself reflected in her female charge, and vice-versa; a tempestuous mix of fondness, favours, and existential threat that keeps us from smashing the patriarchy we operate beneath.

"Are you sure you suffer with imposter syndrome?", I ask sweetly. "Because you appear to be someone who's pretty comfortable with, and confident in, the world. Someone pretty certain they were the right person for that role, and would excel in it. So, putting aside all the office politics and expectations people have of you... if I were in your shoes, Jaz, I'd probably just be really, really, *really* pissed off."

A human reaction shimmers beneath Jaz's corporate veneer, but I can't place the thoughts and feelings running through her mind. She glances at the wall clock behind her, noting that we're now 33 minutes into her 90-minute first session.

"My feelings aren't important," she spits back. "I just want to... need to... get my shit back together. Work well with him, Si––. On this project, with him as my manager. Get it done. Then, move up, or on and up, in a new role, new place. But my head's... Can you help me or not?"

I can't say I much care for Jaz or her company, but I admire her ability to mask and suppress—my thoughts and feelings always had a bad habit of bursting out of my seams... 'Imposter syndrome' has excused the slip of her mask, and it's clear to me that she's unwilling to unpack her true feelings about the injustice she believes she's suffered—not consciously, anyway.

I bet she thought she was being clever choosing a hypnotist to go through the modern corporate 'self-care' motions. The general uselessness of my professional peers, coupled with the lack of personal content oft required for hypnosis, is perfect for someone striving to be impenetrable. I feel like a small child wondering whether to squash a snail beneath my foot. Do I really want to know what icky secrets hide inside her? Will I feel sadness, or something else, at smashing her pretty and protective shell..?

"Sure," I reply. "Sounds like a simple case of... exorcising some demons."

"What? Oh. You said... I thought you said 'exercising'. Like..." She mimes 'exercising' as one might do at a gym. "Yeah, sure, 'exorcising'."

I pause to mull Jaz's dismissal of her feelings; her fixation on power dynamics and her perceived rightful, awesome, lofty place in them; and this friend-turned-foe male project manager whose name she can't bring herself to utter...

"'Exorcise'. 'Exercise'. They're not called Freudian slips for nothing! I suppose the main distinction is whether something is being worked out of you, or if you're working something out."

Jaz shoots me a blankishly impatient look. How foolish, though, of her not to pay heed to the devil in my detail! I shall have to remind her, whilst she's under hypnosis, not to be surprised or resentful when she soon finds the remaining two of the trio of sessions she's booked insufficient for her inevitable workings out.

"Shall we begin, then?", I say with a smile. "The hypnosis?"

She flicks her eyes up to the ceiling for a split second and takes in a short snort of breath: oh, how wonderfully her micro-aggressions are observed and deployed! But her immediate compliance by settling back into the recliner rather undermines her air of superiority.

Such is Jaz's impatience with me, and such is her deference to her manager-mentor in seeming to address her 'imposter syndrome', that she is quick to comply with the hypnotic process. And so I decide to spend the remainder of today's session bringing themes of power to the forefront of her subconscious mind. My ambition is that, by the end of our 90 minutes together, I shall pry out the icky secret I suspect is hiding beneath Jaz's hard shell and thus find a suitable way forwards.

I share, next, Dear Reader, that same hypnotic script with you, so that you, too, can enter into Jaz's mindset—and better appreciate where her mind subsequently went to... It's a little trite for my tastes, but it's amazing what a creative-genius hypnotist can knock up on-the-fly with ChatGPT while a client's eyes are closed.

***

"As you settle into the comfort of the recliner, take a deep breath, and relax. With each breath, feel the tension leaving your body, and feel all preconceived notions leaving your mind. Let your body slip deeper and deeper into a state of deep restfulness. Let your mind slide into a state of delightful, open curiosity and wonder.

"Imagine yourself standing at the top of a majestic spiral stone staircase. The walls surrounding the winding stone steps before you are adorned with the symbols of an ancient mysticism, and are gently illuminated by a soft, mysterious light. You wonder what secrets lie at the bottom.

"You take a first step down the staircase, the feel of the cool solidity of the stone beneath your feet giving you grounding and courage as you proceed into this enigmatic moment. With each step further downwards, that solidity beneath your feet seems to change into something less sure —though still safe—sending soft ripples through the fabric of your perception, and leading you deeper and deeper still into the realm of uncertainty.

"Notice the dimly flickering torches that line the walls, further revealing the ancient symbols and casting intriguing shadows across the ancient stone. Perhaps you brush your fingers and hands against the bumps and grooves carved into the stone, wondering more at the texture and solidity than at the symbolic meanings. The dance of light and darkness all about you heightens your curiosity and piques your senses yet more.

"With each step, you can sense the atmosphere shifting around you. The air thickens with a mysterious energy; it is as if the very walls of the staircase are whispering their ancient secrets to you. Your mind opens to the possibilities that await—for you are about to enter an ancient temple, a sacred space; a place of secrets and untold power. But you are safe and protected, for you are the seeker of knowledge, embarking on a journey of self-discovery.

"As you descend further, the boundaries of your mind begin to blur. Reality melds with imagination, and the staircase itself seems to morph and twist, defying the laws of physics. You are no longer sure if you are walking or floating, but it matters not, for this is a place where illusions, and illusions within illusions, hold sway.

"You near the bottom of the staircase—floating or walking, as you prefer—and notice a faint glow emanating from its depths. Descending the last step now, and still feeling grounded and courageous, you follow a flickering, dim torchlight through a corridor—towards a grand stone door. You take a deep breath, yearning to know the secrets behind this imposing door—ready to enter this strange, alluring, secret place.

"The door swings open, and you step through the archway into a dark chamber bathed in an otherworldly glow. Before you is a cavernous, glorious ancient temple bedecked with intricate symbols and statues that seem to move and glitch. The air is thick with the scent of incense; its intoxicating aroma seducing your senses and soothing your inquisitive mind. You can feel the presence of the ancient ones who have come before you; their knowledge, wisdom, and power lingering—pulsating—in the air.

"You are drawn to the centre of the temple, where a circle of cloaked figures await your arrival. These figures wear flowing robes of deep purples and gold; their faces obscured by golden masks. Their presence exudes an air of secrecy and authority, leaving you both apprehensive and beguiled. Are they fellow seekers or mischievous tricksters? Through whispers, they will you to join them.

"As you take your place in their circle, you feel a surge of anticipation course through your mind and body. The leader of this clandestine gathering emerges from the shadows; a figure shrouded in a long, flowing, ornate cloak. They speak of ancient wisdom and esoteric knowledge, but the words seem to meld and blur, offering contradictory insights that tantalise and bewilder.

"Your initiation into this mysterious order commences, but there are no straightforward rituals here. Instead, you find yourself engaged in a web of paradoxes and nonsenses. The boundaries between illusion and reality cloud, and you are swept up in a whirlwind of confusion and enlightenment. It is a psychedelic symphony of chaos, designed to shatter your preconceived notions and open your mind to infinite possibilities.

"As the initiation nears its crescendo, you realise that you stand upon the precipice of revelation. The secrets you are uncovering are but fragments of a larger puzzle; a cosmic joke that challenges your perceptions. Yes, you realise with a grin: *it is only true if it makes you laugh.* You hear the melodious, teasing voice of the leader demanding a cosmic joke of a truth from you—a truth that will unlock the power and wisdom that so elude you.

"Their words come like a whisper from beneath their mask. 'Tell me the truth. About he who you call 'Si'. And with your truth, you will be granted unto our ancient order.'"

***

This power-themed mind-guide led me to Jaz's truth: she'd liked 'Si', she'd longed and lusted for him, and, now, she loathed him. I empathised that these unwanted, base, icky *emotions* were getting in the way of her forging her professional reputation and path.

Armed with this information, I wondered what, then, to do with her—what post-hypnotic suggestions to leave her with and where to lead her via her next two sessions..? I reflected on all I'd learned of my witting, and unwitting, hypnokink adventures; of what Alice, Theo, and C had taught me of leaving *my own* preconceived notions firmly behind me.

And so I decided to do nothing. I simply instructed Jaz's subconscious mind to mull on that truth, and to willingly and excitedly return to this chamber of secrets next session to exorcise—or exercise—her demons.

***

Jaz returned to me a week later. The moment I returned her to our hypnotic temple for her to self-direct her therapy, I realised the perils of abstaining from using my divine powers. For, in leaving Jaz alone with her own unconscious wants and whims, I had unleashed a beast!

What follows is Jaz's firsthand account of what took place in that chamber of secrets, where she has taken up an important role both within the temple's order—and within her fantasy as the narrator. (Btw, it was also polished up by my own fair hand, of course; I cannot stress enough how hopelessly maundering hypnotic subjects are, Dear Reader.) Over to Jaz...

***

Our Sentinels light the beacons to signal that he, the Seeker, has breached the boundaries and comes ever closer to our hidden chamber—to this nexus of esoteric knowledge and power—to this place where I await; where I rule. His coming was foretold to us by the Oracle, but, still, the cool, staid air of our secret sanctum seems to surge with that powerful, primal force of these most rare of nights—an initiation.

From the darkest corner of our grand temple, I watch and wait for the Initiate. I can see him, in my mind's eye, a shadow among the recesses of this ancient city—his heavy cloak clasped around his broad shoulders, his puny silver dagger holstered at his hip; searching, searching for us, closer, closer. I feel his hunger for power, knowledge, freedom, release. My skin ripples beneath my bejewelled robes as I savour the ritual to come. It is rare that a Seeker finds our elusive order—we have taken such great, careful measures throughout history to evade fools and pretenders. But the coming of a new Initiate is a sacred moment—the death of the mind, as it is... or the death of the body, should the Initiate prove unworthy. And the power and pleasure of either is all mine.

Six Sentries troop through the archway and close the heavy stone door behind them, awaiting the Seeker—the door closed, but not locked, as is the custom with magick. One Sentry throws himself down prostrate on the flagstones, begging his fellow guardians for clemency, having played some role in our Seeker's success in finding us out. He is dragged off into the antechamber by the Alchemist, our master of transmutation and spiritual evolution, who presses a steaming goblet of liquid against the man's lips. This Sentry, who failed to protect us, shall pay a heavy price for his negligence.

From behind leaden gold masks, all eyes glitter upon the five cloaked figures at the head of the chamber. In their centre is the Hierophant. He sits upon an ornate throne on a small platform and will lead the initiation ceremony, bridging the realm between the mystical and the ordinary— and perhaps breaking a Seeker who is unworthy in mind or body. The Hierophant looks at the Oracle who chants and gazes into the glimmering waters of a divination bowl, their trance causing them to convulse and fit until this hunched figure draped in white collapses in a stupor beside the spilled bowl's slick waters.

The Seeker—the Initiate, as he is now—is here. I can only see, not fully hear, the proceedings from the cloister from which I will later emerge. I watch as the five remaining Sentries draw their fiercesome swords from their harnesses and wait beside the stone door. The Hierophant and the four Brethren that flank him turn their blankly resplendent gold masks towards them in wait. The Alchemist returns from the antechamber with a tray bearing a flagon and cup, and is joined by the Scribe carrying parchment and quill. The Oracle motions as if to rouse, but swoons again at the sounds of desperate footsteps and pounding on the other side of the stone door. We wait. Indeed, the temple itself seems to hold its breath, as if aware of the descent into an abyss of carnality that is to come.

The Initiate bursts through the stone door, dagger drawn, ready to fight and kill for what he desires. It is always the way with these men. Why do Seekers not approach with humble curiosity? No matter; he shall come to regret his shows of male bombast—and perhaps other such acts—in time.

The Sentries stand firm and still in the face of the Initiate's frenzied entrance. The Initiate is further taken aback as the Alchemist and Scribe convivially invite him inside our sanctum instead of fighting him off. A Sentry relieves the Initiate of his dagger, while the Scribe unsheathes him of his hood so as to take his particulars down. I see a pleasing, handsome male face shining back at me—the man is overwhelmed by what he has penetrated: the symbols and texts inscribed on the stone walls; the mysterious objects of ritual; the glistening eyes of the cloaked, masked spectres that surround him. I throb with anticipation in the knowledge that he knows not of my eyes upon him, and impatiently stroke the implement of my coming role in his initiation.

The Alchemist proffers the man a refreshment, which he thirstily and naïvely gulps down. He is escorted towards the belly of our temple where the Hierophant and his Brethren await, and where—at the Scribe's direction—the Initiate must make his case. From the man's swagger and animated gestures, I know he is making the usual grandiose claims to his rights to power and wisdom. He shall be humbled, humiliated, havocked here tonight if there is to be any hope of his joining our order.

The Hierophant stands and approaches the Initiate, towering over him as he appraises and circles him. With one quick swipe he rips the cloak from about the Initiate's neck, dropping it to the floor, and exposing our infiltrator's strong but compact build. The Hierophant's gold mask gazes down upon the empty leather holster at the man's hip. He beckons for one of his Brethren, who presents him with the man's small, shining dagger. The Hierophant returns the dagger to its holster before he returns to his throne. This is the signal for the Sentries to return with their failed fellow protector—now nude, begging, sobbing from beneath a black full-head hood. The Initiate watches in bewildered trepidation as the disgraced Sentry is chained to a post erected at the side of our proceedings. He wipes his brow with his shirtsleeve as the Scribe ushers him towards the Sentry, his slight stagger indicating that the potion is working.

I watch—tense, tantalised—as the Initiate is handed a long, cruel whip. He surveys it in his hands and makes weak protests of confusion and objection. Our gathered order waits stonily, silently—the disgraced Sentry's bare, quivering buttocks and sobbing, shaking head from beneath the heavy hood say all. As all Initiates do, the man realises he must mete out this dreadful punishment.

Scwiii-thwack! Scwiii-thwack! Scwiii-thwack!

The fall of the whip dances up behind the Sentry's soft flesh before the braided cracker end bites into his buttocks. More screams, cries, protests from our betrayer. The Initiate goes easy on him at first, but the surrounding figures remain stony silent; without a 'no' or a 'stop', all these men understand only to continue and to escalate, and to exorcise their discomfort and oppression on another. And so he lashes and flicks the whip against those white-to-pink-to-red-to-bloody-bleeding-raw buttocks, again and again, crack after crack, til the Sentry collapses into a whimpering, welted heap.

The Initiate yells and protests: what more do they want from him?! Yes, see how quickly we lead him to thoughts of death; of killing! He unholsters his dagger and waves it about—is this what they want from him?! He approaches his sunken victim, holding the blade to his throat—protesting that he will not do such a thing. But I have witnessed many such ceremonies and know just what men are capable of with only the smallest morsel of permission from a master. In this Initiate's case, the Alchemist's potion is taking hold of his body and mind before the Sentry becomes yet another causality of our grand scheme. The Initiate stumbles, and lets out a hysterical cry-laugh. He raises the dagger in his hands up to his face to look at it, fascinated, horrified, regarding his reflection in its glinting blade, cackling manically, before dropping it to the stone floor with a clink.

The Alchemist approaches the Initiate, whispering words of comfort and instruction as the potion works to rob the man of reality, reason, and perception. The Oracle, who has now roused, leads the gibbering man away to the antechamber to continue their preparations. His mind—should it survive this glimpse into the abyss of true and total madness—is now a mere vessel, an instrument of illumination. And, should he survive me, his body will follow.

***

The Scribe bows reverently to the Hierophant and each of the Brethren in turn, before taking his place at a grand oak desk in the corner of our temple. Here, he will chronicle all that follows. The five remaining Sentries, however, are not permitted to set eyes upon the next phase of the initiation. The Hierophant allows them their spoils, though—with but a flick of their master's gloved hand, they set upon their former defender, pleasuring themselves orally and anally in an orgiastic frenzy. They must be treated like the base animals they are until they evolve up our esoteric order. I watch disinterestedly as they thrust and grapple and howl at one another, a tangle of cloaks and nakedness—their outcasted watchman a tired, ragged but enthusiastic recipient of these attentions; a reminder of his own mind- and body-blowing initiation, I don't doubt.

The final two Sentries fight to spend their seed inside the beaten man's gaping mouth just as another pumps his last into his asshole. Our defenders collapse like animals who have just devoured a satisfying meal, the subsidence of their grunts and shunts giving me a delicious insight into the fate of the Initiate, out of sight in the antechamber. The Alchemist will be purging both his body and his mind, before feeding him intravenously with a stabilising and strengthening formula for the next phase. I hear gasps, and cries, and howls. I can only wonder at what secrets and truths and possibilities the Oracle is divining in him while he undergoes these ordeals. As our conduit for messages from

271

higher planes of existence, only the Oracle can know if the Initiate is mentally and physically strong enough for me to play my sacred role.

A gong is sounded from the antechamber, its deep tone rippling out through the temple and signalling for the Sentries to leave us. They jostle the disgraced man away between them; it will be a long night for them til they resolve whether he is still friend or foe to the order back in their sleeping quarters. If the mind is weak, our way is to test that the body is strong.

The Hierophant and Brethren are thus alone in the temple when the Oracle walks ceremoniously into the room, wafting musky incense from the thurible hanging between their hands. They take their seat at the head of the stone altar, whispering incantations and communing with our higher plane. Then follows the Initiate, now clad only in a loincloth, and accompanied by the Alchemist carrying a small bottle of oil. Fortified by the concoction coursing through his veins, the Initiate seems vacantly strong and ready—I am hot and heartened that his mind and body seem so open after his initial disappointing shows of bravado and brutality.

He is a lion—our symbol of power, strength, and divine privilege! As such, we must adorn him with our symbolism. Per the ritual, the Alchemist leads our lion up onto the altar and pushes him down into a kneeling position. I watch as the willing but naïve man kneels before the Oracle at the head of the altar, wondering, no doubt, what ritual comes next. But instead it is the Alchemist behind him who acts. The Initiate forces himself to keep his eyes front and his body calm as his loin cloth is lifted by our Alchemist, exposing his naked rear. Warm oil is dripped and drizzled down the man's crevice and I watch as the Alchemist slides his hand between the Initiate's cheeks to massage the slickness in.

One of the Brethren retrieves a wooden box from the oak table where sits the Scribe, takes it to the altar, opens it carefully, and presents its contents to the Alchemist. With his spare hand, the Alchemist triumphantly lifts from the box a fine, long lion's tail—preserved from a once-living beast. The Hierophant beats his staff on the stone floor in a faster and faster rhythm, with the Brethren taking their staffs to join the pulsating, rousing beat. The Alchemist grasps the hilt of the lion's tail where sits a flared plug. I watch the Initiate's face carefully as the Alchemist plunges the plug slowly but surely into his pink, purged rectum, his mouth and eyes reacting as the Alchemist expertly waits for each ring of muscles to welcome the next part of the plug inside. Once he is fully stoppered by the plug, and the tail sits proudly outside his body, the beating of the staffs ceases as the Alchemist gives it an exultant swish with his now free hands.

The Initiate is encouraged up from the altar by the Alchemist and must parade before the Brethren. He stumbles at first, confused, cowed. But then he stands taller and begins to prowl up and down before those he believes are judging him. It is I who will judge him, though. It is I who sees him reveal every facet of himself to us—known and unknown—through this ritual. I care not for his machismo, but he is a fine specimen of man, I must admit. I long to stroke his fine tail, running my hand from its fat protrusion down to its fine, downy tip... and to see what might be stirring beneath his loincloth. But instead the Alchemist ends the lion's parade by pushing the Initiate down onto the ground before the first of the Brethren. I see with sadness that the man is still wearing his mask of socialised superficialities, momentarily pretending, protesting that he does not know what is required of him next. And yet the intimidating swelling from beneath the Brethren's robe tells all.

***

The Initiate must submit. He must submit willingly, completely, utterly if he is to become a vessel of illumination. My eyes shine with expectation and excitement as I watch the Brethren pull his velvet robe aside, exposing his naked manhood standing stiff before the face of the Initiate. To question, to protest, to cry out now will spell the end of the Initiate's quest for power—he will simply be left to the Sentinels and their base aggressions before he is thrown back onto the streets, living or dead, come sunrise. He must gratefully take any chalice of power our order seems to be offering him, and drink it down without question, if he is to progress to the true test.

I wonder what is running through the Initiate's mind in the split seconds before he acts. It is such a thrill to see how such men, when they submit—for most do—decide to drink from this first chalice. Some are clearly familiar and happy with the act, gobbling up the Brethren gladly and expertly. Others are so timid and meek with their tongues and mouths that the ceremony lasts for hours. This Initiate strikes me as unfamiliar with another man's sex, but desirous to impress the wise ones before him. I gasp quietly as he kisses the Brethren's penis with his sumptuous lips; respectfully, regally, as one might kiss the ring of a king. Then, his mind set, he kisses his first cock again and again, soon gripping it in his hand and lavishing it with nuzzling kisses. I start to wonder if he thinks he can cheat true submission, instead stimulating the Brethren with his lips and fingers alone. But then I see—I *feel*—the Initiate submit. He swallows the penis into his mouth, sucking deeply and meditatively on the shaft, lost in his task.

The temple is still yet expectant as all eyes watch the Brethren's pleasure building. He runs a gentle, fond hand through the Initiate's hair in encouragement, prompting our lion to move his attention to his superior's engorged tip. He tongues and licks and sucks the most sensitive parts, still taking his time—I do so hate to see these Initiates rush us. The Brethren's masked head falls back a little as he focuses on his coming climax, stroking the Initiate's hair, panting and moaning with each motion of the lion's head. On the brink, the Brethren lightly pushes the Initiate's head back so that only the tip of his penis is now inside his mouth. The initiate sucks passively upon its bulbous end until the Brethren ejaculates into his mouth in a melodious cry. Much to my satisfaction, the Initiate gulps the cum down, unthinkingly, before the Brethren's softening member slips out of his doused mouth.

The Initiate kneels back from the Brethren. Will he make a show of assuming his task is now complete? I do so hope not! He glances at the next Brethren in the semi-circle and sees a larger protrusion peeking from his purple gown—then he crawls upon bended knees towards his waiting groin, his fine tail swishing from between his buttocks. Oh, I am pleased to see him submit so obligingly. This next Brethren is not so tender a teacher as the Initiate's first, but he bears it well. Soon he has sucked out the flaming seed of all four Brethren, and swallowed their sacrament with gratitude and grace. His submission to the idiosyncrasies of the sizes, shapes, movements, and kinks of each of their fine members pleases me. I watch his lion's tail flicker and swish in time with the bobbings of his head and lappings of his tongue, longing to tug upon it and distract him from his work.

***

Finally, though—at least in this phase of the initiation—he must submit to the Hierophant. Our lion crawls into position at our imposing master's knees, ready to receive him into his lips and to drink him in. But the Hierophant senses his by-now presumptive ease and confidence—to plot is not to submit. The Hierophant strikes him angrily across the face, before rising onto his feet. The Initiate clutches his shocked face as our liege pulls aside his robe with a gloved hand, revealing a long, thick, hard, throbbing member waiting just as angrily for satisfaction.

Tentative lips approach its glistening tip, but, instead, the Hierophant grabs at the Initiate's hair with his free hand and mashes his wet, used lips down onto his cock. The Initiate struggles, gags, chokes as the master plunges himself ever deeper into the man's mouth and throat, the two locked in a battle of wills and reflexes. The master insistently forces the Initiate's head back and forth against his monstrous cock, caring not how deep and hard he thrusts; this moment is only about his carnal release—the Initiate is but a vessel. Perhaps this realisation clicks inside the man's head, for then he becomes a lamb instead of a lion, his lips, mouth, tongue, and throat yielding to work in tune with the Hierophant's lunges, wide eyed and wet lipped as his face is fucked and fucked and fucked by our liege.

Having been accepted so completely and beautifully by our submitting student, the master pulls out from his yawning mouth before cumming. Instead, he waits to see what our Initiate will do—what creative way will he show his desire to fully satisfy his superior? The man snaps out of the face-fucked trance he's been in and, childlike, cups his hands beneath the master's bloated, purpling tip. The Hierophant stimulates his own shaft with his gloved fingers and spills his creamy essence into the man's waiting palms, sitting back down upon his throne to watch as this humbled Initiate hungrily laps up the hallowed offering with his weakened tongue.

The Initiate pants feebly on his hands and knees upon the stone floor. But this is nothing compared to the test to come, for now it is my turn to probe and stretch and bend his body—and mind—to my purposes. The Oracle chants and lights a new incense to mark the transition to this next phase, while the Alchemist scoops the man up and brings him to the altar. The Hierophant and his Brethren snuff out the candles illuminating their half-circle, plunging them into a darkness from which they can see but cannot be seen. Then they begin to strike their ceremonial staffs on the ground in an eerily pulsating rhythm, heralding my entrance.

***

The temple is heavy with pungent incense, the altar aglow in its centre and all else dark aside from the dim dot of light beside which our Scribe chronicles tonight's rituals. As I move silently from my lair, I see the Initiate standing beside the altar, looking all about him, his body slick with sweat and his lion's tail draped regally at his feet. The beating of the staffs on the floor gathers pace as I approach; I can see the man start to detect the swoosh of my heavy bedecked cloak across the ground, and the soft padding of my bare feet on the stone. Next, he places the sounds from the shimmers of my cloak as it meets the chamber's glow. I thrill at the thought of the fear and anticipation in his mind as he starts to comprehend my magnificent shape move towards him—the iridescence of the hundreds of jewel-beetle wings sewn into my cloak; the gold thread and filigree; the pearls, rubies, turquoise, corals, sea shells. Emerging, resplendent, from the darkness.

The light is now upon me proper, revealing my form to the Initiate. He makes a silent 'O' as he beholds me. I am the Illuminatrix; the order's divine feminine; the embodiment of the forces of intuition, wisdom, and sensuality. I see the man look over my exposed breasts and mound of hair, and am gratified by the stirrings beneath his loin cloth in response. But I also wear the mask of Baphomet, representing the union of opposites, and the synthesis of spiritual and earthly realms—the balance between feminine and masculine. And so, despite the allures of my human body, he shrinks back in apprehension at my otherworldly head and gown.

I stride up to <u>my</u> Initiate—for he is mine to initiate—and stand before him. I allow him to fully look upon me, from the curling horns of my fearsome goat's head mask, down and across my breasts to my outstretched bejewelled wings of my grand cloak, then down, down past my belly and pudenda, down my legs and my taloned toes. The man's rod stirs yet more from beneath his modest sheath of cotton, like the proverbial snake. But I am no Eve and he is no Adam; an illumination the Alchemist will help us to achieve with the elixir he now passes me.

I press the goblet of heady brew to my lips, exposed beneath the snout of my mask, and drink half of it back. The remainder I proffer to the Initiate, who knows by now not to hesitate and so gulps the liquor down in one. Almost instantly, the temple and all those within it seem to vibrate and bend and morph and meld—as if reality is but made of clay to be manipulated as one pleases. The man is also feeling the elixir's effects, staring wide-eyed from his hands to my breasts to all around his surroundings. Unused to the heady effects, he does not notice the Alchemist relieve him of his loin cloth, exposing his now flaccid and shrunken manhood beneath it. Nor our master of transmutation aiding me in stepping into a leather harness that he fastens at my hips.

The Initiate's fascination with his hands is transferred down his body, to where he now sees and feels only a small sagging mound of skin, his sex having retreated into his body, thanks to the potion. Since we have already cleared him of his identity and memories, he is simply puzzled, rather than panicked, by this. He looks searchingly into my face—into my mask's shining red gauzed eyes from behind which mine are concealed—and sees, comprehends, I know not what. As he beholds me fully, he reacts to what is now nestled in my mound of hair—a magnificent erect penis, of some 12 inches long, plus a fistful in girth, intricately carved from bull elephant ivory by our founders for this, my Illuminatrix test.

The man gasps—not in fear or shock or delight—but in some natural, primal response to such an awesome sight... and possibility. He looks so innocent and ready that I cannot resist gifting him a kiss from my hungry mouth. I take his chin in my hand and press my lips to his, sliding my tongue inside his warm, salty-sweet mouth and dancing it insistently against his. He kisses me back yearningly as I pull away—a promising sign that he is ready for this experience. I nod for the Alchemist to prepare him. He then guides the man by the arm to face the altar, placing his hands on the cool ledges of the stone and kneeling upon a velvet stool on the floor, his asshole—still plugged by that fine tail—at my hip height. I stroke and tug at his tail playfully while the Alchemist now tends to me, drizzling sacred oil upon my ivory member and working it across the shaft. The Initiate moans as his plug pulls inside of him. Then, in one slow, gentle but resolute move, I grasp it by the hilt and ease the plugged end out from inside him.

The Alchemist's elixir works its magic as I gaze into the Initiate's winking hole—I feel as one with my ivory rod, which seems to thrum with yearning. I position my glossy oiled tip against the gaping orifice, probing, nuzzling its pink ruches, wanting solely to be inside; to connect; to feel. I press myself against the shy hole a little more firmly, wanting to be welcomed in rather than to force entry. The Initiate responds by pushing back a little against me, exhaling as he feels the ornate tip of my rod prod the inner crevices of his chasm. I hold his hips with my hands to stop him rocking forwards again, keeping us in this delicate union whilst his tight, virgin sphincter muscle relaxes and draws me inside. I stroke the downy skin of the Initiate's back and buttocks to help his body yield. He trembles a little as he takes a breath in and out—then I feel the inner ring softening against my persistent tip before opening and swallowing in a couple of inches of my length.

I hold my Initiate steady by his hips as he acclimatises to the feel of me inside him. He gasps and moans as he tries to rock and writhe, his prostate swelling and throbbing against my ivory. But I demand to be deeply and completely inside of him, and for our pleasure to be as one. And so I begin to push slowly further inside of his hot, stretching ring, my widening girth and peculiarly carved bumps, curves, and grooves invading his body. I see his hands grasping at the corners of the altar as I push myself deeper and deeper. I hope he keeps the lesson taught to him by the Hierophant in mind as I still and sooth his tense, bucking, buzzing body—he will deny himself the power, wisdom, and pleasure of true illumination if he fails to submit completely.

I feel I am so, so close to being fully connected—only when we are as one can I make my pleasure, my energy, my climax his. My soothing gestures still the last of the twitches and jerks his body reflexively makes, and as my fullness slides inside of him he becomes pliant and calm, free, as he is, of all preconceived notions of what does and doesn't constitute 'the' 'natural' sex act between two souls. I gasp and grind my hips against his buttocks, now able to stimulate my own sex whilst savouring the soft, velvety folds of his innocent ass. Inside of him, truly and completely.

I see before me the Oracle, seated at the other end of the altar, communing with our higher ones in tongues whilst swinging the incense. They—the higher powers—will guide our united act, and so I gaze into her dark black pupils from behind my fiery red eyes, putting myself, my cognition and consciousness, aside. I am but an instrument of illumination as my magnificent ivory rod starts to work back and forth inside this burrow of flesh, clitoris and prostate massaged and pressured and rubbed and thrusted in sync... Our movements become as instinctual as the ebb and flow of the sea, as the rotation of the earth. Driving us on, on, on—until—-!

My climax is beyond words—an eternity in a moment, a symphony of the senses, a sex-magick that makes two people both as one and yet so much more. A power and wisdom that only the ancient order of the Illuminati knows how to manipulate and harness.

I rouse, as I always do, lying upon the altar in a swoon, with the Alchemist removing my harness from my closed legs. I see the red, slick face of my Initiate at the foot of the altar, panting back at me, the pupils of his eyes like saucers and his mouth set in a blissful smile. A large pool of opalescent semen has been spilled from him—from me. He sees me regarding it and knows to lap up this gift from our bodies—he shows great promise in progressing to far higher forms of sensual sorcery, which pleases my mind.

But, finally and most crucially, he must please my body. The Alchemist completes his final preparations. He lays the objects of ritual beside me: a bound bundle of owl feathers to represent wisdom, night, and superior perception; a hunk of ice and hot burning candle for the rebirth, immortality, and transformation of the phoenix; and a smooth glass baton topped with a serpent's head, to represent knowledge and the awakening of the consciousness.

With these symbols of our great work, both mythical and real, and with his own imagination and ingenuity, my

Initiate's final test is to give me pleasure as I have never felt before.

I splay my legs open wide in front of his eager, open face, showing him all of my feminine secrets.

I hope he does not disappoint me. I hope, I hope...

***

I write these notes from my marital bed at gone midnight while lying bedside Addy. I have just recounted what Jaz described to me whilst in deep hypnosis earlier today to his eager ear.

I appreciate that you, Dear Reader, may have purchased my scribblings to forward your knowledge of hypnotism; perhaps, even, your career as a hypnotherapist. The most promising among you will, of course, deduce that I cast myself as the Scribe in Jaz's subconscious mind. And so, after the oath of silence I made following my encounter with Alice, I have no shame in sharing this account with my husband. Freud's contemporary Carl Jung founded analytical psychology, creating meaning and resolutions from the nonsensical swirls of people's minds and dreams. Since I have used my knowledge of archetypes and the collective unconscious to give Jaz's stumblings in the dark narrative and form, I figure it belongs to me, Addy—us—as a collective, rather than simply to Jaz, whose penchant for power will be woefully incomplete until she learns of the myth, lore, legend, and Illuminati mess that got us here.

I don't quite know why I write this—this *what?* This 'journal'? (Ugh, no!) These 'field notes'..? This 'casebook', perhaps. Or: this *confessional..?*

Yes, perhaps that is it, for I must confess: what if, in Jaz, I've now blurred the lines between the internal and external world? My previous experiments seemed clearer cut in both place and purpose: the revivification of a memory that one can tap into; a fantasy to fuel a real-world ambition; my own sordid peek into someone's innermost mind-space to which they're none the wiser. Theo and Alice are consenting adults, already on the path towards making their fantasies realities. But, in Jaz, I fear I have opened a Pandora's Box... What if she acts upon her lust in the workplace? Or, worse, her loathing? Her next appointment is in two weeks, and I feel impatient to see her. I like her more now that I've seen her selfish, twisted darkness.

Oh, but on the subject of impatience, Addy is keen to play the role of Initiate to my Illuminatrix in spite of my commitment to my clients and professional growth. I am grateful to be in correspondence with Dr Charlotte Karoly—such a luminary of psychiatry, psychology, and (it must be admitted) vintage CIA mindfuckery—to provide academic sense-making and a sheen of professionalism to my escapades!

So. Until our next session, then, Dear Reader...

CASE #216 / THEO (AGAIN)

Going through the hypnotic 'looking glass' world with Theo—and Addy—with my own fantasy. But do I ever dare to make it reality..?

"It's me now, Lilith. <u>The Hypnotist</u>. *Your* hypnotist. That voice, that presence, in your head that's always watching, waiting, willing. Am I the one turning the cogs in your mind; you the mere mechanism for my ticks? Or do we turn the wheels together, with only the distinction between the passing of seconds, minutes, and hours, as we comprehend and liaise and act, creating the illusion of our separation? Or perhaps we tick along in perfect time to the workings of something beyond both our comprehensions?

"Whatever 'freewill' is or isn't, *I see you* watching him. Theo. He lounges there, in your fine tan leather recliner, updating you on his progress and problems since he saw you last, you both keeping your pacts of silence about the Alice rabbit hole. His quest to conquer his sexuality and identity is, as you well know, a grand, open-ended one, and you have both crossed lines in pursuing if and how hypnosis can help. And now here he is again, wondering whether hypnosis can help him break down the walls of his self in singular ways that singularly appeal to your—to our—ego and imagination.

"Theo is becoming addicted to your powers; to hypnotism's abilities to grant him his deepest desires and dreams. You are like two magnets, attracted to one another above and beyond mere sex; repelled by the professional, personal, and societal boundaries that govern us all. Hear him ask for book recommendations; hear him make those knowing little observations on your hypnotic techniques and tricks. We are sure he has started to learn your art and science from small slips of his tongue—his familiarity with key names and experiments that you mention. Soon, he will ask you to teach him. Will you teach him? Knowing that he will likely use it for desires as natural and innocent—yet as sinfully, ignorantly harmful—as sex?

"And what of your desires, Lilith, in that respect? You did well to close your mind to Theo and C while watching Alice. But I saw Theo. Saw his body. His sex. His essence. Yes, I feel your body shifting in your chair, recrossing your legs, clenching your thighs together, feeling the wetness start to ooze from your cunt into your panties...

"Imagine how easy, how sweet, it would be. He sleeps upon your command now. You could instantly place him into hypnosis and make him your plaything. Remember Ian? Where this all started? Imagine having Theo unbuckle his belt and unfasten his jeans at your swift command. Imagine him easing them down along with his briefs, exposing himself to you. We never saw him soft and vulnerable, did we? It would be so nice to have him show us his nakedness—and to be none the wiser for it; our puppet on a string.

"But we want to see him grow, don't we? Yes, yes—don't think I can't feel your clit swelling at the thought; that I can't sense the other parts of your mind flitting back to your fantasy of Theo, gazing into your pussy, then easing his long, agile fingers inside your slit. We'd command him to touch himself, to make himself hard; watch him engorge from root through to tip. We'd compel him to make himself as big, as stiff, as impressive as possible—til his balls swell, and his veins pop, and his tip leaks—but detached from desire and the compulsion to cum. Let's see him in all his desperate, physical glory.

"But what then..? Ah, yes—you bite your lip, betraying your urge! You want to take him in your mouth. To get down on your knees and savour him. Imagine sucking and tonguing at his sex knowing you're working only a machine —his mind, his consciousness, closed off while you worship him. How delicious it would be to kiss his shaft and tickle his frenulum with your tongue knowing it is only your physical actions taking effect; that there is no cognisance enhancing the experience for the recipient, pre-empting your actions, embellishing you and what's happening with intrusive, competing fantasies, getting out of sync with your command over their body with their own thoughts and feelings. What a sensuously meditative task that would be, to bring a cock to climax by your mind and body alone.

"But what if Addy should discover you! You share fantasies and flirt with such adventures, but you, Lilith, cannot fathom how to make power, spontaneity, and risk consensual and planned. Should he discover you with your lips wrapped around Theo's ample cock, let's imagine you stop sucking to glance back at him, your shocked husband, taking in this scene at the open door of your therapy room. You hope you would share a knowing, permissive look between you—before you continue working at that delicious cock.

"And next you feel your skirt being roughly pushed up from behind as your husband kneels behind you. You hear him unbuttoning himself before pulling your sodden knickers aside. You're losing focus on Theo's body as Addy drives his cock deep inside your cunt—or your ass—you can't decide—gasping and rasping against the bloated tip of your client's penis as your husband starts to ram you from behind. You rarely cum from this position, but your body is so enflamed by this new taboo that you start to feel the pleasure and pressure building more and more and all three of you rock back and forth, the force from Addy's pounding hips forcing your mouth and throat deeper, harder, and faster onto Theo's quavering cock. You explode in an orgasm more powerful than you've known in years. Your pleasure is like a chain reaction for your husband, who shoots hard and deep inside of your pussy—ass—pussy—mmm—can't decide which. He pulses inside of you as you slurp on Theo's cock, the hypnotised man delivering a blasting but strangely silent orgasm into the back of your throat. You picture your husband staring at the man in front of him as you feel the slick, cummy, satisfying mess at your mouth and hole—and...

***

"Hmph. Fine. Pretend you have a pressing urge to put the kettle on and make a coffee, Lilith. But don't think I don't feel that burning between our legs. That I'm not already dreaming up one hundred ways to relieve it the moment Theo departs from his appointment.

"You came to this world of hypnosis as a curious visitor, didn't you, Lilith, proffering cures for habits, phobias, and pains in exchange for cash and a sordid glimpse inside many a personal wonderland. But this internal 'looking-glass' world has a habit of turning itself inside-out—of making the internal external. Thoughts become Things; Things become reality. I am the hypnotist and you are my subject. What shall WE make real?"

-END-

Disclaimer #3

Thank you for reading the first *Mine Control* book. Already my client notebook is filling with yet more confessions of my hypnotic, erotic adventures, and so I hope you'll join me, Dear Reader, in future casebooks. Follow or bookmark my Amazon author page, and/or visit www.ipsissimus-press.com for updates.

Oh, one final thing before I put down my pen... Despite Disclaimer #2, upon finishing this book, you feel strangely moved to now recommend it to a friend, or to post about it on social media, or to write a glowing review on Amazon. Don't believe me? Hmm, well—do you feel that little tickle, that irritating little... *itch*... on your nose..? Yeah, that—*that* tickle, *that* itch. (It's okay, go ahead and scratch—it's just the power of suggestion working its magic on you.) Well, *that* tickle, *that* itch will continue to irk you til you do just one of those things. Just one, Dear Reader—and then it will go away and bother you no more.

Should you be sufficiently charmed by my suggestions to oblige me by doing two of those things, though, then you shall be rewarded with a particularly sound and peaceful night's sleep tonight. And you shall awaken tomorrow well rested and filled with a renewed vigour for life.

For those of you who do all three: well, you will additionally be visited in your dreams by whatever pleasant thoughts, fantasies, and ideas most appealed to your subconscious mind within these pages for as long as you'd like. Such are the perks of being an exemplary hypnotic subject, for which you have my very warmest thanks and regards.

- Lilith

Printed in Great Britain
by Amazon

26085255R00175